T0246447

FOR THE
STOLEN FATES

ALSO BY GWENDOLYN CLARE

FOR THE

Stolen
Fates

GWENDOLYN CLARE

FEIWEL AND FRIENDS
NEW YORK

A Feiwel and Friends Book
An imprint of Macmillan Publishing Group, LLC
120 Broadway, New York, NY 10271 • fiercereads.com

Our books may be purchased in bulk for promotional, educational, or business use.
Please contact your local bookseller or the Macmillan Corporate and Premium
Sales Department at (800) 221-7945 ext. 5442 or by email at
MacmillanSpecialMarkets@macmillan.com.

Library of Congress Cataloging-in-Publication Data is available.

First edition, 2024
Book design by Sarah Nichole Kaufman and Megan Sayre
Feiwel and Friends logo designed by Filomena Tuosto
Printed in the United States of America

ISBN 978-1-250-23076-8
10 9 8 7 6 5 4 3 2 1

FOR CHRIS

Never let the future disturb you.
You will meet it, if you have to,
with the same weapons of reason which
today arm you against the present.
—MARCUS AURELIUS

1

WILLA

1891, countryside south of Bologna

THIS IS A terrible idea," Willa said as she picked the lock on the front door of the villa house.

Saudade looked faintly amused. "Yes, you've said."

"It bears repeating." She felt the last tumbler click into position and twisted the torsion wrench. "You know, I'm only about eighty-five percent certain this is even the correct summer cottage we're breaking into."

Saudade raised their eyebrows, taking in the two-story stone house with its leaded glass windows and red tile roof. "You consider this a cottage?"

Willa held back her shrug until after the lock popped open. This was only one part of what had once been a multi-structure villa owned by some fantastically wealthy Renaissance aristocrat, before it fell into disrepair and was sold off in pieces. "It was probably the villa's guest house originally."

"It looks like it could accommodate a family of ten in extravagant comfort."

Willa straightened and tucked her lockpicks away inside the boning of her corset. "You don't have much experience with extravagance, do you? Trust me, the conspicuous displays of wealth get much worse than this in the pre-cataclysm centuries."

It was a strange turning of the tables, to be back here in 1891 where Willa was the expert and Saudade had only their local database of historical knowledge to lean on. Despite the modestness of her living conditions since her familial estrangement, Willa's parents had raised her to be a marquis. She was intimately familiar with aristocracy, and she might have worn the title comfortably if only it didn't require living as a man, which she most decidedly could not do. She was used to getting by on her own, but her room in the boardinghouse was no longer an option, both because she no longer had a university stipend with which to pay for it, and because multiple people would know to look for her there.

Never mind that Saudade's chosen appearance was rather memorable. They presented themself with curly dark hair and medium brown skin, and while they wouldn't be the only person of color in nineteenth-century Bologna, the other residents of the boardinghouse would've certainly taken notice. Willa was fairly certain that Saudade—being an android from the future—could alter their appearance to blend in, but she couldn't bring herself to ask someone else to compromise their identity for her convenience. That would be the worst kind of hypocrisy, coming from Willa.

She turned the doorknob and let them both into the summer cottage. The entryway was somewhat narrow but two stories high, with a stairway leading up to balcony railings on the second floor. The house was clean inside but only sparsely furnished and decorated—her mentor, Augusto Righi, had occasionally spoken of how much work he still needed to put into his summer property, and how he could never find the time to make it presentable. Willa felt reasonably confident that none of his colleagues from the University of Bologna or from the Order of Archimedes would have been invited for a visit, so no one would think to check for Willa here. And with no children to inherit, Righi's estate would likely be tied up for some while, as the lawyers of distant relatives argued over his holdings.

Willa said, "Fine, I'll admit it: So long as we don't get arrested for trespassing, I suppose this will do well enough."

Saudade grinned. "I've always wanted my very own secret lair."

Willa took a long, steadying breath. Despite everything that had happened since learning Righi had died, his absence still hit her like a sharp spike between the ribs. "I feel as if I'm taking advantage of his death."

Saudade let their grin fade. They understood whose

house this was. "Even just from reading his journals, it's clear Righi cared for you. I can only surmise he would have provided what assistance he could to our mission, if he'd lived to make that choice himself."

"I don't know that he would have trusted me with this." Willa's gaze was drawn to the satchel hanging from Saudade's shoulder, which contained the book that would end the world. "Righi never wanted me anywhere near his secret society of science cronies."

"Don't confuse his desire to protect you from the Order with a lack of trust." Saudade paused. "Riley and Jaideep trust you with this. Does that count for nothing?"

"Right. Riley and Jaideep." Her throat went tight around the names. Two more fresh losses to add to her collection—not lost to death, at least, but left behind in an uncertain future, when it proved impossible for two twenty-first-century humans to travel to 1891 with the intent of changing history. Now it was all down to Willa and Saudade—an apprentice mechanist who'd lost her mentor, and with him, the laboratory she'd once had access to at the university; and an android time cop who'd rebelled against their own organization, risked everything to help three upstart humans, and was now cut off from whatever incomprehensible network and processing resources they'd once taken for granted. Neither of them at their best, and now they had to protect the very fabric of spacetime.

Willa couldn't help but feel a pang of abandonment, despite the fact that she was the one who left the future behind. She knew Riley would have stuck with her, would have seen the mission through to the end if it were possible. Willa grimaced, angry at herself for this irrational sense of hurt. She often found her emotions to be less than convenient, but now in the wake of Riley, they were harder to bottle up, too.

Saudade set a comforting hand on her shoulder. "Come. Let us settle in and take a look at this prize book we've chased after so diligently."

The sitting room of the summer house was furnished with only a single settee, a pair of wooden chairs, and a standing lamp that with Willa's luck would probably not have any oil in it. The two of them sat side by side on the settee, and Saudade pulled the leather-bound volume from their satchel and handed it to Willa, as if deferring to her authority in this matter. Willa blinked, thrown for a moment—she was no scriptologist, hardly an expert in the creation of artificial worlds despite having visited a few of them, but apparently Saudade felt that she was in charge of this mission nonetheless.

Willa opened the book to the first page, but found it empty. She flipped forward, a small nugget of panic turning in her stomach. "It's blank! The whole book is blank. What is this?"

Everything she'd lost couldn't have been for *nothing*—this book was supposed to be the key to stopping a global catastrophe before it ever happened. If it was worthless . . .

"Hm." Saudade leaned closer, eyes scanning the pages intently. "Interesting. There is ink, it just doesn't reflect in the visible spectrum."

Willa put a hand over her chest, trying to calm her pounding heart. "Can you read it?"

Saudade flipped back to the beginning, and a frown creased their brow. "There are portal coordinates here."

She felt faintly ill. "Please don't tell me we stole the *wrong book*."

What they'd *meant* to steal was a scriptological artifact that did not itself code for a new world, but instead could be used to edit the real world as if it were artificial. The editbook should not have coordinates for entry.

"Let's not despair just yet," said Saudade. "Not before we investigate the contents of this worldbook, at least."

Saudade stood and Willa followed them, leaving the book on the settee. Using whatever internal machinery allowed them to open a portal, Saudade generated a black disk as tall as a person, limned in iridescence where it cut through the air. The two of them walked through into a void of cold nothingness, and then on the next step, into a different world.

Willa found herself standing in a stone pavilion, Greek-style columns circling the margin of a smooth-paved platform. Beyond the pavilion floor, stone cliffs dropped sharply into a sea of swirling purple mist, the same mist surrounding them at a distance on all sides, marking the edges of this small pocket universe. In the center of the pavilion stood a broad stone pedestal with a large, leather-bound tome resting on it. And in a sphere around the book, some kind of electrical field sparked and glowed with eerie blue light.

Willa peered through. "So that's the editbook, do you think?"

"Hm." Saudade tapped their pointer finger against the barrier, which sparked brightly and made them wince and pull their hand away. "Someone has already gone to great lengths to ensure the editbook is not accessible for use."

Willa rubbed her hand against her face, thoughts racing. "This doesn't make sense. Let's run through what we know again: In spring of this year, there was a conflict between several parties for control of this editbook. Then in summer, something triggers a paradox in northern Italy, which gradually spreads across most of the planet, destabilizing the laws of physics and rendering the Earth uninhabitable. Only the editbook could do that."

Saudade nodded. "But the editbook was already well protected before we stepped in to interfere with the course of events."

Willa chewed her lip. The events leading up to the cataclysm were supposed to become clear once she returned to her time and acquired the editbook, but she felt less certain now than ever. "Let's head back to the summer cottage. If there's any chance we're going up against another time traveler, we'll need to set up some defenses."

"Certainly. I do have some ideas on that front."

Willa offered them a wry smile. "I was hoping you would."

Saudade nodded. A portal irised open at their invisible command, and Willa followed them through. "Do you have human matters to take care of? Eating or sleeping or some such?"

"Well," she said dryly, "I do have to do both of those activities every day, as boring and repetitive as that may seem, although neither urge is pressing at the moment. I suppose I should unpack."

Saudade waved open a smaller portal, reached inside, and produced Willa's carpetbag from the pocket universe they'd stashed it in. While Saudade examined the downstairs for security concerns, Willa carried her luggage upstairs. Only one bedroom had any furnishings at all, and those consisted of only a bed and a cedar chest. She was relieved to discover linens in the chest, so she could at least put sheets on the bed. But there was no wardrobe to hang her clothes in, which rather defeated her intent to unpack.

Willa sighed and rubbed her hand over the back of her neck, where it felt stiff from her cybernetic implant. The metallic material was smooth and oddly flexible under her fingers, like a silver starfish suctioned to her upper back.

When she'd rejoined Riley after getting the implant, the other girl had run tentative fingertips over the same place. "Does it hurt?"

"It's a little sore," Willa admitted, "but that's supposed to pass."

They were standing by the wall of windows in the A-frame chalet they'd been using as a safe house. Riley pulled her hand away from the implant to gnaw on her thumbnail instead, and she shifted her gaze to the forested mountains beyond the glass. Willa was too busy watching her to appreciate the view. Riley's brows were pinched with guilt and worry; despite the desperate little ball of tightness in Willa's chest at the idea of Riley blaming herself for this, Willa wasn't sure what to say to make it better.

"Riley . . . *everyone died* the first time around. Saudade, Jaideep. *You.* This is the technology I needed for rewriting that failed timeline. I don't regret it."

"I never wanted to corner you into making a choice like that. It's your body, and you shouldn't be coerced into modifying it—not even to save the planet."

Earnestly, she said, "I know what it's like when some aspect of my body feels incorrect, and this isn't it."

"But does it feel *right*?" Riley persisted.

Willa quirked her lips and answered dryly, "Well . . . I can't claim that I've always identified as a cyborg, but I suppose some aspects of one's identity can be flexible."

Riley cracked a grin despite herself. "You jerk. I'm trying to wallow in my guilt here, and you go breaking out the snark."

"I thought you were enamored with my 'snark.'"

Riley took Willa's hand with an unhesitating ease that

still surprised her every time. Lifting their clasped hands together, Riley planted a kiss on her wrist, where one branch of the implant ended. "I like every part of you."

In the half-furnished bedroom of the summer cottage, Willa scrubbed her palm against her hip, banishing the memory of touch. The last thing she ought to do was stand around their "secret lair," dwelling on the absence of lost loved ones while she waited for some unknown enemy to make the first move. No, she and Saudade needed to remain one step ahead, to do what they could to stay pro-active instead of reactive. She ought to be putting together a plan of action.

She would go into town tomorrow to pick up some supplies and hopefully hear some news. It was possible the events leading up to the cataclysm were already in progress. She needed to find out what kind of trouble her pazzerellone contemporaries had been cooking up, and mad scientists weren't exactly known for subtlety, so with luck it would be the noticeable kind.

Willa nodded to herself, drawing comfort from having a plan. There was work to do, and if she focused hard enough, it would leave no room for pining.

2

ARIS

1891, Firenze

ARISTOTELE GARIBALDI DOES not appreciate being locked in a cell with nothing but his own thoughts to keep him occupied, not in the least. It's a comfortable sort of imprisonment, as cells go—the basement level of the Order of Archimedes's headquarters has blessedly little in the way of squalor and rats, as might be expected to come standard in a city jail. A barred slit of a window high up on the wall allows him to judge the time of day, and he has a cot with a blanket and a privy alcove, both of which help to preserve some modicum of dignity despite how far he's fallen. But this is still a prison.

Two days ago, he was the son of the man who defeated the Kingdom of the Two Sicilies and was bringing the Kingdom of Venezia to heel, and soon would accomplish what no one had done since the fall of the Roman Empire:

uniting the disparate states of Italy into a single, glorious nation. Two days ago, he had a purpose, and he had his freedom, and he had a father. Now he has nothing.

Despite the late hour, Aris hears the other prisoner shifting around in her cell perpendicular to his. The wall between them is solid, so he hops off his cot and leans against the bars to see if he can get a glimpse of her. "Elsa!"

Still out of sight, she huffs and refuses to answer. Elsa is, ostensibly, his enemy, but the bottom line is that Aris is terribly bored and no small bit curious about how she came to find herself in a cell right beside him.

"You wound me, Elsa. Would simple conversation be so terrible?" It irks him, being ignored like this. "So you're forcing my hand, then, hm? I have no choice but to annoy a response out of you."

Elsa releases a put-upon sigh and shifts, coming into view as she approaches her own set of bars. Her black hair is a bit messy from attempted sleep; when she looks at him, her green eyes stand out in sharp contrast against the sienna tone of her skin.

"I have no doubt you'd excel at coercing my attention," she says. "What do you want, Aris?"

He smirks, enjoying the warm little seed of victory despite her cutting rejoinder. "I was only wondering how we came to find ourselves in the same position. It seems rather ungrateful of the Order to throw you in a cell after letting you do their dirty work."

Elsa rolls her eyes. "Retrieving the editbook from you

was my responsibility; my mother scribed it, and I am its steward. If I accomplished anything that the Order of Archimedes approved of, it was by coincidence."

"After everything you did to foil our plans—after turning *my own brothers* against me—now you refuse to come to heel when the Order snaps their fingers?" Aris carefully schools his face, showing only cool amusement where otherwise rage might boil. He does not have the luxury of allowing his temper to flare when they are trapped together like this.

Elsa, ever ready with a riposte, says, "I like to believe there's a middle ground between the Order's policy of abdicated responsibility in the guise of so-called 'political neutrality'—as if such a thing even exists—and your own brand of political activism, which involves rather more wholesale destruction of cities than I am comfortable with."

Aris opens his mouth to reply but is interrupted by a muffled sound from outside the cellblock. Elsa makes a shushing noise at him and leans into the bars, listening intently, her body tensing. With a soft *clack*, the door to the basement stairs opens, and in walks the tall, confident form of his once ally and now enemy: Vincenzo. He steps almost silently down the short hall of the cellblock, his hand hovering ready near his holstered revolver. Aris can feel Vincenzo's gaze land on him like heat from an open flame, but he says nothing and turns instead to face Elsa. Aris watches with helpless want; Vincenzo always had a rakish profile, even more so since his aquiline nose healed slightly crooked after a fight. A confusion of feelings he'd rather not examine churn in Aris's chest. Emotion never did him any favors.

"Vincenzo," Elsa says, relieved. "What is going on? I thought Porzia had a plan to get me out of here, but I've heard nothing from anyone."

"She was going to bargain for your freedom with the editbook, but . . ." Vincenzo winces. "It was stolen."

"Again?! For the love of—well who took it this time?"

"Wasn't me," Aris offers, and Vincenzo shoots him a look. "What? It wasn't! If I had minions at my beck and call, do you think I'd still be locked behind bars?"

Vincenzo turns back to Elsa. "Porzia didn't recognize one of the thieves. The other's a mechanist named Willa Marconi, who until recently was apprenticed to Augusto Righi."

"Righi? Oh." Elsa's eyes widen. "*That* Righi? So they're after revenge, then?"

"Dunno. Unlike some people"—Vincenzo glances meaningfully at Aris—"they didn't stick around long enough to monologue."

Aris suppresses an eye roll as Elsa apparently feels the need to inquire about the location and status of every person she's ever met—her mother, and her mentor, and her childhood friend whose name Aris hadn't bothered to remember before and certainly isn't going to store in his brain now, taking up valuable space where something useful could go instead. He tunes them out until they get back around to the escape plan.

Vincenzo solves the problem of Elsa's locked cell door in the most inelegant fashion possible: He jams an awl into the keyhole and simply breaks the lock with brute force. Aris almost laughs, except now the cell door is swinging open and there's nothing further to delay them, and a spike of genuine panic hits Aris in the chest.

"Vico, wait! You're not just going to leave me here, are you?"

Vincenzo finally turns to face him and addresses him directly. "Do you honestly think I'm going to let you out of there after what you did to Napoli? I was stationed with the Napolitano Carbonari rebels for more than a year! I had allies and friends in the city. Had, *past tense*, thanks to you."

"Come now, Vico—you can't truly believe that I *meant* to destroy the entire city. It was supposed to be a show of force, a threat, nothing more. It just . . . got out of hand. Controlling a volcanic eruption with the editbook was trickier than I anticipated."

It isn't a lie, exactly. The editbook is incredibly difficult to use with any degree of accuracy. And anyway, Aris has never had much use for objective truths—the truth is whatever he can get everyone in the room to believe, starting with himself. So, sure, if Vincenzo needs to believe him innocent, then he'll just have to be that.

"It *got out of hand*? That's your excuse?"

"Vico, please," Aris says, softening his tone. "I can't redeem myself from inside a cell."

Elsa snorts. "Since when are you interested in redemption?"

But Vincenzo looks torn. He wants to see something good inside Aris; he always has, and Aris is not above exploiting that fact, no matter how bittersweet Vincenzo's expectations may feel. And who knows? Maybe Vico truly can save him from his own darkness.

"I have been my father's weapon my whole life; I don't know how to do otherwise. But I could learn, you could teach me. You know I am adaptable."

Vincenzo glances at Elsa, a wordless plea in his eyes, but she says, "Don't look to me for permission. I'm not your commander. But if you set him free, whatever he does next—good or bad—is on you."

two weeks earlier, Trentino

Aris meets Elsa for the first time when she brings Vincenzo back to him.

His father's stronghold is a cold, impregnable fortress in the mountains. After years of separation, Leo has been home with them for only a few short weeks. His little brother is unsettled, unhappy at having to leave behind his friends, and for Aris it is a trial not to be short with him—is Aris not enough for him anymore, that he pines after others?

Then Elsa and Vincenzo brazenly stroll up to the front

gates, claiming to seek an alliance. In the years when Aris was in hiding with his father, Vincenzo has grown into a man. His cheeks hollowed a bit in his narrow face, jaw darkened with stubble, his once lanky, too-tall frame filled out with lean muscle. Aris thinks, smugly, that despite what his father might say about necessary sacrifices, it *is* possible to have everything he wants.

And yes, fine, so Aris also flirts outrageously with Elsa. She's sharp-witted and easy enough on the eyes, and it's an entertaining game to see how close he can get while trying to dig under her armor to find her true motivations for being here. He knows there's some sort of romantic entanglement between Leo and Elsa, but Leo belongs to Aris, and therefore anything that is Leo's is ultimately his.

Aris doesn't truly understand there's a problem until he lets himself into one of the guest bedrooms only to walk in on Vincenzo packing his bag.

"What are you doing?" Aris says, stunned into asking despite the obvious answer.

"What does it look like I'm doing?"

Aris steps into his personal space, almost close enough to physically impede him. "Vico, you're overreacting. Wait."

Vincenzo's hands keep working, folding a shirt and rolling it into a tight bundle with quick, angry movements. "Wait? Wait for what, exactly—for you to just once in your life discover a shred of sympathy? I'll hold my breath and die suffocating."

Aris shamelessly scrambles for an excuse. "I was try-ing to make you jealous. Isn't it obvious?"

"I shouldn't be surprised that Garibaldi's son can't tell the difference between loving people and toying with them." Vincenzo avoids meeting his gaze, as if to hide the real hurt pinching at the corners of his eyes.

A small seed of panic threatens to germinate inside Aris. "But you're the one I really want."

"I know this is going to come as a shock, but the world doesn't revolve around what you want," he retorts bitterly.

"I beg to differ." He rests a hand possessively on Vin-cenzo's hip, feigning confidence. "You're not going to leave me again. You love me."

Vincenzo plucks Aris's hand off his body and drops it. "You don't truly want me, and you certainly don't want Elsa. You just want to watch everyone around you dance to whatever tune you're playing."

"How can you think such things? You were my first."

"First kiss?" Vincenzo says. "Or first attempt at romantic manipulation?"

There is a chance here—Aris can see it so clearly—a chance to reveal something deep and true and intimate, to make himself vulnerable, an opportunity to give Vin-cenzo the power over Aris's heart that he so obviously desires. Aris does not take it.

"Fine. Walk away from me, then, and see what it gets you. As if you have *any relevance* aside from that which we provide. Ungrateful street rat," he lashes out, then stalks angrily out of the room. If it's over, let Vincenzo be the jilted party. Aris is untouchable, as his father taught him to be.

1884, Venezia

Aris is twelve when his fencing instructor brings a strange boy to their palazzo.

The boy is scrawny, with messily cropped hair and worn, poorly fitted clothes. Aris has never interacted much with other children, aside from Leo and Pasca, and certainly not one who looks like he should be sweeping chimneys instead of standing awkwardly in their expensive fencing salle, with its carefully maintained wood flooring and racks of beautiful weapons.

"This is Vincenzo," Signora Rosalinda says. "He'll give you a challenge at saber and foil."

"Hi!" says Leo, with that ten-year-old guilelessness.

Ignoring his brother, Aris holds his head high and sniffs. "We'll see about that."

Rosalinda selects a pair of foils from the rack, and Aris grinds the sole of his shoe against the dusting of fine sand atop the wood floor to test the footing. Signora Rosalinda does not favor the use of a planche indoors, as it puts too much limitation on one's footwork. Aris accepts a foil, pulls on a wire-mesh mask, and squares up against the chimney sweep, confident of his impending victory—until Rosalinda says allez and the bout begins.

Vincenzo fences like it's a *fight*, with no care for elegance or presentation, no energy wasted on making his form look pleasing to an audience. Aris is almost tempted to think of it as sloppy, except for the speed and precision of each movement. They trade lunges and ripostes, each of them feeling out the other's technique. Then Vincenzo crouches low and extends his leg, catching the top of his foot behind Aris's heel, and jerks his foot out from under him. Aris staggers and recovers his balance, but the tip of Vincenzo's foil has already touched his padded jacket, right over his heart.

Aris rips off his fencing mask and throws it down in a fit of anger. "You cheated!"

Vincenzo speaks for the first time, his voice soft but with a hint of teasing. "If you're dead, you can't complain I broke the rules."

The burning flash of Aris's rage smooths out into something warm and fond, and without really meaning to, Aris lets out a bark of laughter. "Two can play at that game, new kid."

As the weeks go by and Signora Rosalinda keeps bringing her protégé to the palazzo, Aris starts practicing more frequently on his own, determined to earn more of the impressed look Vincenzo gives him when he manages to surprise the other boy during a bout. Aris likes being the center of attention, though the only attention that *matters* is that of his father and brothers—or at least, that used to be true, before Vincenzo. Aris tries not to think about what it means, this unexpected desire for a friend. Aris has been raised to believe that his aptitude for mad science, just being a pazzerellone, makes him better than regular people; Vincenzo is clever and savvy in his own way, but he is not *one of them*, has no talent for mechanics or alchemy or scriptology.

Still, Aris wants to bask in Vincenzo's regard. He wants to claim Vincenzo for his collection, the way little Pasca hoards pretty pieces of sea glass. Aris finds excuses for the two of them to sneak off together—not *playing* exactly, since they are too old for such childish behavior, but in a city the size of Venezia there's plenty of trouble to get into and out of. And they do.

When Aris is thirteen, he starts to feel an odd sort of tension in the air when they're together, be it in or out of the fencing salle. It's not a *bad* feeling, exactly, but he doesn't understand what it is, and that irks him. All he knows is that the curve of Vincenzo's mouth is fascinating, and so are his long, dexterous hands. Sometimes Aris has dreams of a type he definitely can't tell his brothers about.

Instinct tells him that Father would not approve, though rationally, he's not certain which part he'd object to. That Vincenzo is also a boy? Or simply that Aris might develop loyalty for someone outside the family. Either way, Aris does not want Vincenzo to be labeled a distraction and sent away.

So he's very careful to make sure they won't get caught the first time he presses his mouth to Vincenzo's lips.

Aris's shoulder twinges with the threat of pain, his arm twisted back in a joint lock by some Veldanese friend of Elsa's. His own brother disarmed him and allowed this peasant to frog-march him into the library, and now Leo has the gall to raise his rapier at their father.

Ricciotti Garibaldi stands, cool and unaffected, beside the control panel with the single, large red button. Despite the indignity of his restraint, Aris feels a flash of pride— for his father's composure and conviction, for the ingenious design of the doomsday device Aris scribed into existence, and even in a small way for the bravery Leo has mustered to oppose their father. They may be at odds now, but one truth remains certain: No one can describe their family as *insignificant*.

"Don't," Leo warns with an edge of desperation, raising the tip of his rapier. "Father. Please. Don't make me do this."

"Don't be absurd," Father says. "You're not going to kill me, Leo."

Father reaches for the button that will collapse the entire city of Venezia into the sea. Dread floods through Aris, along with the sudden certainty that neither his father nor his brother will capitulate.

It almost doesn't look real when Leo lunges forward and sinks his rapier into Father's neck. No, this can't be happening . . . but Father's eyes widen and he makes a terrible, wet choking sound.

"I tried to tell you, Father: You don't know me anymore," Leo says, and pulls the blade out.

There is blood on Leo's steel, and panic kicks Aris hard in the chest. "Noooo! Father!" He thrashes against the hold restraining him and pain shoots down his arm. "Father!"

Father stumbles and clutches at the wound in his throat, unable to breathe through the flow of blood. He goes to his knees and slumps bonelessly across the carpet. But Aris is a pazzerellone of incomparable skill, and he'll be damned if he lets his own flesh and blood perish from so simple a wound, when science can surely fix this.

"Listen to me, Leo! There's still time, I can fix him, it's not too late," Aris says urgently, his mind racing ahead to the challenge. He will need access to an alchemy lab at the very least, though the editbook might also suffice as a tool for reviving the dead. "Leo, Leo! We can make this right. We can put our family back together. Just let me go!"

Leo turns to face Aris, his gaze hollow and shocked, but with no hint of the wavering regret Aris expects to find there. "I'm so sorry, Aris, but I don't want to fix him. Don't you see? Nothing could ever make our family right."

No, it can't end like this, after everything Aris has done to hold on to his family. *No!* The feelings are so awful he cannot even put names to them, so he just screams.

And where is Vincenzo, when Aris's whole world falls apart? He's not there with him; Vincenzo is never there when Aris truly needs him.

Vincenzo wavers, glancing between the just-freed Elsa standing beside him and the bars still imprisoning Aris. He flips the awl in the air and catches it, fidgeting as he struggles to decide. Then his wrinkled brow smooths out with resolve, and he steps over to the cell.

Despite Aris's ironclad self-confidence, he feels *surprised*. A quick self-examination reveals that he really didn't believe Vincenzo would help him. He thought—some part of him still fears—that he burned the bridge between them too thoroughly, and Vincenzo would abandon him to his fate now. Vincenzo apparently didn't think it was important enough to show up for that fateful confrontation between Leo and Father, and his absence proved there is only one person Aris can rely on: himself.

Vincenzo pauses with the awl poised against the keyhole and pins Aris with his gaze. "We're going to Napoli, and you're going to use that giant brain of yours to help with the relief efforts. Repair some of the damage you caused. Try to weasel out of it, and I'll put you back in your cage myself. Understand?"

Well, that's taking the whole *redemption* thing a bit more literally than he expected. But such a deal will achieve his immediate goal of getting the hell out of this basement. "I place myself entirely in your hands, Vico."

Vincenzo snorts, eyeing Aris as if to gauge whether the innuendo is intentional. Where the sleeves of his shirt are rolled up, the muscles in his forearm visibly tense, and the lock breaks with a metallic *crunch*. Then he pulls the barred cell door open with one hand while the other reaches behind him to tuck the awl away in the small satchel he wears strapped across his back.

Aris steps out of his cell with as much dignity as he can muster, moving to stand just a little too close to Vico. "Thank you."

Aris lets his gaze flick down to the other man's lips. He feels adrift in the world, cut loose from the mooring of his former purpose, alone and directionless. Perhaps Vico can give him a purpose; perhaps Vico can *be* his direction.

Vincenzo swallows thickly and whispers, "Don't," before Aris can lean in for a kiss.

"I can be patient," Aris replies, intent and undeterred.

At that, Vico huffs out a laugh. "Patient. *You*. Now that I'd like to see."

Elsa rolls her eyes. "Can we go now? Need I remind you both that we haven't actually escaped yet?"

Vincenzo shakes himself and strides past Aris, leading the way up the basement stairs. On the main floor, he pauses at a junction between two hallways, holds up a hand for silence, and listens. Aris inches forward and peers around the corner. Given the length of the hallway, he can catch only a narrow view of the lobby beyond—just the sitting area with its leather armchairs, empty as far as he can tell—but he can hear the metallic clanking of at least one bot on patrol.

"What now?" Elsa whispers. "We can't exactly stroll

out the front door, unless you've found a way to disable the Order's security bots."

The corner of Vincenzo's mouth quirks a little. "We don't have to go out the front."

Instead, Vincenzo leads them farther back into the rear of the building and up a narrow stairwell. *There must be roof access*, Aris concludes, his mind already leaping forward to how they might escape from there: *Zipline to a neighboring building? Rappel down the side?* From his confident stride, Vincenzo must have a plan already in place. Sure enough, they crawl out a hatch and emerge onto a shallowly sloped red tile roof, the night breeze bringing fresh air to the city. Aris inhales deeply, the air tasting of freedom in the back of his throat.

From his satchel, Vincenzo pulls out a curved brass handle that Aris briefly mistakes for a flintlock pistol before he recognizes the short muzzle of a Coston flare holder. Vincenzo tucks a flare cartridge into the end and pulls the trigger to ignite the fizzing red chemical glow, then raises his arm, the holder spitting red light against the darkness.

There's not much city noise at this late hour, so as soon as Aris thinks to listen for it, he can make out the thrum of an approaching airship. He scans the sky, his night vision still adjusting, until his gaze lands on the familiar silhouette of two flexible wings flanking an oblong gasbag.

"That's my airship!" Aris says, affronted that someone else would dare appropriate his invention.

Mildly, Elsa says, "If it offends you so, you're free to invent your own way off this rooftop."

Except he manifestly is *not*, since his agreement with Vincenzo requires that he travel with them. Aris shoots her a glare.

The airship taxis to a stop above them, and the access ramp at the rear of the gondola cracks open, spilling light from the interior. At the end of the lowering ramp crouches a brass-haired, amber-eyed young man, ready to toss a rope ladder down to them. Aris's chest feels suddenly tight; strange, how even now a part of him is still expecting his brother to somehow be ten years old forever. But he looks so grown up.

"Leo," Aris croaks through a throat stiff with unexamined emotion.

His brother's eyes land on him and widen in shock at his presence. Leo turns to Vincenzo and, over the thrum of the airship's steam engine, shouts a single word: "No!"

3

FARAZ

1891, Venezia

FARAZ HUNG BACK by the wrought-iron front gate of the palazzo and eyed the funeral gondola dubiously as the crew of four oarsmen maneuvered the ponderous vessel to a stop at the dock. Aside from being larger than strictly necessary, the gondola was downright gaudy, with a gold-painted angel at the prow and an intricately carved awning to shade the coffin. Leo didn't even *have* a coffin to put the body in. This was going to turn into quite the headache, Faraz could already tell. He shouted down to the gondola crew that they'd be ready in a moment and went back inside.

Ricciotti Garibaldi's Venetian palazzo had been lovingly reconstructed after the fire in 1886 that had convinced Leo he was an orphan, and Faraz couldn't help but wonder if it felt haunted with childhood memories, despite not truly being the same home. He crossed the airy entry hall with its grand staircase and let himself into the library, where Garibaldi's blood soaked the carpet and Garibaldi's corpse lay wrapped in a bedsheet. Leo stood over it, just staring; he'd moved the body onto the improvised stretcher by himself, instead of waiting for Faraz's help.

Faraz wanted to be supportive, but it was difficult when he felt so conflicted about his own role in all of this. He had always considered himself a person of strong morals, but his best friend had been cornered into choosing the lesser of two evils, and Faraz had stood by and let Leo commit patricide to save the city. Faraz had tried to pray for clarity, but how could he know if they'd done the right thing in a situation where every option was terrible? And in the absence of pure remorse, how could he seek absolution for his complicity in Garibaldi's death?

Softly, Faraz said, "It's time."

Leo nodded, dazed. "All right."

Faraz was taller, but Leo was strong for his size, so Faraz took the feet end of the stretcher, and they shuffled slowly out the front entrance. The crew at the dock tried to argue about the absence of a coffin and grumbled that it *simply wasn't done* for mourners to ride in the same gondola as the deceased. Faraz smoothed it over with a modest increase to the transport fee, while Leo stood by silently, staring into the water as if he couldn't even hear the argument.

Soon enough, they were gliding through the canals of Venezia. Strange—only yesterday, these same canals were infested with sea monsters created by the editbook, and today the city was back to business as usual. They rowed underneath a construction crew evaluating the damage done to a footbridge. To Faraz, it seemed almost disrespectfully resilient, the rest of the city moving on like nothing happened.

Leo was terribly quiet, numb and unresponsive in a way Faraz had never seen in their years of friendship. Faraz didn't know how to help such a hurt. He hardly understood it, let alone had any clue how to find the words that would lessen it.

Faraz could barely recall his own biological parents, and he had no siblings—none that he knew of, anyway—so Leo was the only person he might call a brother. To him, family were the people he chose to be with, to rely upon and place his trust in: Leo and Porzia most of all, but more recently, even Elsa. The same was not true for Leo, though, who had lived as the middle child of three before his separation from his father and brothers, and for whom family was such a confused concept. By Faraz's definition, family *couldn't* betray you, but in Leo's idea of family, the betrayal was practically the defining feature.

So Faraz let Leo have his silences and didn't push him to explain the emotional minefield he must be trying to navigate. Faraz showed his support in the way he knew he could: by handling the logistics while Leo stared at the world around them like he wasn't sure any of it was real. He didn't feel like he was doing enough, but Leo was the brother he'd chosen for himself, and after everything they'd been through, he wouldn't lose Leo to grief. Faraz could be patient and wait for Leo to talk, whenever his friend was ready to open those floodgates, and he could keep his own doubts to himself.

His gaze lingered on the wrapped corpse. Was it too late to seek guidance from Allah with the deed already done?

The cemetery island of San Michele sat in the lagoon as if it were a foreign object dropped there, the water going right up to the low stone wall that delineated the island's margin. Green shrubbery and the tops of a few buildings seemed to peer over the wall at them. The gondola crew docked, and Faraz asked them for directions to the crematorium.

In the last decade or so, cremation had become popular among very different groups of people: the poor who couldn't afford better than a pauper's mass grave; the rational, scientific-minded portion of the upper class who felt public health should be a larger concern than the funerary dictates of the Catholic church; and, ironically, the paranoid anti-scientific social movements who feared there were alchemists lurking in every cemetery waiting to rob the graves of fresh corpses for their nefarious experiments.

Faraz himself wasn't the sort of alchemist who worked on humans, but even for those who did, it was rarely if ever necessary—let alone desirable—to raid corpses for raw materials. Unlike Leo, none of the people who got the vapors over imagined grave robbing had an older brother who was both very brilliant and very angry, and actually might try to revive their father from death given half a chance. Leo hadn't said as much, but Faraz could tell he needed this to be over; he needed the destructive finality of incinerating that horrifying possibility. So to the crematorium they went.

Privately, Faraz didn't see how disposing of the evidence would provide meaningful closure. The truth of what they'd done—both good and bad—would not go up in smoke.

The crematorium looked like a Greek monument—a narrow but tall building fronted with columns, the only real indication of its purpose being the smokestack jutting up toward the back, ominously dark against the blue of the sky. That, and the scent of ash carried in the air.

Inside, Faraz had to once again argue with the workers. No, it wasn't good enough to leave the body and trust they'd get around to burning it eventually. Yes, he really did insist on seeing Garibaldi go into the cremation chamber himself. Fine, they would leave right afterward instead of waiting several hours for the process to complete, and the ashes could be delivered to the palazzo when it was done.

Faraz sighed. Inshallah, this was the last of the day's troubles.

* * *

Faraz stepped out onto the open-air arcade on the second floor of the palazzo. He went up to the railing between two columns and leaned over, the Grand Canal stretched out below him, and he stuck two fingers in his mouth to blow a piercing whistle. The sound echoed a bit against the buildings on the opposite side of the canal. He waited.

After a few minutes passed, a small silhouette wheeled against the blue sky. The creature swooped in and caught a perch on the iron railing right next to where Faraz rested his hands. Skandar's body was composed of two wings, lots of tentacles, and one giant eye. Faraz smiled down at his alchemical creation.

"There you are," Faraz said. "Been keeping busy, patrolling the city for krakens to screech at?"

Skandar gave a slow blink of that single, expressive eye.

"I'm sure you've been doing a very good job," Faraz continued. He nudged the creature with one hand, and Skandar took the signal to crawl up his arm, releasing the railing so they could head inside. But motion below caught his attention, and Faraz paused long enough to look down on a gondola pulling up at the palazzo's front entrance. He sighed. "Let's go see what that's about, shall we?"

He made it halfway down the grand staircase before the bell chimed. Leo came shuffling into the front hall, looking a bit bleary, and Faraz felt a spike of annoyance that his friend had barely managed to lie down for half an hour before some inconsiderate interruption summoned him up again.

Leo rubbed at his face with one hand. "What is it now?"

"I'll handle it. Here, take Skandar," Faraz said, passing the creature to Leo's shoulder.

Leo looked a little nonplussed at being made into a perch for a tentacle monster, but it was hardly his first time. In Faraz's opinion, Leo really needed to be hugging a puppy or something right now, but he didn't have any puppies or kittens, so his own companion creature was the best he could offer. Skandar, being a good sport and surprisingly perceptive about human emotions, gently poked Leo in the cheek with one tentacle in an attempt at comfort.

Faraz let himself through the front door and opened the wrought-iron gate beyond it. A small boy in short pants and a newsboy cap was standing on the front dock; behind him was a delivery gondola with a gray-bearded man handling the pole. The boy looked up from the thick cardstock in his hands and eyed Faraz skeptically.

"Telegram delivery for Leo Trovatelli?" the boy said. In the hall behind Faraz, Leo let out a soft, wounded noise at the sound of his old alias, the surname that he hadn't known was a lie until a month ago.

"That's us," Faraz replied firmly, taking the telegram and dismissing the boy.

Their friends wouldn't have bothered sending a telegram unless something went wrong, and his heart already felt heavy before he even looked at the words. Faraz scanned the contents of the telegram quickly before passing it to Leo. The message was written in the sort of vague short-hand that would be meaningless to a stranger, but clear to them: The editbook was back in play, Porzia was pursuing it, and Vincenzo needed an exfil strategy for Elsa.

"Oh" was all Leo said when he finished reading it.

Faraz tucked his hands into his trouser pockets, reluctant to push Leo but equally aware that he didn't have much choice now. "Think you can figure out how to operate that airship we've got docked on the roof?"

"Do you even need to ask?" Leo replied, showing a flicker of his usual confidence for the first time since Garibaldi's death.

The corner of Faraz's mouth quirked. "If you want to take it as a challenge to your skills as a mechanist, that's entirely up to you."

Skandar reached curiously for the telegram, eager to participate, and Leo relinquished it despite the fact that tentacles weren't really meant for holding cardstock, and the telegram folded and crumpled in Skandar's grip. Quietly, Leo said, "It could be good. Having something else to focus on."

"Sure," Faraz agreed. Privately, he thought what they actually needed was to catch a damn break—to have just one uninterrupted day in which to process guilt and grief. But that was not the hand they'd been dealt, not today.

*　*　*

Leo left Faraz at the controls in the pilot's cabin as he went astern to open the gangway. Faraz had watched him pilot the airship all the way from Venezia to Firenze, and all he really needed to do was keep a hand on the wheel, but even that made him a little nervous. Skandar was no help, clinging to his shoulder and occasionally fanning wings in his face with excitement. At least manning the wheel didn't require him to look *down*; his fear of heights was mostly under control, so long as he maintained a polite fiction for himself about how they surely weren't hanging in the air high above the ground.

"Hold her steady!" Leo called, the words muddled beneath the roar of the steam engine that sat between them in the midship.

"What do you think I'm trying to do?" Faraz muttered to himself.

How difficult was it to pick up two people off a roof? This was taking too long; they were floating low over the building, entirely exposed, and now it sounded like they were shouting at each other? Faraz couldn't make out the content of the argument from where he was stuck holding the controls.

Finally, it was Elsa who squeezed past the engine into the cockpit to relieve him.

"What is going on back there?"

Elsa rolled her eyes—a habit she seemed to have picked up from Porzia. "Aris talked Vincenzo into bringing him along. Leo seems to think we have time to put Aris back down in his cell, which we manifestly do not."

"Fantastic," Faraz said dryly. "Can you get us out of here?"

She took the wheel from him. "On it. Can you talk some sense into Leo?"

"When have either of us ever succeeded at that?"

Elsa smirked. "What's that phrase they have in English? 'Hope springs eternal'?"

Faraz shuffled down the narrow passage alongside the engine and out into the rear of the airship, which was set up more like a mobile laboratory than a passenger compartment. Vincenzo was cranking the winch to close the gangway while Leo and Aris got in each other's faces.

"You *belonged* behind bars!" Leo shouted.

"At least I didn't commit *patricide*," Aris spat.

"The two of you were going to sink the city of Venezia into the sea! I had no choice but to play the numbers game. He forced my hand."

Aris narrowed his eyes. "You still did it."

Faraz's stomach dropped as the airship lurched into motion, gaining altitude.

Leo glanced up, the sudden motion interrupting them, and transferred his ire from Aris to Faraz. "What's Elsa doing? We can't leave! Tell her to take us back down."

"We don't have time to argue about this here," Faraz said, trying to inject some reason into the heated moment. "Even at night, we're not exactly inconspicuous, floating right above their headquarters. Let's not find out the hard way if the Order has defenses that can shoot down an airship."

"I can't believe this." Leo tossed his hands in the air and spun away from them, but there wasn't much room for pacing within the confines of the gondola. "What are we even supposed to *do* with him now?"

Vincenzo folded his arms. "I'm headed back to Napoli. There's a humanitarian crisis going on, thanks to him," he said with a nod toward Aris, "and he's going to be put to work saving some of the people he endangered."

Aris's expression shifted from furious to sour and he grumbled, "I'm standing right here."

"And we're going to talk about you as if you aren't," Leo snapped back, "because I can't even stand to *look* at you! None of this would've happened without you helping along his mad schemes."

Faraz's eyes went wide with realization. *Oh*, so Leo was coping with what he'd done by blaming Aris for the whole thing. Assigning fault did seem to be the unofficial national pastime for Italians, or so Faraz had observed in his years of residence. Not that Aris was exactly blameless, but it didn't seem like a productive strategy for moving toward healing.

He set a quelling hand on Leo's arm and could feel how tense his friend was. "Why don't you go relieve Elsa?" Swapping control of the airship was a good excuse to get Leo away from Aris without it feeling like a retreat.

Leo huffed, spun on his heel, and stalked down the narrow passage to the cockpit. Faraz moved to follow, but then hesitated, turning back to Aris. It was still a little strange, seeing Leo's unusual amber-colored eyes looking out of someone else's face. Aris had dark brown hair instead of Leo's and Pasca's blond, but the resemblance among the three of them was undeniable. *Like they belong together,* he thought with a small pang.

Faraz said, "Friendly bit of advice: Maybe try *not* to escalate every conversation into a duel?"

"Don't tell me how to handle Leo. He's *my* brother."

Right, well, no one could say Faraz didn't try to broker for peace. "Fine, do what you like," he said mildly. "You're the one who's losing him."

Aris jerked, almost as if he'd been slapped. If looks could start fires, Faraz would surely combust under Aris's glare. Faraz just shook his head, resigned to accomplishing nothing here, and followed Leo into the cockpit.

"But you're good at managing Aris," Leo was saying to Elsa, who was still piloting the airship.

She winced, clearly hating to deny him anything. "Leo . . . the editbook is missing. It's my responsibility to ensure no one uses it. Someone else will have to keep an eye on Aris."

"I can't deal with him right now," said Leo. "And we both know Vincenzo is compromised when it comes to Aris. Please."

Elsa turned to Faraz as if she was hoping for an alternate volunteer, but Faraz showed his palms. "Don't look at me. I barely know Aris—I'm hardly the best candidate for someone to keep him in line."

Leo's brow lowered with determination. "The edit-book is not just your responsibility, Elsa. I know I've . . . made some mistakes, trying to protect you instead of trusting you can handle things. But Porzia and Faraz have never wavered in their commitment to securing the edit-book. It's our fight, too. We can handle it."

Elsa took one hand off the controls and grabbed Leo's shirt collar, pulling him in for a quick, hard kiss. "You're going to owe me for this, you know."

Relief loosened the set of Leo's shoulders at her capit-ulation, but Faraz chewed the inside of his cheek. Avoid-ance was a temporary solution at best. The Aris problem wasn't going away, and Leo would have to confront his feelings about his brother sooner or later. Which meant Faraz needed to work up a strategy for making peace. He might not know how to repent for his role in what hap-pened, but if he could nudge these brothers onto a path toward forgiveness, that would be a good start.

Faraz had his work cut out for him.

4

WILLA

1891, countryside south of Bologna

WILLA TRUDGED BACK up the dirt road to the summer cottage, feet sore in her low-heeled walking boots. The town of Riolo was only a couple kilometers away, but her satchel was weighed down with groceries, lamp oil and candles, soap, and other odds and ends they'd need. Maybe she should have risked asking Saudade to do the shopping. By stashing things in a pocket dimension, Saudade could carry effectively unlimited weight without being burdened. Except Saudade wasn't familiar with the worth of a lira in 1891, or when and how to barter for a better price, which—on top of their coloring and too-tall android height—would make them memorable.

Long walks through the country had not been a common activity in her urban life before. More than anything else, these fields and woods reminded her of the trek across

East Germany in 1988 with Riley and Jaideep. Dresden and the surrounding countryside had been recently evacuated into scribed worlds, so they'd traversed an eerie landscape of empty buildings, abandoned cars, and fallow fields.

"What was it like?" Willa had asked. "Growing up with no access to the real world, I mean."

Dryly, Jaideep said, "Well, the horizon's a lot closer, when there are literal edges to the world you live in."

Riley lightly smacked his arm. "Wiseass. Greater Bostonia is thirty miles wide, it's not like you run into the edge every day. And there's a transit system for portaling between worlds."

"Anyway," said Jaideep, "you don't notice the fake parts when it's all you've ever known. The programmers actually put a ton of effort into replicating parts of Earth as closely as they could—so much so that nobody tried to innovate. The whole scientific field still has a depressing amount of conventional thinking."

Riley kicked a pine cone off the road as they walked. "Hey, at least it means a programming degree gives you actual job prospects. Experimental physicists don't really have marketable skills outside academia, as my mother regularly reminded me."

"You make it sound so normal," Willa said. "But the—what did you call it?—the 'servers' with the script had to be anchored in the real world, where they could be eaten up by the cataclysm if the stabilizers failed. Weren't you afraid all the time?"

Riley shrugged. "How much do you worry about, I don't know, cholera epidemics on an average day? You can't spend your whole life stressing about something you have no control over."

Jaideep snorted and shot Riley a wry glance. "Well, *you* can."

"Okay, yeah, but I have an exceptional talent for maintaining anxiety. It's basically a marathon sport for me."

Willa missed that about Riley—how easily she talked about anything, how entirely unashamed she was to show herself. Jaideep had been more reserved with Willa when they first met, but that was lingering grief making him reluctant. Now Willa understood, all too well, how impossible it was to contemplate letting in new people when all you wanted was your old people back. Even the limited interaction of haggling with the market vendors in Riolo had exhausted her tolerance for strangers. Willa sighed and adjusted the stack of newspapers in her arms; the summer cottage coming into view as she approached was a relief.

Opening the front door, Willa called out, "Saudade?"

"Sitting room!"

Willa followed the sound of their voice. Saudade was running a hand along a windowsill, as if examining the cottage's weak spots for potential points of forced entry. They gave a satisfied nod and turned to Willa. "You recall Petrichor's early-warning system in the safe house? I've set up something like that."

"Doesn't that involve temporal manipulation? I thought we wouldn't be able to do any time travel now that we've got the editbook." As Willa understood it, a person or object that was critical to maintaining the current timeline had a vanishingly low probability of time-traveling—a temporal portal would simply refuse to open in its proximity.

"You and I are stuck in the now, so long as we want to hold on to the editbook. But that doesn't stop us from cheating a little by receiving hints from the near future. My supplies aren't infinite, but I did bring a few tricks in my metaphorical sleeves." Saudade's gaze flicked to the stack of newspapers Willa carried. "What's the news?"

Grimly, Willa said, "Someone had a busy week with the editbook."

She dropped her armload on the settee. She'd managed to wrangle a few recent issues of the two premiere daily newspapers—*Corriere della Sera* and *La Stampa*—both published in the Kingdom of Sardinia and distributed throughout the Italian states. The papers had headlines like VOLCANIC ERUPTION DEVASTATES NAPOLI, KRAKENS INVADE VENEZIA!, SARDINIAN MILITARY MOBILIZED, and even POPE CONDEMNS ATTACKS AS HERESY. Saudade came over and pawed through the stack, eyebrows rising as they skimmed the ledes.

"This is worse than I anticipated."

"It's certainly not good." Willa pulled one of the wooden chairs closer and slumped into it, letting her satchel slide off her shoulder to the floor. "At least there's no evidence that anyone has tried to use the editbook for temporal manipulation yet. Did you have a chance to examine the script in the worldbook we stole?"

"Yes." Saudade picked up the lockbox worldbook from where they'd left it on the settee and stroked their fingers down the spine, like petting a cat. "The loopholes written into the script that allow access to the editbook are fairly specific. From context, I'd presume the scriptologist responsible is Porzia Pisano."

To Willa, Porzia was only a passing acquaintance, but she'd been present in the conference room when Willa and Saudade stole the book from the Order of Archimedes. Willa wished she could recall more about the other girl. Porzia was around the same age—seventeen or eighteen, she thought—and a scriptologist from an old-money, old-influence pazzerellone family based out of Pisa. Privileged in quite a different way from how Willa had been raised, brought up in the ivory tower instead of the aristocracy.

Willa said, "Could you get through the energy barrier protecting the editbook if you had to?"

Saudade tilted their head to the side, considering. "I could probably do a spectral analysis and determine a frequency that would act as destructive interference to dampen the energy field."

By the standards of her time, Willa was an expert on electromagnetic radiation, but devising a way through a scriptologically created barrier could have kept her occupied for weeks even with access to proper laboratory equipment. "So whoever is responsible for the cataclysm has skills comparable to an android time agent native to the twenty-first century, or they're the person who put the editbook inside that world to begin with. Namely, Porzia."

Saudade held up the newspaper edition with the headline about krakens. "This seems apocalyptic enough to catch the attention of an unscrupulous time traveler."

Willa unpinned her hair to run her fingers through it, fixing the slight mess her walk had made of it. "I think we should look into Porzia—see if we can determine if she belongs on our list of suspects."

"We have a list of suspects, now?" Saudade replied, sounding amused.

"We'll have the start of one if Porzia's name is on it."

"All right." Saudade set down the lockbox worldbook and the newspaper. "If we're going sleuthing, I'd better get changed for the occasion."

Saudade stepped into a portal and returned a minute later, having exchanged their futuristic blue jumpsuit for brown trousers and a waistcoat over an off-white work shirt.

Willa raised her eyebrows. "Look at you, with the sartorial subtlety. I didn't realize you were acquainted with the concept."

"What is the point of having a pocket universe full of

my collected historical costumes if I only ever get to wear the boring ones?" Saudade sighed and looked down at themselves. "But on occasion, sacrifices must be made."

Willa fixed her hair into a properly modest updo again while she considered what supplies to bring along. Her lockpicks, certainly; Saudade had only a middling comprehension of mechanical rather than electronic security measures.

Glancing over at the settee, Willa chewed her lip. "Should we take the editbook with us?"

"Hm. Best not, in case we get ourselves into trouble. And it's not precisely unattended here—I'll know before anyone breaches the house."

"Then I suppose we're ready. How's your mental image of nineteenth-century Pisa?"

"Easy. Leaning Tower." As part of their android design, Saudade had the incredible advantage of being able to open a portal anywhere in the world, except that for the portal to connect correctly, they required sufficient knowledge of the destination. And Saudade had no prior experience with this century, since the Continuity Agency always avoided sending its agents so far upstream, and in fact had been actively deceiving them all about the nature of the cataclysm. The Agency's founder, Norn, had been committed to preserving this precise timeline, spatiotemporal devastation included—so much so that Saudade's best friend sacrificed himself to stop Norn.

Saudade touched Willa's shoulder. "Are you all right?"

"Sorry." Willa shook herself. "Just thinking about Petrichor and Norn."

"Ah." Saudade fidgeted with the buttons on their waistcoat, avoiding eye contact. "Some things are easier if you simply don't think of them." When they looked up, their smile was weak and pained.

Willa recognized that was her cue to drop the matter entirely, but her thoughts kept spinning onward like well-oiled gears. "It just . . . still doesn't really make sense, you know? Why was Norn so determined to protect a timeline in which a major paradox occurs? Who gave her that directive?"

Saudade's brow furrowed and they sounded troubled. "I don't know. Perhaps her calculations worked out differently from mine, and she concluded that an attempt to correct the cataclysm might actually make it worse."

"Perhaps," Willa allowed. That answer didn't sit right with her, but she didn't wish to argue in circles, especially not with the loss of Petrichor still raw for Saudade. Was Petrichor's sacrifice more palatable if it turned out Norn had been well-intentioned but wrong, instead of driven by selfish or petty motivations? Willa didn't see how either option would be comforting, but it wasn't her grief, and she had to let Saudade deal with it in their own way.

Pisa was a small city, only half as populous as Bologna, but Willa still felt some tension in her spine unwind at the familiar bustle of the narrow cobblestone streets and wide-open piazzas. The rattle of carriage wheels, the smell of roasting coffee from a nearby café, a loud argument over the price of a delivery. *Familiar.* Willa may not have been much of a people person, but she was a city person—she liked this odd combination of anonymity and connectedness. Both were sorely lacking in the future cities she'd seen in her recent travels, especially Kairopolis, the scribed homeworld of the androids. Kairopolis was more akin to a fever dream than a recognizable city. Pisa practically felt like home by comparison.

"If I'm not mistaken, that is it," Willa said, pointing to a building on the opposite side of the street. "The ancestral home of the Pisanos, called Casa della Pazzia."

Saudade narrowed their eyes, but responded only with a noncommittal *hmm*. Even Willa had to admit that the place was a bit much. Despite the name, Casa della Pazzia did not look much like a house. With its Greek Revival facade and prominent domed roof toward the back, it seemed more akin to an academic building belonging on a university campus.

"I have no idea what kind of defenses they might have," Willa continued.

Saudade cocked their head to the side. "I'm not detecting any wireless transmissions."

"You better not be," she grumbled. Before she was accidentally drafted into being a time traveler, wireless telegraphy had been the focus of Willa's research, and she would've felt really irked if some other pazzerellone had figured out how to implement alternating current technology for practical use before her.

"All right, let's go then." Saudade set off in a sudden burst of decisiveness, striding around the side of the building.

Willa scrambled to catch up with them. "What are you doing? Do you have a plan to get inside?"

"Yes." Saudade grinned. "I'm going to ask nicely."

While Willa sputtered an incoherent protest, Saudade located a discreet side door that opened onto an alley smelling pungently of urine. The servants' entrance, assumedly.

Saudade rapped on the door. "Delivery!"

"You're not even carrying anything," Willa hissed.

"Easily rectified." Still grinning, Saudade reached their arm into a small portal and withdrew a large package wrapped in brown butcher paper.

Willa just shook her head, her ability to be astonished long since exhausted. "You just had that ready to go, did you?"

"I've talked my way into a lot of buildings in a lot of eras."

They both waited. Willa wrinkled her nose at the reek and was silently grateful that she'd put on ankle-length working skirts that morning—it was not worth the added propriety to have her hems dragging. Saudade stood tall and unaffected, but after another minute, they knocked again. No one answered the door.

"Lockpick time?" Willa said.

Saudade deflated. "Oh, very well, you win."

Willa took out her lockpicks and bent to get a closer look at the lock plate. Saudade made the ridiculous package vanish into a portal, peered down the end of the alley to make sure they were unobserved, and then made their palm glow with electric light so Willa could better see what she was doing. It was a lever tumbler mechanism, and she eyeballed the size of the keyhole to select a torsioner and lever pick of the proper length. A little fiddling with depressing the levers and a twist of her torsion tool, and the bolt surrendered.

On the other side of the door was a short, poorly lit hallway leading into a kitchen beyond. Willa paused in the open doorway, listening for sounds of movement inside, but heard no one. She shot a questioning glance at Saudade close behind her, but the android shook their head, not hearing anything, either. Willa snuck forward, and then her breath caught in her throat—the kitchen was unlike anything Willa had ever seen. The stoves and counters and washbasins were obscured within a mess of mechanical arms, all of them motionless, as if the room itself were waiting for its cue.

"It's fully automated," Willa said, swallowing down her irritation that someone had invented such an incredible mechanism, and then used it for nothing more than running their private kitchen. She couldn't help but imagine possible applications for the machine tool industry, or even textiles. The Kingdom of Sardinia was lagging sorely behind Britain and Germany in terms of industrialization, and the Order of Archimedes just sat on inventions like this, doing nothing meaningful with them.

While Willa stewed in her frustrations, Saudade walked the margins of the room, tapping on the walls until they found a hidden panel to pry open. They mucked around with the wires and cables they found inside the wall, and then—much to Willa's consternation—pulled a wire out of their own wrist and plugged themself into the house.

"Is that safe?!"

"It's fine, probably." Saudade shrugged. "Anyway, we're in luck: The whole house is wired for audiovisual detection."

"A surveillance system?"

They *hmm*ed doubtfully. "It's wired more like a nervous system, as if the house itself has a sentient construct built into the walls. Though it appears to be inactive at the moment. Come look at this."

Saudade held up their other palm and projected a two-dimensional holographic viewscreen into the air. Willa stepped closer to stand at their shoulder. Despite everything she'd witnessed in the future, a spark of awe still struck Willa when she saw Saudade make such casual use of advanced technology.

"Here's the foyer," Saudade said as the image resolved to show them a large, round room.

The camera angle looked down at the space from high up on one wall, so it took Willa a moment to make sense of what she was seeing. The plaster was destroyed in several places around the room where wall-mounted guns had apparently burst forth, though the weapons seemed to hang quiescent now. The inlaid tile floor reflected the light as if it had been mopped to clear the plaster dust, but there were mottled, red-brown stains permanently soaked into the grout between the tiles.

Willa squinted at the image. "Are those *bloodstains*? What happened here?"

"Hrm. Perhaps something that would explain why the internal systems have been deactivated."

Saudade flipped through a series of rooms, each proving just as empty as the foyer: a dining hall with one long table, but no place settings laid out; a children's dormitory with a dozen small beds in two neat rows along the walls; a warmly lit, multistory octagonal library. Saudade paused, cocked their head to the side.

"We've been there."

Willa had to mentally tilt the image a bit before the familiarity clicked for her. "Oh! That's where we came out when we portaled back to the real world from Veldana."

To reduce temporal resistance, they'd executed the time jump upstream to the nineteenth century from within the scribed world Veldana—the oldest continuously populated artificial pocket universe. And here it was, the Veldana worldbook in the possession of the Pisanos. A coincidence? Willa was not comfortable with the extent to which their mission seemed intertwined with whatever Porzia Pisano was up to here and now.

After a moment, Saudade went back to cycling through the security feeds. Finally, they landed on a cluttered office with two people inside. Porzia sat across a desk from an older woman who looked like she could be a relative, with the same prominent cheekbones, small mouth, and olive complexion, but with gray in her dark hair. Porzia wore a slightly rumpled but perfectly fitted mauve dress that seemed a bit incongruous when compared against the grease-stained smock worn by the older woman.

Porzia was saying, "If we bring the children home now, what are you going to tell them about the house?"

"We'll tell them Casa is asleep for maintenance," the older woman countered. "If you find the Marconi girl, what will you tell her about Righi?"

Porzia heaved a sigh. "I don't know. That it was an unfortunate confluence of events? It's not like we *meant* for Casa to kill three people."

Willa went cold. The university staff person who'd informed her of Righi's death had known nothing about how he passed, and Willa had tried not to dwell on it much; it wasn't terribly unusual for pazzerellones to die in laboratory accidents, and while he'd been away on business for the Order at the time, she'd assumed it had been something of that sort. She certainly hadn't guessed that he'd been murdered by a sentient construct owned by the Pisano family.

Willa forced herself to tune back in to the conversation as Porzia was saying ". . . can't imagine what she plans to do with it, given that she's a mechanist by all accounts."

The older woman pursed her lips. "You mentioned she's not working alone. Perhaps she has recruited the help of a scriptologist."

"Not that it matters much. Regardless of their plans, I have to get the editbook back." She rested her elbow on the arm of the chair and propped her cheek against her palm. "Elsa's exasperation is going to be . . . just epic to behold. Maybe we should've tried to destroy it when we had the chance."

"And risk more collateral damage?" the older woman said.

Quietly, Porzia said, "It seems no matter what we do, the bodies just keep piling up."

"That's enough," Willa croaked. "I don't—I don't want to hear any more."

She turned away from Saudade's screen and pressed the back of her hand against her mouth. Willa had maintained her stoicism through losing her employment, and getting sucked through a temporal portal into the future, and being chased around the timeline by murderous androids. She was *not* going to start crying in her enemy's kitchen in the middle of a reconnaissance mission.

Saudade closed their palm, the holographic display winking out. They watched Willa for a moment, stewing in uncertain silence, then unplugged themself from the house system.

"The Pisanos don't seem to be actively plotting global destruction," Saudade offered.

"Can we just go?" Willa said tightly. She was hit with a strong desire to be anywhere else but here.

Saudade nodded and opened a portal.

Willa was accustomed to ignoring her feelings, reflexively boxing them up in the back of her mind and focusing on her work instead. So it wasn't until they'd returned to the summer cottage that Willa even recognized how *angry* she was. Saudade kept shooting her worried glances, like they were wondering what in the world to do with an upset human, and Willa had removed herself to the solitude of the bedroom she'd claimed upstairs. That was where the fire burning in her gut finally made itself known.

She wanted to get justice. No, more than that, she wanted to exact vengeance. Her impotent fury clawed at her, desperate for an outlet. She wanted to . . . to *do violence*, which was not at all a familiar impulse. She was mad at the people responsible, of course, but her anger was bigger than that. She was mad at the whole world, the political conflicts and societal norms that set the stage for all of this to happen, and she was mad at the indifference of the world, at the ultimate insignificance of Righi's death. She wanted everything to burn the way she burned.

It was dangerous, feeling this way—she could recognize

that with some distant part of her mind responsible for self-examination, as if she were watching her own emotions occur in a dark mirror. And with that clinical detachment, she could follow the trajectory of her feelings to the future actions at which they pointed.

Willa unbuttoned the wrist cuffs of her dress and rolled up one sleeve so she could run her fingers over the curling vinelike metallic implants fused to her skin. The implants formed a network across her whole body that unmoored her from the timestream, allowing her to operate outside of it the same way the android time agents were designed to do. She could effect changes to the course of the timeline with less risk of those changes propagating into her present self and updating her in a way that would cause a localized paradox. No nineteenth-century pazzerellone would even think to ask if such modifications were possible.

Willa, herself, was a futuristic, cyborg time agent. And she had access to the editbook. And she was so very angry at everything.

What if the person fated to destroy the world was *her*?

5

ARIS

1891, in the air over Tuscany

THE DISTANCE FROM Firenze to Napoli is around four hundred fifty kilometers as the crow flies, so even with Aris's ingenious airship design, the journey will still take them the rest of the night. Leo refuses to let Aris pilot *his own airship*, which is just insulting, and Elsa keeps asking how far they've come and sighing impatiently. Even Vincenzo seems reluctant to engage with Aris, perhaps deterred by the brittleness of his mood since the confrontation with Leo.

Aris peers out one of the round porthole windows along the side of the gondola, but the dark sky beyond yields nothing of interest. He folds his arms and taps his fingers impatiently against his opposite biceps. With this infernal waiting, the confines of the airship are hardly an improvement over his cell. He intended this space to serve as a mobile laboratory, not a passenger cabin, so there aren't even any seats (Vincenzo's sitting on the floor, long legs stretched out in front of him in a way that Aris is deliberately trying not to fixate on).

Enough is enough, he needs something to occupy him. Aris opens the cabinet built into the side of the airship, expecting to find his scriptological supplies immaculately organized as he keeps all of his equipment, but he has to swallow a growl at the mess within. He should have known his brother couldn't resist rifling through his things. Apparently confiscating a few of his worldbooks, too. His machine lab is still there, at least, but his portal device is gone. Aris glares into the cabinet, disliking this thwarted feeling.

"Looking for this?" Vincenzo says dryly. He casually lifts one hand, holding up the rectangular brass case of Aris's portal device.

Aris sputters. "But—*when* did you even steal that?" Leo had plenty of time to muck about the airship unattended before picking them up in Firenze, but Vincenzo has only been on board in Aris's presence.

Vincenzo smiles, a bitter twist to the curl of his lips. "I'm not fourteen anymore, Aris. I'm a highly trained rebel agent, and you doubt that I can confiscate a portal device without you noticing?"

"Give that back," Aris says, then scowls at himself because now *he* sounds like he's fourteen.

Elsa sighs, reluctantly inserting herself into their conversation. "What do you plan to do with it?"

"Get to work on this whole redemption thing, obviously."

"And how are you going to do that, exactly?" she says. "We're not even in Napoli yet."

"Vico didn't bring me along for my dashing good looks," Aris points out. "What you and I can do that your average plebeian can't is provide equipment."

Elsa blinks, processing this. "You want to build an excavator to speed up the rescue attempts."

"Obviously." What did they expect Aris to do, dig people out of collapsed buildings with his bare hands? The Napolitanos may think a shovel is the height of technological sophistication, but Aris has no intention of relying on manual labor to get this done.

"Elsa?" Vincenzo prompts, sitting up a little straighter, as if her consideration might require him to be on guard.

"It's not a terrible idea," she admits. She holds out her hand, and Vincenzo reluctantly passes the portal device to her. "Don't worry, I won't let him so much as pick up a wrench without supervision."

"I am not a child to be supervised," Aris sulks.

Vincenzo leans back against the wall of the airship, but there's something affected about his casual lounging now. "No. You're much more dangerous than any child."

Aris tells himself that Vico's mistrust does *not* cut him like a scalpel. Aris was made to be dangerous; it is only good sense for Vincenzo to recognize it. Aris can be patient and work to prove himself.

Elsa says, "I assume you have a laboratory world? Show me the coordinates."

Aris tenses his jaw, biting down on the urge to snap at anyone who dares order him around, since he is supposed to be playing nice with her. He plucks the leather-bound volume from the shelves and flips open the cover, the paper vibrating under his touch with the subtle hum of readiness that indicates a functioning world. Elsa leans over to read the first page, then twists the knobs on the portal device to input the coordinates. When she's done, Aris leaves the worldbook on the counter built against the wall aft of the cabinet.

He raises a challenging eyebrow. "Shall we?"

"Fine, let's see what we have to work with." She flips the switch, and a portal irises open.

Aris walks through first to prove this isn't some sort of trap, but she soon joins him inside the laboratory. It's a cavernous room reinforced with steel girders, pulleys and cables hanging from the ceiling, hydraulic arms bolted into the floor—everything they'll need for constructing a large mechanized vehicle. A set of carriage-house doors on tracks separate the main lab from the stockroom, and a sturdy writing desk stands against the wall nearby.

Aris taps his fingertips against the scriptology book sitting open on the desk. "I can describe whatever components I need here, and they'll coalesce in the stockroom behind these doors. So no need to worry about raw materials or forging."

Elsa makes a soft, unimpressed sound in her throat, but holds her tongue.

Aris takes a deep breath, tells himself to let it go, but can't help snapping, "What?"

"Nothing," she says. "Just wishing we could've recovered my laboratory book from the Order. I scribed it with predictive stockrooms."

Aris can practically feel his hackles rising. "Don't act like you're the first person to think of scribing mechanical components instead of manufacturing them in the real world. I've been doing this since I was eight years old. No one's going to give you an award for reinventing the wheel."

"Yes," Elsa says dryly, "and by the looks of it you're still using an eight-year-old's methodology."

"Rude." Aris scowls. "I think I liked you better when you were playing spy."

"You mean when I had to pretend to stroke your ego to get what I wanted? Yes, that must've been nice for you."

Aris used to wonder what it would be like to have someone around who's as smart as him. Now he knows: It's annoying.

"Are we here to build an excavator, or argue about whose laboratory is better?" he huffs.

Elsa tucks Aris's portal device away in a leather pouch hanging from her belt. "You're right, you're right. What were you thinking in terms of mobility? I suppose we could portal the excavator from one building to the next, but it would be more expedient if we could drive it through the ashfall."

"Continuous track propulsion would be best. We could manage to modify a steam walker, of course, but it would take some fiddling with the gyroscopic balance to handle uneven terrain . . ."

And so, with only a small amount of assistance from Elsa—hardly enough to merit a mention, really—Aris gets to work building his excavator. The challenge of designing the machine and optimizing for both function and expediency of construction is quite absorbing. Even arguing with Elsa helps to distract from his inconvenient emotions, replacing them with the certainty of work. He could not guess how many hours pass while they're focused on the task.

By the time they finish and take a portal back to the gondola, the airship is approaching Napoli, and dawn breaks the darkness in a stunning cascade of reds, enhanced by the volcanic dust still hanging in the air. The rising sun silhouettes the twin-peaked, conical shape of Mount Vesuvius to the east and casts long shadows from the jagged rooftops below. Aris presses his lips together tight, watching out a porthole as the airship scouts for the best place to dock, taking a slow circuit over the city. It . . . does look bad down there. He can admit that, at least in the privacy of his own thoughts. Napoli is blanketed in gray, ashfall clogging the streets and weighing down many roofs to the point of collapse. The eastern districts were swallowed entirely in ashflow—nothing to be done about that, those residents were cooked in their homes like the ghosts of Pompeii.

Regret is for the weak, the voice of his dead father reminds Aris. *Never apologize for the great and terrible things you can do.*

Is that right? Is that who he should be? Father is gone, his approval rendered irrelevant, and Vincenzo wants him to regret. He isn't sure he knows how to do that, and he feels seized by a sudden, frightening self-doubt. What if he is incapable of the compassion Vico demands of him?

When Aris was little, Marianna—the woman swollen with the as-yet unborn Pasca—would try to tell him bedtime stories, ludicrous stories about princes and the unlikely circumstances in which they fall in love with inappropriate girls. Young Aris had no patience for such tripe. It wasn't until much later that he came to understand that when other people talked about their hearts, they meant they actually *had* something—a tangible something, instead of the little black devouring pit that lived inside his own chest. He always thought "happy" meant that momentary flash of smug satisfaction when you've won and someone else has lost.

His father's approval fed that empty hole in him. Never enough to sate his hunger, of course, just enough scraps to keep him focused like a hunting falcon. Now Father is dead, and his brothers hate him, and there is absolutely nothing left to quell the emptiness. Aris suspects he could devour the whole world and it still wouldn't be enough to satisfy his unfillable void, and the thought of continuing to exist like this gives him a dull ache he can't quite identify. What if he can't learn to be something Vico will reward with pride?

Aris, Elsa, and Vincenzo are unceremoniously dropped off at an old watchtower near the northeast margin of the city. Leo doesn't even bother to emerge from the cockpit to see them off, which leaves Aris with an unsettled feeling of incompleteness in his stomach, despite the rational part of him that knows a proper farewell would've just turned into another argument. No matter what else may be driving them apart, the need to keep his brothers close is too deeply ingrained for logic to sway Aris. He hates Leo for killing their father. But if Aris allowed instinct to drive him, he would grab Leo and pull him close until they destroyed each other, rather than letting go.

Vincenzo leads the way down the watchtower stairs and shoulders open the door, pushing against the heavy drifts of ash. Napoli is an overcrowded city with hulking five- and six-story-tall tenements, most of which are evidently still in use from the trails of footprints and cleared doorways—even some of the buildings with roofs that have collapsed into the top floor are still occupied on the floors below. Aside from the initial rush to evacuate, the Napolitanos don't seem eager to abandon their homes, now that the worst has come and gone, although the normal urban activities seem to have ground to a halt. There are no street sellers hawking wares from their stalls, no laundry hanging from balconies. And while the streets are not empty, the people they encounter wear cloth over their lower face and do not engage with one another.

The air scratches at Aris's lungs and throat—they're going to have to fashion some face coverings, too, to work in these conditions—and the ashfall crunches and shifts like sand beneath his boots as the three of them make their way to the nearest relief outpost set up by the Carbonari in the aftermath of the eruption. Vincenzo takes charge of coordinating their efforts with the teams of volunteers who've been on the ground already. Elsa tweaks the controls on the portal device and holds open a particularly large portal for Aris to drive the excavator through from the laboratory world, and then it's time for the real work to begin.

And it is *work*, too. Despite the massive arm of the excavator scooping away rubble and volcanic debris and propping up unstable roofs, the task of freeing people trapped inside half-destroyed buildings is still dirty, sweaty, slow labor. The heavy vibrations of the excavator seem to sink into his joints and bones, and Aris has little choice but to switch off mastery of the controls with Elsa every couple hours. When he's not driving, he's careful to orchestrate the rescue so that it's Vincenzo's face the victims see first; their gratitude makes Aris acutely uncomfortable, and he prefers to fade into the background rather than be exposed to it.

When they lose the light, they make their way through the settling gloom of evening back to the relief outpost, parking the excavator in the middle of the street and allowing its engine to cool for the first time in almost fourteen hours. Aris has grown short-tempered with fatigue and discomfort. Grit clings to his skin, and he's starting to doubt he'll ever feel clean again. At the outpost, he has to wait in line like a refugee for a sad-looking bowl of pasta and beans, and he's too hungry to complain about the culinary offerings. Vincenzo, who is apparently tireless, has gone off to coordinate with the leaders, so it's just Elsa babysitting him over dinner.

"Reduced to eating peasant slop," Aris mutters. "Father would never stand for this."

Elsa just raises an eyebrow and pointedly forks a bite into her mouth.

"Oh, what do you know," he snaps, as if she'd responded aloud. "Despite whatever my traitorous brother has told you, Father only ever wanted the best for us. We had the finest tutors, state-of-the-art laboratory equipment, anything we wished for."

Elsa sighs, like she's trying to keep her opinions to herself for the sake of not starting an argument she's too exhausted to finish, but after a minute, she gives in to the urge. "If you want to remain forever angry at your brother for doing what had to be done, that's your prerogative,

I suppose. But this fiction of Ricciotti Garibaldi being the perfect parent is a story you'll have to peddle to someone else. You're forgetting that I saw how he was with you and Leo."

"Father had exacting standards. And your surprise arrival certainly didn't help with Leo's ornery behavior."

"Oh, so it was only Leo he smacked around then, was it?" she says, her tone falsely mild.

"I don't expect you to understand," Aris scoffs. Elsa grew up in a hovel in Veldana, isolated from the real world; she knows nothing about being the progeny of a revolutionary.

"You were never his sons, you were his experiments. He only cared about what you could do for him."

"So what? Everyone wants something. All relationships are exploitative."

Elsa stares at him, blank-faced and frozen mid-chew for a moment before swallowing. "I don't even know where to start with that."

Aris squirms under her scrutiny and fakes a sudden dedication to sopping up the last of his bean sauce with a slice of stale bread. He has that feeling again, like he's missing something critical that's obvious to everyone else. He hates that feeling.

1880, Venezia

Aris is eight years old, and he doesn't know what to do because Leo won't stop crying. They're alone now in the cozy second-floor study where they have their lessons, but if he doesn't convince Leo to quiet down, Father might come back and cuff him again just for being a crybaby.

Leo has been struggling to read, even though he's five years old already. (Aris was reading on his own at five—*Le memorie di un pulcino* and even *Pentamerone*.) Father asked for a demonstration of Leo's progress, and then he got angry and yelled and fired the governess. And now Leo is sitting frozen in his little desk chair, red-faced and sobbing, and Aris telling him to *shush* doesn't help at all.

Aris hates feeling afraid. Eight is old enough for Aris to understand that he and his brothers are meant to be *useful*, and Leo is failing to keep up with Father's expected developmental timeline. His fear of what might happen is a nebulous, undefined thing, but eight is also old enough to understand that the world has a cache of fresh new horrors to blindside him with.

Aris will just have to be better—more brilliant, more noticeable, quicker to impress. When Father is pleased with Aris's performance, he forgets to punish Leo. Aris will be a distraction, or failing that, a shield, because either way, his brothers are *his* to protect.

1874, Venezia

Aris is two and three-quarters years old. He should not be able to remember this, but he can. It is the earliest moment he can return to in his mind.

Aris is not quite three, and the woman with the big belly who he's not supposed to call Mother is screaming. Aris stands in the cracked-open doorway and no one tells him to leave, no one notices him. The man in black—called the *doctor*, whatever that means—is arguing with Father. The white sheets are wet and turning very red.

Father takes a tiny knife and cuts open the screaming woman's big belly, like splitting the skin on an enormous peach. There are wet sounds and so much red, and Aris doesn't really understand what he's seeing, only that it makes him feel woozy and like there are ants crawling over his skin.

The woman isn't moving anymore, but her head is leaning to the side and her eyes are open and she's staring right at Aris.

Father says, "Don't look at that, it doesn't matter."

(Later, Aris will understand that the woman *wasn't* anyone's mother, only a paid study subject, a living incubation chamber for Ricciotti's experiment. But in the moment, those blank eyes seem to pin him with their gaze.)

Father crouches down in front of Aris, blocking his view of the bed. Father is very large, and now he's all Aris can see. He has a tiny baby cradled in one arm. "Come here and meet your brother."

1891, Napoli

In the morning, the relief organizers send them to the Spanish Quarter. The streets are so narrow that it's a challenge to navigate through with the excavator, and the combination of the tall buildings looming over them and the volcanic haze still hanging in the air plunges the street level into an eerie, perpetual twilight. After a frustratingly slow morning, Aris decides to try for a better view of their surroundings. He does *not* need Vico's help getting onto the roof of one of the tall tenement buildings, but neither does he bother to argue against it when Vincenzo comes along with him.

The open air is a relief even if it is not exactly fresh, with all the particulates still hanging in the air. Aris can see clear down the slope of the hill, across Old Town and all the way out to the port. The port, where a whole armada is sailing in—steam frigates, gunboats, at least one ironclad warship. Aris has to squint to guess at the details from this distance, but the larger picture is clear: The Royal Sardinian Navy has arrived. The sudden tightness in his lungs is not from the dust, a knot of emotion tangling up his diaphragm.

It *worked*. Decimating Napoli has given the Kingdom of Sardinia the opening they need to oust the Bourbon dynasty and annex the Kingdom of the Two Sicilies. A unified Italian state is no longer a lofty dream, but well on its way to happening, because of what Aris did here. Yet it is hard to take any joy in the victory, when Father is not alive to see his dream realized.

"Tell me the truth, Vico: If you had been there, would you have stood by and let Leo murder my father?"

Vincenzo sighs, gazing at the distant ships while taking

long seconds to consider his answer. "What does it matter what I might have done?"

Aris tightens his throat to keep the words from quavering. "It matters to me."

Vincenzo chews his lip, then finally looks at Aris. "It grieves me to see you in pain. But Garibaldi was a madman driven by misplaced anger and thirst for control, and he dragged you down into that darkness with him."

"He was . . . imperfect, I'll admit. But he was all I had left." *And now I have nothing*, Aris doesn't add.

"He was all you had because he carefully isolated you to keep you dependent on him!" Vico says, exasperated. "Has anyone ever asked you what *you* want to do with your life? With him gone, you get to decide that now for yourself."

Aris clenches his jaw, biting down on the instinct to verbally lash out at him. He feels exposed, as if Vico cracked open his rib cage to peer inside.

"Your father doesn't own you anymore, and that is a change I certainly do not mourn."

Aris's rage boils over, his own hurt turning inevitably into a need for someone else to hurt. "It just burns you, doesn't it, that *Father's plan worked*. This was a major victory for Italian unification."

Vincenzo eyes widen as if he was struck. "Aris, this was a *war crime*."

"No war is won without collateral damage."

Vincenzo scrubs his face with his hands. "An *entire city* is not what I would call acceptable losses."

I did what Father told me to do, Aris wants to argue, *I didn't have a choice*. But somehow, all the counterarguments he can think of are words that Vincenzo would turn back around on him. If he can form no unimpeachable defense of his actions, then Aris must acknowledge—if only to himself—that perhaps his defensiveness is little more than denial. The possibility that Father may have been *wrong* feels like a horrible gaping maw capable of devouring him. If Vincenzo is right, and Aris has spent his whole life unquestioningly following a madman, then everything he has lost, everything he sacrificed, was for nothing.

1886, Venezia

"Close the door," Father says.

Aris tenses as the latch clicks into place under his hand. Father often uses the library as a private study, so it feels like trespassing to step inside, even at Father's insistence. The walls are lined with tall shelves, and a large, sturdy table dominates the center of the room. The wooden surface is practically buried in Father's work—a regional map of Venezia with pins in it, and stacks of progress reports, and encoded communiques from his associates.

Father finishes writing a note while Aris stands there, growing nervous. Finally, he sets aside the fountain pen and turns his full attention to his son. "I've heard from multiple sources that Austrian agents are inciting unrest. Tensions are likely to turn violent soon, so I'm afraid this Venetian political experiment is drawing to a close."

Aris twists his hands together behind his back, where Father can't see. "We're leaving Venezia?"

"Yes." Father stands and skirts around the table, coming closer to Aris. "Operating out in the open like this hasn't yielded results. We've got to rethink our strategy— leave behind this failed cover identity and start anew."

He nods. "I'll tell my brothers. How soon should we be ready?"

"No. Leo and Pasca will remain in the care of Signora Rosalinda."

"What?" Aris croaks.

Father rests a comforting hand on his shoulder. "Your brothers aren't ready to be effective agents. Pasca is only nine, and Leo still hasn't developed proficiency for any science beyond mechanics. You'd mastered the basics of all three major disciplines by his age."

Aris's stomach drops with sudden dread. In trying to protect Leo, did he only succeed in rendering his brother irrelevant? He swallows against the dryness in his throat. "We can take them with us. They can learn."

"That is not the plan."

"Father, we can't leave them behind. Leo and Pasca are a part of this," he argues, not entirely sure whether he means *this family* or *this mission*, if there even is a distinction to be made there.

The set of Father's jaw hardens, and the hand on his shoulder tightens in reprimand. "I've made my decision, Aris. Don't forget your place."

Panic gnaws at the margins of his mind. Losing his brothers is unthinkable; it is not meant as a punishment, and yet Father could not have devised a worse one if he tried. Aris feels like he might shatter. But he holds his tongue, the dutiful son.

Eight years later, Father dies in that room, standing in almost exactly the same place.

Aris knows his place. At every age, in every time, Aris knows his place—except when his father is dead. Which part of losing one's purpose is supposed to feel like freedom?

6

FARAZ

1891, Pisa

IT WAS MIDDAY by the time they docked the airship in Pisa, and Faraz was grateful to be back in familiar territory. For the whole flight, Leo had alternated between being twitchy and closing himself off. Faraz carefully held his tongue and resisted the urge to point out that this arrangement was by Leo's design, and if he wanted to switch places with Elsa, it was within his power to do so. He hoped returning to Casa della Pazzia might have a calming effect on Leo's nerves, but it was disquieting to step through the front doors and not be greeted by the disembodied voice of the house, as always used to happen.

Instead, Porzia met them in a swirl of skirts and brisk effectiveness. "You're here, finally!" She immediately steered them down the hallway, and Faraz found himself swept up in her wake, Skandar's wings fanning to keep balance on his shoulder as Porzia strode fast and talked faster. "Casa is still deactivated and looks to remain so for the immediate future. Mama took a break from the repairs and went up the coast this morning to retrieve the children—she should be back with them on the afternoon train. I would've lent her Elsa's doorbook, but I thought I'd better keep it with me so we can get to work immediately now that you've arrived. Did you sleep at all? No? Well, wouldn't be the first time any of us worked through the night."

Porzia shouldered her way into the octagonal library and beelined for one of the reading tables where there was a spread of scriptology supplies. She began sorting through the books and shoving a few into a knapsack. "We'll need the tracking worldbook, obviously. One thing I can say for all that time spent chasing after Garibaldi—we invented some damn useful tools, wouldn't you agree?"

"Hold on, hold on," Faraz finally interrupted. "Did you drink us out of espresso in a single day, Porzia? Let's take a minute to breathe and plan before rushing off half-cocked."

Porzia huffed and set her hands on her hips, but at least she stopped the frantic packing. "I've been planning. Nothing half-cocked about it. I've been sitting around waiting for you two, and you didn't even manage to show up with Elsa. Though I note you brought the tentacle monster, Faraz—very helpful." She looked to Leo. "Tell me Elsa isn't still locked in the Order's basement, please."

"She isn't," said Leo. "We flew her and Vincenzo to Napoli, to help with the relief efforts."

Faraz side-eyed Leo for his avoidance of mentioning his brother, but he decided not to correct the glaring omission. Either Leo would come around to sharing the truth on his own, or Porzia would extract it from him like a surgeon pulling out a bullet. At least with Leo and Porzia, Faraz did not need to play mediator.

"Hm." Porzia narrowed her eyes, unsatisfied with Leo's explanation.

"Anyway," Leo said, "tell us about our megalomaniac of the week. Who stole the editbook this time?"

Porzia paused, giving him a look that said as plain as words, *I know you're trying to distract me and I'm letting you get away with it, for now.* Then she caught them up on what she knew of this Willa Marconi. Faraz didn't recognize the name, but Leo frowned as if it sparked something for him.

"So we'll start at Righi's laboratory," Leo said. "She won't be there anymore, unless she *wants* to get caught, but we should be able to track her from there."

Porzia nodded. "That's what I was thinking, yes. I've already scribed us a door to Bologna." The doorbook was an invention that, instead of creating a new pocket universe, allowed them to make portal connections between places here on Earth, the book itself serving as a directory of locations. Porzia really had prepared.

Nonetheless, Faraz managed to talk them both into

sparing enough time for him and Leo to change into fresh clothes and eat a quick luncheon. He coaxed Skandar onto the perch in the alchemy lab, where the creature gave him a watery-eyed abandoned look, but Faraz held strong against Skandar's pleading. A winged tentacle monster was *not* a subtle accessory when they might be interacting with common folk.

The three of them—sans Skandar—portaled into an impressive library with shelves lining the long walls on the ground floor and balcony levels. The architecture had the feeling of a cathedral; white columns held up a high, vaulted ceiling, and rows of tables flanked the central aisle like pews designed for a different kind of worship. A few students glanced up from their studies, startled by the sudden appearance of a portal in their midst, but they went back to their books quickly enough. The university must have enough of a scriptology book collection for portals to not be entirely unheard of here.

"The library? Really?" said Leo.

"What?" Porzia said. "It's the only university building I spent any time in when I visited Bologna. I remembered what it looks like well enough for the doorbook to work, didn't I?"

"Of course you did. It's a *library*," Leo teased.

"Hmph. If we relied on the sort of details *you* pay attention to, we'd probably have to crawl out from underneath a train or something. Is there a single piece of architecture in *any* city that you could reliably describe?"

Faraz pressed his lips together to hide his smile. It was good to hear their verbal sparring again. He remembered when Leo had first arrived at Casa della Pazzia at the age of twelve and had fallen almost immediately into a pattern of bickering with Porzia. The apparent discord had upset him. Faraz himself had been apprenticed at such a young age that he could no longer recall his own mother's face, just the confusion and heartbreak of being abandoned into the care of a stranger. Then he lost his whole world again when his mentor sent him to live in Pisa. Slow to trust after this fresh pain, he'd been withdrawn and politely distant with the other children for months after his arrival—he certainly hadn't instigated arguments at the first opportunity.

With Leo and Porzia, it took him several weeks to realize that they both enjoyed sharpening their words against each other, and that neither came away from it with ill feelings. Now, Faraz understood all too well that silence was worse.

Porzia had no shame about interrupting a student to ask for directions to the science building. The campus they walked through was an architectural study in arched windows and baroque arcades. It was the oldest university in the world, founded in 1088, and it sprawled through the city in the somewhat disorganized fashion of an institution that had grown slowly over the course of centuries. When they finally found their way to the correct research building, a rather mousy administrative assistant insisted that he could not let them into Professor Righi's old laboratory where Willa Marconi had worked until recently. After a fair bit of cajoling, Porzia managed to talk him into providing them with the address of Willa's residence, at least. They were dear friends who had traveled all the way from Pisa to check up on her after the tragic death of her mentor! Thanks to the combined acting skills of Porzia and Leo, it mattered very little that Faraz couldn't lie to save his life.

The boardinghouse was a short walk away, a three-story row home with a faded stucco facade that may have once been a bright peach color. Porzia knocked, and the door was answered by a short, middle-aged woman who must be the boardinghouse matron.

"Need something, dear?" she said.

"Only a minute of your time, if you can spare it," said Porzia. "Might we come in?"

The matron gave her a quick up-and-down glance. Porzia was dressed down in a travel-appropriate skirt and matching jacket, but everything Porzia wore had the precise fitting of custom clothes, which gave her away. The matron likely could tell that Porzia had more money than the sort of young working girls who were her regular boarders, but luckily, this seemed to pique the woman's curiosity. She opened the door wider and ushered them into a narrow entry, and then through an open doorway into a somewhat roomier communal dining room.

Porzia said, "We're looking for Willa Marconi. I believe she rents a room here?"

"Oh dear, I'm afraid you've just missed her. She was scarce for a few days, then she came around with that new *friend* of hers just the day before last. Packed up her things and turned in her key—no warning, mind you! Practically up and vanished on me, with hardly a by-your-leave."

Leo said, "Do you know where she went?"

"Oh, I'm sure I couldn't say, with her leaving so suddenly like that. Mixed up with the wrong sort of company, is she? And after months of acting so standoffish with my other girls—all perfectly respectable young ladies, mind you. Now that you mention her, I always had a bad feeling about Willa," the boardinghouse matron said, obvious in her attempt at fishing for gossip.

"Sure you did," Porzia muttered under her breath. Faraz shot her a quelling glance, hoping the matron hadn't heard the sarcasm.

"Wrong sort of company?" Leo asked, feigning ignorance of her meaning.

The last thing they needed here was a well-intentioned escalation. "Leo . . . ," Faraz beseeched.

"What?" said Leo, with a flawless impression of innocence. "I just want to know what the nice lady meant."

"Oh, you know," the matron said. Then her eyes landed critically on Faraz, seeming to weigh his well-made clothes against his skin tone. "Or maybe you don't," she concluded to Leo.

"Ah. Yes, can't have the *wrong sort* loitering around your . . . very fine establishment." In a power move that must have made Porzia swell with pride, Leo let his gaze linger on the draperies, which were two or three decades out of fashion.

The matron flushed red, clearly recognizing both that she'd been insulted and that she had no recourse to respond. Even if Leo had given overt offense, the difference in their relative stations would give her pause. She sputtered, "Well—I don't—if there's nothing else you need of me, I must get back to—"

"Actually," Porzia interrupted, "may we see the room Willa rented, assuming it is still vacant?"

The matron puffed up a little, as if gathering the shreds of her pride. "I don't see what you think to learn from an empty room."

Porzia produced a small stack of coins and pressed them into the woman's hand. "The rent for the week, to compensate for Willa's abrupt departure."

"The room hasn't been cleaned yet," the matron said reluctantly, but she counted the coins.

"That's fine."

"There are no men allowed on the upper floors. House rules."

"The boys can wait here while I go up," Porzia replied with forced patience. "Now, the key?"

The matron finally produced a key and gave her directions, and Faraz and Leo lingered at one end of the dining room while Porzia went upstairs to search the room. The matron vanished briefly through a door at the back that must lead into the kitchen. Faraz could hear muffled yelling as the matron took out her embarrassment on whatever poor underling was back there working the stove.

"The *wrong sort*," Leo mocked under his breath.

"I don't need you picking fights for me," Faraz said, exasperated.

"Maybe if you'd start more fights for yourself I wouldn't have to," Leo grumbled. "I don't understand why you put up with people talking to you that way."

Faraz closed his eyes for a moment and reminded himself that Leo meant well. "I have to pick my battles. Otherwise, it's like trying to drain the Adriatic with a bucket: exhausting, endless, and nobody's paying me to do it."

Then the matron came back with a stack of plates and silverware, and she began setting the long table as a blatant excuse for keeping an eye on the male interlopers in her dining room. The silence in the room felt weighted with her suspicion.

Faraz leaned closer to Leo and muttered, "Awkward."

The corner of Leo's mouth cracked into an almost-suppressed grin. Voice low for his ears only, Leo replied, "I'll have to protect the respectable young ladies from your corruptive influence."

Faraz made a sound like he was choking as he did his best to swallow the bark of laughter that wanted to escape. Faraz was the one always pulling Leo *out* of the trouble he got himself into. Alhamdulillah, it was good to hear Leo joking again. But at the sound of returning footsteps, Leo drew up in sharp attention, like a hunting dog anticipating the moment he'll be let off the leash. He'd always been like that, too—ready to switch from insouciant to on guard in a second—and it hurt Faraz to know this was probably a trait that Garibaldi had trained into Leo as a child.

Faraz realized with a shock that he was actually *glad* Garibaldi was dead. What did that say about him, that his heart could be so full of hate?

"Get anything?" Leo was saying as Porzia descended the stairs.

"Success," she reported, holding up a single, unmatched glove. "The room was pretty well cleared out, but I did find this left behind under the bed."

Leo frowned. "Are you certain it belongs to Marconi?"

"Well I can't tell just by looking at it, can I?" Porzia snipped. "We'll just have to try tracking her with it and see if it works."

"Right, sorry." Leo deflated a little. "We can always go back to the university and break into the lab tonight, if we have to."

Porzia sighed and looked down at the glove in her hands, her expression turning pinched. "It was a sad little room. Not the sort of place you live if you have family to go home to instead."

Careful to keep his voice mild and free of criticism, Faraz said, "Porzia . . . I doubt Signorina Marconi has any use for your pity."

Porzia had grown up with her parents, three biological siblings, and a gaggle of pazzerellone orphans who might as well be brothers and sisters—Faraz and Leo chief among them—not to mention the considerable resources of generational wealth. It must be hard for her, having to confront what it might be like to lose all that, the way Willa did. Faraz decided not to point out that being able to afford her own room was actually quite a cushy arrangement for a single working girl. Nonetheless, it would be a mistake to assume they understood anything about their current adversary based on an empty boardinghouse room.

The matron had retreated again to the kitchen, so Porzia said, "Might as well try it now."

She dug around in her bag and produced a portal device and the tracking worldbook. On the former she twisted the dials to input the coordinates, and the latter she handed off to Leo, who scowled but accepted it without argument. The worldbook served as an anchor in the real world, so they could portal back to this exact place, but that meant someone had to stay behind with the book. Then Porzia bent to unlace her shoes.

She glanced up at Faraz. "You coming, or staying?"

"Right," Faraz said, and scrambled to take off his boots and socks, too.

Barefoot and skirts hiked up in one hand, Porzia flipped the switch on the portal device, and the black hole irised open to swallow them. Faraz followed her through that chilling moment of nothingness and stepped into the tracking world with a splash. The floor of this world was a scaled-down model of Europe, with West Asia and North Africa around the margins. The Adriatic Sea was ankle-deep; the Alps were just tall enough to bang one's shins on, Faraz knew from experience. Holding her skirts out of the water, Porzia waded to shore and stepped across the continent. The podium with the controls stood on the other side.

Faraz stepped up onto the map of Italy, while Porzia set the glove on the tracking machine and pulled a lever. As far as Faraz understood it, Porzia and Elsa had scribed the tracking world such that ownership was a measurable physical property here, as objectively real as color or temperature. The ownership property of an object would point back to the location of its owner. Porzia had become much more inclined to creative and seemingly impossible applications of scriptology since Elsa came along, and at this point, Faraz didn't bother questioning it.

A red dot began glowing on the map between his feet, and he called out, "It's working! Got a location."

Porzia detaches the tracking compass from the controls and joins him. "Where?"

"Not too far from Bologna, actually," he said. "Out in the country to the southeast. Near Riolo, it looks like."

Porzia allowed herself a smug smile, holding up the compass that would continue to target their quarry even in the real world. "Willa Marconi doesn't know who she's messing with."

They portaled back to the boardinghouse and shared what they'd learned with Leo while they hurried back into their shoes. Before they could wear out their welcome, the three of them retreated back out to the streets of Bologna.

Porzia had never visited Riolo, and without a location description, the doorbook could not get them any closer than they already were. Instead, they would have to rely on more commonplace methods of transit, but by that time, it was too late in the day to catch a train. Faraz proposed that they retire home to Pisa for the night, get some actual sleep, and return to the chase refreshed tomorrow. With only a moderate amount of grumbling about the delay, Porzia agreed.

In the morning, they portaled back to Bologna and took the Piacenza-Ancona rail line southeast out of the city. Porzia spent the train ride trying to extract the truth from Leo with regard to his evasiveness yesterday, and Leo spent the train ride lying extravagantly to cover said truth with transparently absurd explanations for his unsettled mood and Elsa's absence. As if they could avoid discussing Aris forever.

The next stop on the rail line was the town of Castel Bolognese, where they disembarked and transferred to a horse-drawn station bus that carried them, along with three other passengers, to Riolo. The rolling hill country they passed through was a patchwork of vineyards, fields, and chestnut orchards, with the rugged profile of the Apennine Mountains as a backdrop. The town itself was home to a hulking medieval fortress and some neoclassical thermal baths, the latter of which were a popular travel destination for the rich and idle.

They climbed out of the station bus, and Porzia straightened her skirts before taking out the tracking compass. "Fair warning: After the week we've all had, if we find Marconi relaxing and rejuvenating in a mud bath, I may have to scream."

Dryly, Leo said, "Once we get the editbook back, you can visit the spa yourself. Smear mud on your skin to your heart's content."

"Oh, if *only*," she lamented.

The compass needle pointed them east, and they left Riolo on foot, following the dirt track of a local road that headed in roughly the same direction. After a couple kilometers, the needle slid northward and took them off the road into an old villa that was converted into a cluster of summer residences, most of which appeared to still be vacant this early in the season. The compass aimed them toward a side building that was not quite so ostentatiously large as the main house, and they headed for it.

"Hold on." Porzia stopped short, staring down at the compass.

Leo blew past her by a few strides before slowing to a reluctant stop, as if stretching the end of some invisible tether. "Ugh, what? Do we really need to stop now to argue about how to handle the approach?"

"Um, no," said Porzia. "Come look at this."

Faraz leaned over her cupped hands to peer at the compass face. Beneath the glass, the needle swung listlessly, no longer drawn in any particular direction. Leo trudged back to them to look at what held their attention.

Porzia said, "We lost the targeting. She's not here anymore."

Faraz glanced at the smaller house in front of them and back to the main house, scanning over the grassy, open landscaping—there really was no way to sneak away from the villa unnoticed. "Given that we haven't seen anyone fleeing on foot, do we think Willa left through a portal? Or was she never here, and somehow tricked the tracker?"

"How would she even know we had a tracking device in need of thwarting?" Porzia countered.

"Let's find out," said Leo, striding away from them and right up to the front entrance.

Leo rapped his knuckles on the door and waited, listening for any sign of movement inside. Faraz supposed that was smart; even if they were certain Willa had left the house, they still had no knowledge of the whereabouts, or even identity, of her mysterious accomplice. He and Porzia hesitantly followed Leo closer to the house. Leo's confidence could only get them so far, when they had no clear idea what they were walking into. There was no sound of footsteps inside, and the door remained unanswered, for whatever that was worth.

Leo took his lockpicking set out of the pocket of his waistcoat, but then he bent to look closer at the lock, frowned, and twisted the doorknob. "It's unlocked."

"Right," Porzia drawled. "That's not suspicious at all."

Leo gave the door a quick shove and stepped back as it swung inward, his stance tense with readiness. Nothing happened.

From behind him, Faraz said, "Are you expecting the house to be booby-trapped?"

"If I lured someone to an isolated building and abruptly vanished before they could catch up with me . . . yeah, I probably would've laid some traps in that scenario," said Leo. "Hey, hand me that stick?"

Faraz picked up the half-meter-long branch from the unkept yard of the villa and handed it to Leo, who proceeded to stick it through the open doorway and wave it around at different heights, then poke the floor tiles just inside the threshold. When his waving and prodding yielded no results, he tossed the branch inside to land in the middle of the entryway. The branch landed with an anticlimactic clatter, followed by no explosions or nets deploying from the ceiling to capture them or whatever it was Leo had envisioned.

Only then did Leo reach his own hand inside the doorway to run his fingers around the doorframe. When he stretched up on his toes to reach along the top of the molding, he gave a slight twitch of surprise and actually pulled something off the wall above the doorframe. "Huh."

Faraz peered over his shoulder. A tiny gray disk no larger than a fingernail nested in the palm of Leo's hand. "What is that?"

Leo poked the disk gently and lifted it to his face for a closer look. "It's vibrating very faintly, as if it's got some kind of mechanical innards, but it's *so small*. I can't even see any seams in the casing. If it is a device, I've never seen its like before. Not even Aris could design equipment this compact."

"Could it be scriptological in origin?" If Faraz had learned anything from hanging around Elsa, it was that a sufficiently innovative scriptologist could find a workaround for almost any physical law imposed by the real world.

"I suppose it must be," Leo said, though he didn't sound satisfied with that explanation.

Porzia tucked the now-useless compass into her bag. "Well, at least we know the tracking wasn't a complete fluke. Someone with access to advanced technology must have been here to leave behind whatever that is."

"Nothing's exploded so far," Faraz mused. "Shall we

search the house? See what we can discover about these people."

Leo stepped inside first, his fingers absently fiddling with the little device as he looked around. He leaned through an open doorway to the left. "Not exactly well furnished. I doubt they've been here for long, if anyone is staying here at all."

Porzia followed Leo. "As if you'd prioritize interior decorating in the middle of executing some nefarious plan."

Faraz wandered in the other direction, giving a door near the bottom of the stairs an exploratory push and letting himself into a mostly empty space that might be intended as a library or a study. He could overhear Porzia and Leo bickering in the other room, but he ignored them in favor of examining the large chalkboard on the wall. It was filled with equations—recent writing, from the sharpness of the white lines—and Faraz chewed the inside of his cheek, trying to make sense of the mathematics on display. Granted, he was more of an organic chemist than he was a physicist, but he was at least passingly acquainted with Newtonian mechanics and this . . . was not that. He could not make heads or tails of it. *Lorentz transformation $ct' = \gamma(ct - \beta x)$ between inertial reference frames* . . . What?

Faraz felt a cold trickling of dread settle in his stomach. Whoever Marconi's shadowy friends were, they were clearly working on something big. Until this moment, he didn't realize he was still holding out hope that Willa had simply taken the editbook as an act of petty vengeance, without caring—or perhaps even knowing—what the book was capable of, beyond a means for seriously inconveniencing Porzia. But the math he was looking at now . . . this wasn't payback, this wasn't eye for an eye, this was a serious leap forward in technical theory.

They finished searching the house but found little else of interest. Faraz hadn't truly expected to discover the editbook lying around unattended for them to snatch up; when in his life had he ever been that lucky? Advanced mathematics and inexplicable devices were enough to firmly plant a seed of worry in his chest, as the three of them reconvened in the entryway.

"I hate to admit it," Porzia said, "but we'll have to leave empty-handed. Perhaps another time we can catch her unawares."

Leo wavered in a moment of indecision before sticking the tiny disk back where he found it. When Faraz raised his eyebrows questioningly, Leo said, "We haven't disturbed anything else in the house. On the off chance that Willa's absence is a coincidence, better not leave evidence we were here."

They portaled back to Casa della Pazzia to regroup. Porzia tried the tracking world again, and at first it could not get a lock on Willa's location, but a few minutes later, it was back to insisting that Willa Marconi was in the countryside southeast of Bologna. Porzia scribed a door directly back to the villa, and they tried a second time to surprise her, but once again the house was somehow empty when they portaled into it. They tried quietly lying in wait to ambush Willa upon her return . . . except she didn't return.

"I can't believe this," Porzia huffed. "If we go home, and the tracking world tells me she's here *one more time*, I swear I really may scream."

They went home to Casa della Pazzia. Faraz took Porzia at her word, and decidedly did not join her when she went back inside the tracking world. She was welcome to get the frustrated screaming out of her system in privacy. And anyway, by that time, Gia Pisano had brought the children home; now that Casa was deactivated, their evacuation was no longer necessary. Faraz went with Leo to check on Pasca, who at the very least deserved an update on what was going on with their eldest brother.

Faraz sighed and leaned in the open doorway of Leo's chaotically messy bedroom, where a cot had been added to accommodate Pasca's arrival. He hung back and watched as Leo sat beside his youngest brother and did his best to muddle through a stilted conversation in the sign language Pasca now used. The boy looked small and tired, and Faraz could relate.

Faraz had built a family for himself out of this odd collection of pazzerellones here at Casa della Pazzia.

Porzia and Leo and Elsa were his kin now, and the younger ones, too—the orphans like him, Porzia's siblings, and now Leo's little brother. He'd be damned before he let some girl with a grudge and a penchant for thievery threaten the family he worked so hard to hold together.

7

WILLA

1891, countryside south of Bologna

WILLA COULDN'T HELP but laugh when she finally explored the study in the summer house. The built-in bookshelves were still unpopulated, looking almost skeletal in their emptiness, but Righi had found the time to install a large slate chalkboard on the other interior wall. There was no desk, not so much as a single chair, but there was a chalkboard. Such had been Righi's priorities.

Amusing as it was, it did give her a serious idea. She'd been worried that she knew just enough about the future and time travel to be a danger to the timeline. There wasn't a way to make herself know *less*, but what if she bet all in on this hand of cards and learned *more*? Perhaps if she better understood the mechanics of the cataclysm, she could avoid getting cast into the role of loose cannon. She'd need help with this plan, though.

"Saudade?" she called out from the entryway.

"In here," came the muffled reply from upstairs.

Willa hopped up the stairs. The door stood open to the mostly empty room Saudade had claimed as their own. Inside, Saudade was dressed in a white sleeveless shirt that must be some sort of undergarment—although not a historically accurate one for this century—and they were contorting their arms around, trying to reach behind their own shoulder blade.

Willa blinked, distracted by their dramatics. "What are you doing?"

"The bandage," Saudade said, sounding halfway to desperate. "It's started itching, but I can't get it off!"

"Stop flailing around, this is just undignified." Willa bit the inside of her cheek to contain her amusement. "Let me help."

Saudade let their arms flop to their sides and showed their shoulder to Willa instead. "Just peel it off. But go slow."

Petrichor's liquid wound sealant had foamed and solidified into a thick crust that felt rough and stiff under Willa's fingers. Three days ago, Saudade had a deep gash in their shoulder from Jaideep performing some notably inexpert field surgery to remove a tracking chip. Now when Willa gently peeled off the bandage, there was a web of fragile new skin spanning across what had been a gaping wound. It really did not resemble how a human would heal—it looked more like patching ripped clothing with ribbon—but the rate of repair was remarkable, regardless of how the android healing process worked.

Saudade let out a relieved sigh. "Much better, thank you."

"It's nothing. Looks like you're practically good as new."

"Mm-hmm. Our bodies are designed to be more physically resilient than a human's. 'Superior in every way,'" they quoted wryly.

Willa knew that Saudade's interest in human culture was anomalous among the androids, at least in its intensity. Petrichor had been casually curious about humanity, but Saudade longed for it. Saudade mourned the losses of the cataclysm. Saudade named themself "Saudade" for a Brazil that will exist only briefly before its destruction, if they fail to change the timeline. But the derisive way they said "superior" made Willa wonder, for the first time, if Saudade felt that they were lacking in some way.

"Are you all right?" Willa said softly.

"Fine." Saudade pressed their lips into a forced smile.

"You're allowed to not be, though." Willa lifted her nose in self-mockery. "We can't both be the rational one, after all."

This time, Saudade's eyes crinkled with genuine amusement. "We can trade off."

"Oh, very well, if you insist."

"Now." Saudade reached into a small portal and

retrieved a shirt to button themself into. "I believe you were looking for me for a reason?"

Willa drew in a deep breath. "Yes. I want you to teach me temporal physics."

Saudade's fingers stilled on the buttons. "We've been careful so far to *limit* your accumulation of future knowledge."

"That ship has sailed. I'm not going back to whatever life I lived in the original timeline. Saudade, I'm a temporally unmoored cyborg with just enough knowledge of the future to be dangerous. But I can be a better partner to you if I understand the mechanics of the timestream."

Saudade raised an eyebrow at her, considering. "You really want a crash course in general and special relativity and quantum mechanics?"

Willa didn't know what any of those subjects were, but that was precisely the problem. She nodded. "I have a chalkboard."

Partway through special relativity, Willa gave in and carried the wooden chairs from the sitting room into the study. This was going to take a while.

Willa settled back in her seat, chewing on her thumbnail as she stared at the equations Saudade had covered the blackboard with. With a spark of surprise, she realized what she was doing and pulled her hand away from her mouth; she must have picked up the habit of biting her nails from Riley. It had been a sort of charming quirk when Riley did it, but Willa couldn't help the spark of irrational worry that her mother was going to pop out of the woodwork to criticize her comportment.

She forced herself to refocus on her physics lesson. "So . . . if time is just another axis of space, are temporal portals and spatial portals actually the same phenomenon?"

Saudade tilted her head back and forth in a sort of *yes and no* gesture. "Anytime you use a portal of any kind, you're exiting and then reentering spacetime. One could even argue that instantaneous transportation *is* a kind of time travel. So you're right, there's no qualitative difference. All portals are cheating—it's just a matter of how much you're cheating, and whether the timestream lets you get away with it. With a temporal portal, the targeting has an additional variable that makes it much more complex, and the energy requirement is higher, but the main difference is just the increased likelihood of tripping the circuit breakers of the universe, so to speak."

Willa had no idea what a circuit breaker was, but at this point she was immune to nonsensical references to future things. She understood the spirit of what Saudade was saying, if not the particulars. "That's what Riley and Jaideep needed the Itzkowitz probability functions for—to decrease the likelihood of exceeding the failure threshold?"

"Essentially, yes."

"Hm." Willa's thoughts raced, grabbing at the fragments of information she had before and working to hang them on this new intellectual scaffolding. According to historical records in the future, the cataclysm will start somewhere in northern Italy, but over the course of decades, it will spread to affect nearly the entire planet. "If the timestream is best modeled as a four-dimensional manifold that includes space . . . is that also why, when the paradox is large enough that the timestream can't compensate and paint over the problem, the zone of damage doesn't stay localized to the original source?"

This question coaxed a pleased grin from Saudade. "Exactly. Just as the paradox spreads downstream to affect the future, it also spreads outward in space."

Willa nodded. "Okay. Let's get back to time dilation . . ."

The two of them kept at it for hours, only breaking so Willa could put together a midday meal for herself before returning to the chalkboard. Saudade was in the middle of introducing mass-energy equivalence when they suddenly stopped mid-sentence and cocked their head to the side, as if listening to something Willa couldn't hear.

"We have to go."

Willa was already standing from her chair as she asked, "What's wrong?"

"I'm getting a strong cumulative signal from our possible near futures. In approximately two minutes and forty seconds, someone will trigger the proximity alarm."

"Damn. All right." Fueled by a sudden flash of adrenaline, Willa dashed into the sitting room with Saudade only a step behind. She grabbed the lockbox worldbook with the editbook inside and shoved it into her satchel. "Anything else we absolutely cannot leave behind?"

"No time to worry over it. Come on," Saudade said, and opened a portal out of the summer house.

Willa spilled out of the portal just behind Saudade, stepping through into a grassy meadow. She frowned in confusion at the forest margin in front of her, a line of juniper and scraggly Aleppo pines that belonged on the coast, not in the foothills of the Apennines. Looking over her shoulder explained it, though—behind her was an opaque wall of swirling purplish smoke, marking the boundary of a scribed world. They weren't in the countryside south of Bologna. They weren't on Earth at all.

"Where did you take us?" she asked.

Saudade said, "This is Veldana."

Willa raised an eyebrow at Saudade. The editbook was supposedly of Veldanese origin, which meant they were unlikely to run into any physics-related difficulties when bringing it back into Veldana. But on the other hand, it seemed like there would be a nonzero likelihood of running into a Veldanese resident who took umbrage with how the two of them stole the editbook.

Saudade huffed a little at Willa's skepticism. "What? It's a decent place to hide off-world. Veldana is securely anchored to Earth, and I doubt our pursuers will think to look for us here. We just have to avoid the locals, it'll be fine."

"The Veldana worldbook is securely anchored in the

library at Casa della Pazzia," Willa retorted. "Admit it: You just enjoy the perversity of hiding inside a world that's literally in the possession of our pursuers."

"I admit nothing." Saudade lifted their chin in a joking show of haughtiness.

It wasn't that Veldana made for an unpleasant hideaway. The sky was clear, the air warm, and an inconstant breeze ebbed and flowed, carrying the salt-scent of the sea. It was a very nice world—a very nice world owned by people who distrusted Europeans enough to create the editbook in the first place.

That was the part she worried about.

Willa huffed and set her hands on her hips. "I can't believe we were found so quickly. Can your early-warning system show you who, exactly, tracked us down?"

"Relax. It wasn't the Veldanese. I wouldn't have brought us here if it were," said Saudade. "It's three young people, one of them Porzia Pisano. No one else I recognize from the conference room in the Order's headquarters, so I'd guess they're operating independently of the Order of Archimedes."

"Well, that's something, I suppose." Willa sighed. "What do we do now?"

"We wait."

It took perhaps half an hour for Saudade's detection devices to signal the all-clear, then they portaled back to the summer house. Willa wasn't sure in what condition she expected to find their borrowed residence, but it surprised her that nothing looked damaged. The front door was shut, her clothes trunk looked untouched, the small collection of foodstuffs in the pantry were undisturbed. The stack of newspapers in the sitting room might be slightly askew, but she couldn't be sure of it. If Porzia and company had searched the house, they'd done so with tact, not with careless anger.

But Willa and Saudade barely had enough time to check over the house before the early-warning system once again set off alarm bells in Saudade's head. Apparently, Porzia wasn't done. They retreated through a portal to Veldana once again and waited.

A few minutes passed, and Willa started pacing to vent some of her worsening nerves. "They already searched the house. Did they think we'd leave the editbook lying around this time?"

Saudade shrugged. Willa paced. The few minutes stretched into half an hour.

"Wait—how are you even receiving signals from your security system when we're inside a scribed world?"

Saudade grinned. "Give your physics lessons another month, and I'll explain it to you."

Willa found a large rock to sit on not too far away, Saudade trailing after her. They discussed twentieth-century physics. They waited.

The half hour expanded into a whole one, and Willa said dejectedly, "No change?"

"I'm still detecting intruders in our not-so-secret lair."

"Ugh, what do they think they're doing?" Willa sighed. "So you were saying electromagnetic radiation has both the properties of a wave and the properties of a particle?"

The Veldanese sun was dipping low over the horizon, the eastern sky deepening into the jewel-toned blue of twilight, before Saudade announced the summer house was finally empty. Evidently, Willa and Saudade had won the waiting game that Porzia seemed so determined to force them all to play.

That night, Willa left the editbook in Saudade's hands when she went upstairs to sleep. It did make her wonder, yet again, what Saudade did all night to keep themself occupied while the human world slept. Maybe Willa should pick up some books for them on her next supply run—given Riolo's status as a vacation destination, the town probably had a bookseller despite its small size. Of course, it wouldn't surprise her if Saudade burned through reading material so fast that it hardly counted as a distraction. Willa stared at the bedroom ceiling and tried commanding her brain to stop thinking and just go to sleep, as if that ever worked.

Despite a restless night in which she kept jerking awake in anticipation of another invasion, morning arrived without the summer house being disturbed again. She and Saudade cautiously settled into their routine, now full of physics lessons. Only once during that day did they have to retreat to Veldana to avoid Willa's pazzerellone contemporaries making a nuisance of themselves.

On their fifth day staying at the summer house, the security system was triggered yet again. Following Saudade, Willa stepped through into the now-familiar Veldanese meadow, but then she froze. Standing right in front of them was none other than Porzia Pisano, flanked by two young men and also a horrifying alchemical creation that was all wings and tentacles. The boy with the tentacle monster on his shoulder was tall and skinny, and looked to be of Middle Eastern or North African descent. The other boy was shorter, darker-skinned, and almost shockingly muscular in comparison; the fingers of his right hand were spinning a sling around with a sort of idleness that could turn into a threat very quickly. Porzia herself was short and curvy and beautiful, with her round cheeks and delicate chin. Willa felt almost as if she'd been trapped into noticing this, though—she didn't want to find anyone pretty right now, and the fact that it was *Porzia* was infuriating.

Riley was who Willa wanted, and she wasn't anything like Porzia. The Riley in her memories had short hair, tight trousers, and no sense of decorum whatsoever. If Riley were here, she would probably plop down on the grass and cheerfully attempt to talk things through. Instead, they were met with Porzia's straight-backed posture and haughty stare. Willa had known it was a bad idea to come here.

She shot a look at Saudade. "I did tell you."

Saudade fidgeted a bit and muttered back, "I'm used to having access to better predictive algorithms."

"Which is why you should listen to me when—" Willa started to say before the shorter boy interrupted her.

"Access to our world is supposed to be restricted," he said. Apparently, he was Veldanese. "You can't just waltz in here like we're a public train station."

"Revan, let us handle this," Porzia said, resting a quelling hand on his arm for a second before taking a step forward. "I'm Porzia, as I believe you already know, and this is Faraz and Revan. We just want to talk."

It was such a blatant lie, Willa could practically see Riley rolling her eyes and saying *oh, come on*. But Riley wasn't here, so Willa said, "I know exactly what you want, and we're not handing it over to you or anyone else."

A flash of irritation passed over Porzia's face before she schooled her features. "The book you took contains something very dangerous."

"I am quite aware of that," Willa said. "What is your plan for the editbook, if you were to get ahold of it again?"

"*Our* plan," Porzia echoed, disbelieving. "You're the one who stole it, and you have the nerve to interrogate us about—"

"We have no agenda," Faraz interrupted. "We only want to ensure the editbook is never used again. That's all."

Willa narrowed her eyes at him, considering. Faraz had an air of earnestness about him that made it easy to believe his claim. But even with the best of intentions, he and Porzia weren't necessarily worthy of the massive trust it would require to let someone else handle the editbook. Willa had been assuming malicious intent on the part of whoever will cause the cataclysm, but it could just as easily be caused by a well-meaning person trying to do the right thing—perhaps by attempting to destroy the editbook, so no one can use it again. There was no way to be sure until it was too late, and even that was assuming Porzia and Faraz weren't outright lying about their intentions.

Willa said, "I'm afraid that's going to be a 'no' from me."

"Pardon?" said Porzia.

"I don't know you all, I'm not even a little predisposed to like you, and I can't think of a single reason to take you at your word. You want me to not only trust you, but to trust you with the fate of the entire planet? As much as I hate to repeat myself, I'll say it again for clarity's sake: *no*."

"And we're supposed to trust you with it?" Porzia turned to her companions, incensed. "I can't believe this! She's a common thief!"

Once, that might have landed as an insult, but now it only amused Willa. "There is really nothing common about me anymore, if there ever was."

"Look," said Faraz, "fighting about who gets to keep the editbook safe when we all basically want the same thing is pointless. Please, come back to Casa della Pazzia with us, and let's sit down and see if we can't arrive at a satisfactory compromise."

Willa crossed her arms and shot a skeptical look at her partner. Saudade tilted their head, considering. "Faraz does have a point. We're wasting time and attention on people who may be merely incompetent"—Porzia made an outraged noise—"instead of actively malicious."

Faraz's gaze had shifted from Willa to Saudade. "Who is your companion, if you don't mind introducing us? No one seems to know him."

"They call themself Saudade. Not him. *Them*," Willa corrected, using neutral pronouns from English, since all pronouns were gendered in Italian.

"It's fine," Saudade said.

"No, you prefer nongendered pronouns, and they all can put in the effort, or just use your name." Willa had learned that when someone wanted something from her, that was a form of currency she could use to demand respect.

"My apologies, Saudade," said Faraz. "So will you treat with us?"

Willa doubted anything *satisfactory* would come of this, to use Faraz's adjective, but Saudade thought it a worthwhile idea, so Willa relented with a begrudging nod.

"Well, at least you're not entirely impervious to reason," Porzia said. She set the dials on her portal device, but paused to address Revan. "Thank you for bringing us in on this."

Revan sighed. "Do try to limit the uninvited visitors from your world, will you? You know I have enough to handle around here without needing to patrol for unexpected incursions."

Porzia reached for his hand and gave it a squeeze—an unexpectedly intimate gesture to be doing in front of virtual strangers, in Willa's opinion, but then again, her trip to the future had proved that standards of propriety were far from immutable across time and culture. Revan leaned in and kissed cheeks with her in the Italian fashion, as if they were close friends, then walked away with barely a *ciao*, presumably returning to the populated area of Veldana. Porzia's gaze trailed after him for a few seconds before Faraz cleared his throat. She shot him a quick glare and flipped the switch on her portal device.

Saudade seemed content to pretend they were reliant upon Porzia to portal them to Casa della Pazzia. Not that Porzia hadn't already seen Saudade's impossible portal skills—impossible by the standards of 1891, at least—when they and Willa stole the editbook in front of her. But Willa supposed it was wise not to flaunt the unexplainable things Saudade was capable of, lest Porzia be reminded to question them.

Willa stepped through Porzia's portal and into the octagonal library room in Casa della Pazzia, with its high, domed ceiling and shelves of books covering the walls on three floors. The light from the chandelier was warm but faint, swallowed up by the large space, and the wrought-iron railings on the second- and third-story balcony levels looked vaguely sinister to Willa's eye.

Porzia took out a small book and checked something inside before fiddling with the controls on her portal device. "I've got to go retrieve Leo," she said to Faraz. Presumably, Leo was the person who tripped the alarm at the summer house.

Faraz looked over the library's reading table—which was buried under a mess of books—with mild disapproval. "I think I'll set us up in the dining hall."

"As you like," Porzia replied, and vanished through another portal.

Faraz sighed, and then gestured to the door. "This way."

Willa and Saudade dutifully followed, pretending they didn't already have a fairly good understanding of the building layout from their intelligence-gathering expedition. As they walked, the alchemical monster perched on Faraz's shoulder waved a tentacle curiously at the newcomers, and Saudade offered their fingers out for the creature to inspect. The sight of those tentacles wrapping around Saudade's extended hand made Willa vaguely queasy, and she shot them a betrayed glare. She and Saudade weren't here to make friends with these people or with their weird pets.

Faraz led them to a dining room with a single long table that could seat a couple dozen people, it looked like. Down the middle of the table and extending into the wall to the left were a set of tiny train tracks, and Willa guessed the door on that wall, as well as the rails, must lead into the kitchen. Willa circled around the table and claimed the side where she could sit with her back to the windows and both entrances in sight, and Saudade took a chair next to her.

Faraz transferred his tentacle monster from his shoulder to the back of a chair on the other side. "The espresso machine probably isn't working, along with most of the kitchen equipment, but I could boil water for tea, if you like?"

"You don't have to play gracious host for us," Willa said. "We're not welcome guests. Let's not pretend."

Faraz tilted his head a little at this, but remained unflustered at her brusqueness. "I did invite you both here. I'd argue that makes you welcome guests."

He looked like he was considering whether to gently force the issue and make them tea anyway, but then Porzia caught up with them, a young blond man in tow behind her as she entered. Porzia, Faraz, and presumably Leo took seats on the opposite side of the absurdly long table, so negotiations could begin.

"All right, we're here," Willa said. "I admit I'm curious as to what manner of compromise you think we can achieve. It's not as if we can split the editbook in half and each keep our own piece."

Leo scowled at them fiercely from across the table. "The editbook is no concern of yours. It belongs to Elsa di Jumi da Veldana, whose mother scribed it. That book is her legacy and her responsibility."

Dryly, Willa replied, "Yes, I can see how very concerned she is from the fact that she's not even present."

"Elsa has been unavoidably detained with the relief efforts in Napoli," he said. "You know, actually *saving lives* while you play hide-and-seek with us."

Willa shot Saudade a sideways glance, expecting them to have a smart retort to someone calling their advanced security measures *hide-and-seek*. But Saudade seemed reluctant to speak up—unusual for them, who has always been rather loquacious in Willa's company—as if they wanted to fade into the background, and then perhaps the other humans wouldn't notice they were an android from the future. Their preferred appearance did look human enough, so long as they didn't accidentally say something anachronistic. Willa could see the logic in this approach, yet it still hurt her heart a little to see confident Saudade acting so unsure in Willa's native time.

The conversational pause Willa had left open for Saudade went unfilled, and Porzia stepped into it. "We're acting as Elsa's representatives. Leo is her paramour, and I am her partner in scriptology."

Willa responded with an unimpressed stare. Did they honestly believe they were going to talk her into giving it up?

Porzia sighed. "By now I assume you've figured out that the book you stole is not itself the editbook, but instead a worldbook scribed to contain the editbook."

"Yes, we did notice that."

"So how can you doubt that we want to restrict its use? I put a lot of work into making sure no one can access it."

"No one except you all," Willa countered.

Faraz held his hand out in a conciliatory gesture. "We can add another level of security—take the world-book Porzia designed and lock it up here in a container designed by you, Willa, so you can be sure it can't be accessed without your cooperation."

Willa shook her head. "Any security feature can be bested with enough time and effort and the right equipment. As soon as you invent a new kind of lock, someone starts learning how to pick it. If you weren't worried about us beating your own security measures, none of us would be here."

Faraz said, "Our library is already entrusted with the safekeeping of several valuable books, among them the Veldana worldbook."

"You honestly expect us to believe it would be safe *here*, of all places?" Willa didn't try to hide the disdain in her voice.

Porzia folded her hands atop the table, visibly reining in her temper. "If this is about what happened to Augusto Righi . . . that was a tragic malfunction of the artificial entity who ran this house, and Casa has been shut off until we can restore the fail-safes to Casa's protocols."

Willa inhaled sharply, feeling the mention of Righi land like a blow. She had no desire to discuss something so personal here. "Oh, don't worry, Porzia—this isn't personal, I loathe all of you equally. Krakens in Venezia and a volcanic eruption in Napoli is a truly impressive quantity of destruction to have accomplished in a few days."

Leo stiffened in his seat. "That wasn't us. We tried to stop that from happening."

"Mm, yes, bang-up job you did there. Your track record of protecting the world from the editbook leaves something to be desired."

Leo looked ready with a furious retort, but then the door to the hallway opened, and a young woman dressed in working clothes let herself in. "Signorina Porzia, sorry to interrupt," the woman said in a French accent, dropping a perfunctory curtsy. "We're going to see about getting the kitchen in working order."

"Thank you, Colette. That's an excellent idea," said Porzia.

Correction, then: The Pisanos apparently had *one* servant to run this entire household. Willa did not envy her. Colette passed around the margin of the dining room toward the door to the kitchen, carrying a large toolkit and followed by a pair of children who looked maybe twelve or thirteen years old. One was the spitting image of a younger, less curvaceous Porzia, and the other . . . well. Before Willa had met an excess of androids and herself became a cyborg, the boy's appearance would have shocked her. His mechanical right eye glowed red from within a brass eye socket, and the newsboy cap he wore didn't quite cover how part of his skull on that side had been replaced with glass. His right hand, too, was a mechanical prosthetic.

Across the table, the angry tension vanished from Leo's face, his gaze drawn to the boy as if he were magnetic. Leo hesitated, half out of his seat for a minute before launching himself away from the table, abruptly abandoning their negotiations in favor of chasing the children and Colette into the kitchen. Left in Leo's wake, Faraz and Porzia shared a silent conversation full of head tilts and raised eyebrows. Willa couldn't catch the meaning behind their private looks and gestures, but the end result was Faraz rising from his seat—with a significantly more subtle and less disruptive energy—and removing himself to follow after Leo.

Just watching how the three of them interacted and orbited around one another, Willa had to swallow down a burning jealousy that threatened to overwhelm her. The bond of friendship and camaraderie was so clear; they were *together* in such a fundamental sense. Not that Willa wasn't grateful for Saudade's companionship, but she'd left most of her team behind in the twenty-first century. God, she missed Riley's effervescence and Jaideep's dry humor—she missed them almost enough for it to cross over into resentment, that they'd passed the baton to her and sent her back without their support. Not that any better choices had been available, but it still hurt, to be doing this *for* them and *without* them at the same time.

Willa shook her head at herself. When had she become so sentimental? That was Riley's fault, too, she decided. Riley cracked her armor open like an egg, and now her old talent for emotional repression seemed permanently weakened.

Willa and Porzia returned to arguing over specifics. What safeguards would have to be in place for Willa to agree to returning the editbook? While the two of them went back and forth, Saudade abandoned their chair to pace idly behind Willa's side of the long table. Maybe they wanted to set Porzia at ease by evening the odds, or maybe they were just restless—Willa couldn't tell without diverting her attention from the debate at hand.

At some point, Willa thoughtlessly rucked up the long sleeves of her dress, accidentally exposing the vinelike silver branches of the implants that unmoored her from her original timeline, allowing her to be an effective time agent. But, not knowing their purpose, Porzia gasped in shock.

"What happened? Who did this to you?" Porzia reached across the table for Willa's arm to get a better look at the implants.

Willa leaned away from Porzia's touch and resisted the urge to pull down her sleeves; she did not need to hide that which she was not ashamed of. "No one did it *to* me. This was my choice."

Porzia's eyebrows twisted up in disbelief. "What in the world would make you desperate enough to submit to that?"

Willa had thought she was beyond caring what other people thought of her. But as it turned out, Porzia looking at her like she was some kind of freak still hit her like a punch to an unhealed bruise.

"It's my body, and I can do what I like with it," she gritted out. "You and that high horse you rode in on don't get to judge me."

"I wasn't—I didn't intend . . ." Flustered, it took Porzia a moment to recover her usual eloquence. "My sincerest apologies, I meant no offense."

"And yet you deliver the offense so well," Willa said snidely.

Before they could get back on track to negotiating a compromise, there was the sound of heavy, approaching footsteps out in the hallway. Something was off about the gait—the pause between thumps just a little too long—in a way that made dread leach into Willa's stomach. Why was that sound disturbingly familiar?

The door flew open, and Willa's pulse jumped. The automaton in the doorway was half organic, half mechanical, with wings and ram's horns, and she walked on just the toes of her too-long feet. She was *Norn*.

"It's a trap!" Willa yelled, but Saudade was already lunging for her with the surprising speed their over-engineered body could muster. In the blink of an eye, the dining room with Norn was gone and replaced with a sunflower field on a hill. Saudade's fingers gripped firmly to her upper arm, helping her stand as the left half of

Willa's chair collapsed beneath her—accidentally dragged along and cut through, clean as a radial saw, when the portal closed on it.

Willa's skin tightened in gooseflesh, belatedly registering the flash of coldness from the portal between one location and the next, and maybe a bit from the sudden spike of unanticipated fear, as well. She pulled in a deep breath, trying to settle her nerves, and looked at their surroundings. The two of them were standing in the bare dirt between rows of crops; they were in the countryside, obviously, the Tuscan countryside she presumed, though it could just as easily be the south of France. Luckily, it was early enough in the season that the sunflowers were just beginning to bloom and not yet tall enough to get thoroughly lost in. Being able to see over the tops of the plants didn't help much, though, since there were no towns within view from which she might identify their location.

Willa said, "We're somewhere Norn would never think to look for us, I hope?"

"This is . . . nowhere of significance. And I don't have a tracking chip in my shoulder anymore, so she has no way to follow us here."

Willa cast them a critical look. "Did you just drop us in the nearest sunflower field without knowing exactly what you were aiming for with that portal?"

Saudade shrugged. "Worked, didn't it?"

She sighed. "Well, we can't stand around here

indefinitely. Let's head back to Bologna. It's a large enough city to hide in, so long as we stay clear of the university." Willa didn't know exactly how Porzia had tracked them down in the first place, but no matter how it was done, she needed time to ponder this latest development.

Once, Riley had said, "It's super weird, when you think about it, to expect *one person* to meet all your needs. That just puts an unrealistic amount of pressure on a single support structure."

"But Ri," Jaideep interjected in a high-pitched, saccharine tone, "what if I want to marry my best friend?"

"Ugh, barf. Get a friend who isn't me, weirdo," she joked.

Jaideep turned to Willa, mock-serious now. "See, you thought it was an accident when we kidnapped you from your century, but really we just needed someone to rescue us from codependency."

They'd been talking about monogamy, but Willa couldn't help thinking the same principle might apply to platonic relationships. She and Saudade had no one but each other. Riley had wanted Willa to meet new people when she returned to her own century, to be open to the possibility of forging new connections. Dio santo, what a bitter joke that turned out to be. She couldn't trust anyone from this century, and she felt foolish for even entertaining the idea of a truce.

Saudade portaled them both back to the bustling,

cobblestoned streets of Bologna, and Willa found a promising-looking café to hole up in while they thought over their next move. The café was mostly empty, with the morning coffee rush long past and the sunset aperitivo crowd not yet commenced. Willa waved for Saudade to pick a table while she went to the long wooden counter to order from the barista. It wasn't quite late enough in the afternoon for ordering aperitivi, but Willa could use a little alcohol to calm her nerves. She and Saudade were soon ensconced at a table in the back with two glasses of prosecco, and on the table between them a small platter of crostini with the usual accompaniment of cheeses, sliced meats, and olives.

The salty, savory appetizers and the crisp, effervescent wine soon had Willa feeling more like a regular human being and less like a temporal fugitive. Saudade tried very small bites of everything, as if it were a science experiment. They both kept quiet for a minute, lost in their separate ruminations, before Saudade broke the silence.

"I . . . do not believe the person we saw is Norn," they said slowly. "At least, she isn't Norn *yet*."

"What do you mean?"

"Norn was first among the androids—our founder who created Kairopolis in the 1940s and designed the oldest of us herself, before we had specialists like Deasil for that task. But what if she, herself, was much older than any of us supposed?"

Willa set down her wineglass. "You're saying that

Norn was native to the 1890s, and we just met her original, younger self? Are you sure?"

Saudade pulled a face. "No."

Willa bit one of the little round crostini in half, toasted bread and prosciutto and parmesan sharp on her tongue, giving her time to think. Surely there must be a way to tell the difference between the Norn who chased them across time and a Norn who had not yet even conceived of building Kairopolis. She dug around in her satchel, emptying out most of its contents onto the tabletop to sort through the random junk that accumulated in the bottom.

"I know you were pretty out of it when we rescued you from the decommissioning facility in Kairopolis, but do you remember how close Norn was chasing us? She actually had a hand on Riley when the portal closed, and her reflexes weren't quite fast enough. One of her metal fingertips was severed and came through the portal with us." Willa found what she was looking for, and handed the mechanical finger to Saudade. "Riley stashed it in my bag. I haven't the fainted idea what she thought I would need it for, but . . ."

"But our Norn from 2117 has only nine fingers." Saudade rolled the metal digit against their palm thoughtfully.

Willa tried to remember the details from the dining room, but the flood of adrenaline obscured much beyond the need to flee. "Can you remember exactly what this Norn looked like?"

Saudade stared off for a moment, their eyelids fluttering, presumably replaying the memory. "You're right. Ten fingers."

Willa nodded. Ten fingers. The same android who spent more than a century deceiving her own kind into protecting and maintaining a broken timeline was, in fact, active since before the cataclysm.

And a new name moved to the top of Willa's suspect list.

8

ARIS

1886, Venezia

ARIS KNOWS HE'LL be late for the rendezvous with Father, but he can't peel his gaze away from the smoking palazzo. The windows on the third story glow with an ominous, wavering light as the flames spread—everyone should be out by now, his brothers are supposed to be out, that was the plan. Aris has a decent view from the balcony of the room he broke into in the hotel a block away, the curve of the Grand Canal making the palazzo's facade visible at an angle. It's not impossible his brothers went out the rear door into the alley behind, but surely they would take the most direct escape route, wouldn't they?

Finally there's movement on the private dock at the front entrance to the palazzo. Through the haze of smoke, a thin, dire woman in men's trousers emerges, pulling along a flailing blond twelve-year-old by the arm: Leo and Rosalinda, but *where is Pasca?* Panic kicks Aris in the chest like a horse. Leo seems to have the same thought—he twists out of the fencing instructor's grasp and makes as if to dash back inside, but she's a trained fighter and quick. She grabs him around the waist and practically lifts him off his feet as she drags him to the waiting gondola.

Rosalina pushes off from the dock with only one of Aris's brothers safely inside the gondola. *Where. Is. Pasca.*

Aris doesn't so much *decide* to go back; it's more that his body hurtles him down the hotel stairs in response to some deep-seated, instinctual determination to rescue his youngest brother. He races up a pedestrian walkway to the arched footbridge that crosses the smaller side canal separating him from the palazzo's block, the strap of his heavy satchel cutting into his shoulder and the bulk of it banging against his hip as he runs. With grim amusement, Aris thinks, *oh, I am definitely not going to arrive on time for the rendezvous now*, but Father's anger at the delay is a problem for future Aris to sort out; the Aris of right now has more pressing concerns. He darts down the alley behind the palazzo and shoulders his way into the rear entrance.

"Pasca!" he shouts, checking the back rooms quickly but thoroughly—no one in the kitchen, no one in the pantries, no one in the servants' hall. Aris makes his way toward the front of the palazzo, calling out as he clears each room.

In the entry hall with the grand stairs, hot smoke billows along the ceiling, and he can hear the muted roar of the fire consuming the floors above. Aris coughs into his sleeve, thoughts racing. There's no way he can check the second floor—logically, he knows he'll asphyxiate before he finds Pasca, even if it takes every ounce of willpower to resist sprinting up the stairs. Think, *think*.

He has all his worldbooks in his bag with him, including his scribed laboratories with all his projects and experiments. If Aris can't search the second floor, perhaps something else can do the job for him.

He fumbles desperately through the satchel for his portal device, dials the coordinates by memory, and opens a portal to his alchemy lab, calling forth the automaton he's been working on. It steps through the portal with its odd, loping gait, a looming beast with more resemblance to a large gargoyle than a human, mechanical parts intermingled with organic in a manner few pazzerellones can achieve. It does breathe air, but it should be able to survive the suffocating smoke of the upper floors much longer than Aris could.

"Your orders are to find a boy," Aris commands it. "Nine years old and human, which means smaller than me but shaped like me. He's somewhere up those stairs right there. Do you understand?"

The clockwork creature cocks its heavy, ram-horned head to the side and blinks at him just once—slowly, almost insolently, it seems to Aris. Then the creature nods and moves away, loping up the stairs two at a time. The billowing smoke swallows it.

There is no time to worry about the creature's effectiveness, and no real point in doing so besides. It's not as if Aris has an overabundance of backup plans if this one fails, so he must proceed under the assumption of imminent success. If Pasca is up there, he has been inhaling smoke for several minutes and is likely incapacitated. He will need immediate—and very skilled—medical treatment, which Aris has no way of providing.

He will have to buy some time in a very literal sense.

1884, Venezia

Aris has always had an insatiable hunger for understanding how things work. When he was small, "why" was his favorite word, and even at the age of twelve he has no inclination to accept the way things are without a thorough investigation of underlying mechanisms. Despite all of Father's strictness, he never punishes Aris for his obstinate questioning; *great minds interrogate the world around them*, Father says.

And so it is just one more inquiry in a lifetime of over-analysis when Aris begins to pick apart the fundamental rules of scriptology. Specially designed ink and paper—these tools make sense. Words arranged in a precise code to elicit a precise effect—this strict syntax makes sense. But when scribing a new worldbook, why is it necessary to specify the basic physical principles of a habitable world? Every scriptologist knows they must scribe gravity, and light, and oxygen, and time, in addition to creating a space. But why, if not because it is possible to make a world that *lacks* one of those core properties?

Like any good hypothesis, this one is testable, and Aris is determined to test it. He does have enough innate caution to realize it would be unwise to portal into a world with no air, but there are other ways to stretch the limits of plausible physics. He scribes a worldbook in which the temporal property progresses slower than the passage of time in the real world.

He spends barely half a minute inside, but when he returns to the palazzo, he has been missing for almost thirty-six hours.

1886, Venezia

Aris rifles through the stack of worldbooks weighing down his satchel and pulls out his experimental world where time passes two orders of magnitude slower. He doesn't have these coordinates memorized—has hardly thought about this project in two years—but now it may just be exactly what he needs to preserve his brother's life for long enough that Aris can figure out how to stabilize his condition. Flipping open to the first page, he checks the coordinates, then twists the dials on his portal device in preparation.

There are a few muffled thumps upstairs, then the clockwork creature emerges from the smoke and retreats back down to the main floor, carrying a child-size bundle in its arms. Pasca is very badly burned, especially on his right side, and he isn't moving. Aris swallows around the lump in his throat; he can't even tell if Pasca is breathing.

Later. Later. This will all be for nothing if he doesn't get himself out of the burning palazzo in one piece. The heat and smoke are rapidly becoming oppressive, and the upper floors could collapse at any moment. Aris covers his face with one sleeve, coughing, and flips the switch on the portal device with his other hand.

"Take him inside," Aris orders the creature, his voice rasping. "I'll hold open a portal for you when I'm ready for you to carry him back out."

The clockwork creature vanishes through the portal with its precious cargo, and Aris dashes for the back door. He spills out into the alley, hacking to clear his lungs. A dark column of smoke blots out the blue sky above; the Venezia fire brigade definitely will have noticed by now, and Aris has to get out of here before their gondolas show up and discover him at the scene. He retreats back to the side canal where his own small gondola is docked, ready for Aris to make his getaway.

Even with fresh air in his lungs, Aris feels like his chest is afire with a chaotic swirl of emotion. Pasca might not survive, Aris could lose his youngest brother, and it was Father's plan that did this to them. Even if he manages to save Pasca, abandoning Leo still feels like ripping out a vital organ and dropping it in the dustbin. (His heart, probably—Aris has never found much use for it, except the tight squeeze of love it manages to produce for his brothers.) But if Aris renews his argument against leaving Leo behind, Father might become suspicious of *why* he's late to the rendezvous, and some animal instinct insists he must keep Pasca a secret.

Aris isn't sure exactly what he's afraid might happen to Pasca—that Father will cast him aside like he's done with Leo, perhaps. Or that Father will decide to keep him. And what does it mean that *both* possibilities make Aris want to hide Pasca away in some secret, protective cocoon forever?

You know this is all wrong, he can imagine Leo saying. *If you don't trust Father, why are you following him?*

A stab of uncertainty goes through Aris, and he pauses, hands frozen over the rope fastening the gondola to the dock. Could he choose to follow Leo, instead? But he can't, he can't.

Aris, the dutiful son, heads to the rendezvous.

early 1891, Trentino

Rage crystallizes in Aris's veins as his hand closes around the doorknob. He can hear Leo's voice on the other side, invading the parlor room of Pasca's secret chambers. For years, Aris has successfully kept their youngest

131

brother sequestered in a place of safety and privacy—but trust Leo to be incapable of leaving well enough alone. Of course Leo and Elsa went exploring until they managed to expose Aris's most important secret. He should have expected nothing less.

Aris throws open the door and catches Leo standing with his hands on Pasca's shoulders, close and proprietary, while Elsa looks on with wide-eyed shock and the clockwork nanny hovers behind them nervously. Aris turns his glare upon Leo first. "You're not supposed to be in here, brother. And you're definitely not supposed to bring guests."

Leo drops his hands from Pasca, turning to Aris with an expression like he's staring at a stranger. "Is there *nothing* you won't lie about?"

Technically, Aris never lied about this. He may have, on several occasions, failed to correct Leo's mistaken belief that Pasca died in the fire. But he has not lied. Still, he can recognize a royal mess when it's right in front of him.

Frustration making his movements sharp, he signs to the clockwork nanny, "You had *one job*."

The nanny bows its head and hunches, cowed, but Aris will not be swayed toward sympathy. The creature is supposed to protect Pasca and keep him hidden, not accidentally tempt the guests visiting Father's stronghold to go investigating in the middle of the night. Unbelievable.

"Pasca, go to your room," Aris signs.

But Pasca just replies, "Don't tell me what to do!"

"Fine." Aris exhales his annoyance, then snaps at Leo and Elsa in Italian, "Come along, you two."

Elsa says, "We most certainly will not." God, she's impossible.

Leo rubs his hands down his face, his posture softening with an exhausted sadness. "Oh, Aris, what have you done to Pasca?"

Aris bristles—why does he say *done to*, like Aris is some sort of monster?—and he can feel the muscles in his back tensing like he's readying for a fight. "What would you have done? I couldn't very well let him die. He's my *brother*."

"Of course not. Not *your* brother," Leo says as if he means the words to cut like a knife.

The cold inside Aris spreads a little, but he doesn't think it's rage anymore. "What is that supposed to mean?"

"You turned Pasca into an experiment!" Leo cries. "We're not your playthings, Aris—you don't own us. Did you even ask him what he wanted first, before implanting all these mechanical body parts?"

"We are, all three of us, experiments. You know that as well as I." Their father wanted the best and brightest young minds to do incredible things for his mission, and he did not leave the matter up to chance.

"Look at what you have done. You tortured him."

"I tried to fix him. I'm still trying! This is your fault, anyway—if you'd kept better track of him, Rosalinda would have gotten him out safely, and he never would've been trapped in the fire. Ugh! I can't believe we're arguing about this, of all things."

Pasca, who has been watching the argument but probably catching only a little of it from lip-reading, signs, "Stop talking about me like I'm not here."

"If you went to your room like I told you, that wouldn't be a problem," Aris signs, before turning back to Leo. "I thought you'd be happy he's alive."

"Then why didn't you tell me?" Leo counters. "Why did you keep him hidden?"

"I was worried you'd overreact. Oh look, I was right."

"Because you kept him locked away like a prisoner!"

"To protect him," Aris insists.

"From what?"

"From Father!" Aris shouts at last, the ugly truth bubbling up from some dark depth inside of him. The admission burns like acid in his throat. He cannot bear to think on it too long; even while he has been, in some ways, trying to prepare Pasca to do the work the three of them were made for, he has never seriously considered giving Pasca back to their father. Because deep down lives a terrible certainty that Father will take one look at Pasca and reject him. Chastise Aris for wasting his time on an irreparable asset.

Leo has been staring at him, expression inscrutable. Finally, he says, "I'm taking Pasca away from here." He holds out a hand in invitation, and Pasca moves toward him.

Aris's heart seizes, and he signs, "Stop."

"You don't choose for me," Pasca replies.

Aris cannot remember how the confrontation ends. There is a blank space in his timeline that he cannot return to. It is strangely one-sided, the slow memory of consciousness resolving as it returns, while the event of getting knocked unconscious is forever erased.

Is Aris pleased that the clockwork creature allowed Leo to abscond with Pasca? Decidedly not. But at least the automaton has enough common sense to realize it ought to follow wherever Pasca goes, and Aris already has safeguards in place. He can monitor Pasca through the clockwork creature—literally keeping an eye on him, even if it is not Aris's own eye. It feels like a pathetic sort of recompense, hardly enough to soothe the sting of both his brothers choosing to abandon him after everything he's done for them.

Perhaps it is time for Aris to admit to himself that he's never going to have what he wants. It's not that Father was right about letting go and making sacrifices; it's just that it doesn't matter how hard you hold on to things. Loss is inevitable. Might as well let the whole world burn.

1887, Nizza

The stasis chamber Aris built has a shape uncomfortably reminiscent of a coffin, but through the curved glass lid, he can see that Pasca's skin is flushed with living color instead of the waxy pallor of death. Aris keeps an eye on the ticker tape reporting his brother's vitals as he gradually dials down the stasis effect. Pasca is alive, and that is what truly matters, that is what he focuses on. Pasca's heart beats, and his lungs draw air of their own accord, and none of his vital organs suffered irreparable damage from oxygen deprivation, as far as Aris can tell.

The burn injuries were . . . more difficult. Aris could keep only the thumb and two fingers on Pasca's left hand, and the left is the good side. He tried to save the right arm, but the burns were too severe and sepsis set in, and there was no choice but to amputate at the shoulder. The right eye was a lost cause, the swelling in his brain nearly killed him, and then the infection from relieving the swelling tried to do the job, too.

Finally, *finally*, Pasca is stable. He can't hold a wrench or even so much as a fountain pen, but he is alive and likely to stay this way. So long as Aris doesn't imagine the expression Father would wear, were he to see one of his sons in such a useless state, he can manage to feel optimism instead of blind panic. Everything is under control. He can fix this. He will never have to hear Father say, *you should have let him die*. Pasca will not be taken away and killed, because Aris will fix everything before Father even finds out.

Aris watches the pen nibs twitching across the ticker tape as Pasca's heart rate increases, as his brain activity wavers but rises toward consciousness. He pops open the chamber lid with a pneumatic hiss and holds his own breath as Pasca's eyelid flutters. And then Pasca is looking back at him.

"Don't try to move—you're injured," Aris says. "How are you feeling, little brother?"

Pasca is awake, his one remaining eye clear and lucid, but he stares at Aris with incomprehension.

A little eel of dread squirms through Aris's chest. "Pasca? Can you understand me?"

"What?" Pasca croaks out, and his eye widens with increasing alarm. He shifts slightly where he lies, then lifts his head to stare in shocked disbelief at the empty space where his right arm used to be. The angle is awkward—he can't get a very good look at his own condition with one eye missing, and Aris can see the rising panic in his expression as Pasca comprehends the cause of this difficulty. He lifts his bandaged left hand to touch the bandages covering the right side of his head.

Aris shushes him, gently but firmly guiding Pasca's arm down to his side and his head back against the pillow. Ignoring the rush of his own unsettled feelings, he quickly retrieves a pen and the notebook he's been recording medical observations in. He flips to a blank page and writes in large letters—*Can you hear?*—then holds it open where Pasca can read it without straining.

Pasca's eye flits across the words, then he gives a small, meek shake of his head.

Very well. This is fine. This is one more roadblock in

his brother's recovery, but it is no reason to panic. Aris writes, *You were caught in a fire. Are you in pain?*

Pasca reads the question, and his gaze goes glassy for a moment, as if he's occupied with performing an internal status check. He shakes his head again, with more certainty this time.

That's good. Aris was afraid the current dose of analgesics would be insufficient, but doping him further would make it difficult to keep Pasca awake and even minimally communicative. He writes, *Everything is going to be fine, I promise. I will make it fine.*

Pasca reads the words and looks at Aris, gaze inscrutable. He does not nod. Aris tells himself not to be concerned with what his brother's lack of agreement might mean.

1891, Napoli

At this point, Aris is fairly well convinced that Napoli must have been a cesspit even before he dumped a million tons of ashfall on top of the city. He and Vincenzo and Elsa have been working for days, and by now they are mostly excavating corpses instead of survivors. What is the goddamned point of that, anyway? Unburying dead people so they can be reburied more *properly* somewhere else. It's a total waste of Aris's talents, that's what it is. Dead bodies don't care anymore where they lie.

A persistent ache has taken up residence in his wrists from the engine vibrations transmitted up through the controls of the excavator, and no matter how carefully he wraps his face, his throat feels like he's been gargling pulverized glass by the end of every day. They usually work until they lose the light, but the sun is not yet kissing the horizon when Aris powers down the engine with a fed-up yank of a lever. He swings down from the operator's seat, throat raw and joints throbbing, his very last ounce of patience spent.

"What are you doing?" Elsa demands as she stomps over to him, the ash crunching under her boots. "We've got another hour at least until we'll have to stop for the day."

Aris briefly considers trying to care less and arrives at the conclusion that it would be impossible to do so. "This is pointless. I want to see Pasca."

Elsa just raises an eyebrow at him. "You've been helping repair the damage you caused for less than a week, and you think you're in a position to make demands?"

"I think we're well past the point of doing anything useful. What are we trying to accomplish here, besides my penance? Well: Mea culpa, mea culpa, mea maxima culpa. There, are you happy?"

"Hardly, seeing as how that means little to me. Is that from one of your quaint Earth religions?"

He stares at her for a second in genuine bafflement. "You're an off-worlder who fancies yourself ready to get involved in *Italian* politics, and you don't know what Catholicism is."

"I got involved when *you* stole the editbook," she says. "Regardless, people who want redemption instead of a jail cell need to learn priorities. Fixing what you broke comes first; taking a vacation to see your family comes second."

"You couldn't possibly understand," Aris scoffs. "You have no brothers."

Elsa's eyes narrow at him. "Revan might as well be my brother. You don't think I'd rather be visiting my home, checking up on him? He's got a lot to deal with, in no small part thanks to you. But instead I'm on villain babysitting duty, since no one really trusts Vincenzo to shoot you in the kneecap if it comes down to that."

"I suppose I should be flattered that the great Elsa da Veldana still considers me such a threat. There's a compliment hidden in there somewhere."

"Don't strain yourself looking," she quips.

Elsa's tendency toward verbal sparring is practically an invitation, and there's a part of Aris that—despite his general state of exhaustion—is eager to rise to her bait. Any kind of victory, even a duel won with words, would be immensely satisfying right now. But what he truly wants from her isn't the quick gratification of an argument, so he smothers that impulse inside him.

"Elsa, I'm serious. I've helped with Vincenzo's little rescue operation, and now I need this." It chafes, having to beg for what is rightfully his. There are few things in the world that he would swallow his pride for, but Pasca is one of them.

"You know you're not getting anywhere close to Pasca without Leo watching you like a hawk," she points out. "Why? Why is this suddenly so important?"

"Vincenzo can hardly look me in the eye for more than two seconds at a time, and Leo somehow blames *me* for his own decision to commit patricide. The only person I have left is Pasca." Aris clenches his teeth, the words sticking in his throat before he can force them out. "I have to see him. Please. If I can't, you might as well put me back in a cell."

Elsa sets her hands on her hips and scrutinizes him for a moment, as if she's trying to dowse for sincerity in the desert of his mind. "Fine, I'll talk it over with Vincenzo, but that's the best I can promise."

Aris doesn't really *do* humble and self-effacing, it's simply not part of his repertoire, but he can at least hold back the instinct to demand the reward he has earned. Entitlement won't get him what he wants right now. "Thank you. That's all I ask."

1882, Venezia

Aris is ten years old when little Pasca comes down with scarlet fever. He is bedridden; Father hires a nurse to care for him and forbids Aris and Leo from visiting, lest they catch it, too. Aris has not seen Pasca in four days. Eavesdropping outside the locked sickroom door tells him nothing—he can hear the nurse reading aloud from a book or holding a one-sided conversation, but never any response. Is Pasca's throat simply too sore for speaking? Or is this a ruse to temporarily conceal Pasca's death from Aris?

Aris feels physically ill just thinking it, like the thought is a poison his body can eject from his system. He needs to see his brother alive the same way he needs oxygen. Father has expressly forbidden him from picking the lock on the door, but that's not the only way into a room.

Aris secures the rope to the heavy, solid wood frame of the bed in the guest room directly above, and he pushes open the creaky, rusted window frame. Pasca's bedroom window overlooks the Grand Canal, so even if Aris falls, he'll probably be fine, assuming he doesn't hit the water at a bad angle. And he has tied knots in the rope to ease the climb.

He tosses the rope out the window and shimmies through the frame, catching the arches of his feet on a knot as he cautiously shifts his full weight onto the rope. It creaks but holds. The climb down isn't too bad, the stone lip of the windowsill letting him hang a couple inches from the palazzo's exterior wall, enough distance to fit his fingers around the rope as he lowers himself hand over hand. There's a harrowing moment as he clings to the rope with only his off hand and fumbles to unstick Pasca's window, but then it's open and he's slithering inside like a particularly uncoordinated snake. Whatever. He isn't trying to make an impressive entrance; it's enough that the venture didn't end in broken bones.

Aris brushes his palms against his trousers to dispel the prickly, sharp feeling of the rough rope, and he pulls out the cloth he tucked in his pocket to tie around his nose and mouth. (If he gets sick, Father will know for sure about his disobedience.) He approaches the bed and pulls back the gauzy canopy curtain to unveil Pasca's tiny body, asleep beneath a sweat-damp linen sheet. Pasca's cheeks are flushed red, his arms speckled with rash. He is clearly still very sick, but also still alive.

Aris dampens a cloth in the washbasin and folds it neatly to rest across Pasca's fever-hot forehead. Pasca makes a small noise of protest and squirms a little at the touch, but does not wake. Aris wonders, briefly, if he oughtn't wake him to make sure Pasca *can* wake—that he isn't insensible with fever—but Aris decides it's better to let him sleep. He probably needs the rest, and it's the middle of the night anyway.

Something settles inside Aris, now that he can watch Pasca drawing breath with his own eyes. The strangest part of learning scriptology is how things—even Earth things—start to seem less real as you peer closer at the inner workings of reality and learn how to replicate whatever you want inside a scribed world. What is the value of anything if you can just scribe more of it? But *this* is real, Pasca is real. Nothing could ever replace his brothers. Sometimes Aris believes that Leo and Pasca are the only real things in the universe.

9

FARAZ

1891, Pisa

THE KITCHEN IN Casa della Pazzia looked more like an abandoned mechanist's laboratory than a room dedicated to the preparation of foodstuffs, robotic arms hanging in the way everywhere like a forest of dead trees. Faraz spent only a couple seconds assessing the problem before his gaze landed on the argument brewing between Pasca and Leo.

"I don't need help," Pasca was signing.

"Everything in here is . . . A-U-T-O-M-A-T-E-D," Leo replied, his signing still a bit stilted and clumsy, relying on fingerspelling for the vocabulary he didn't know yet (not that Faraz could do any better). "It's run by Casa, but now we need to work everything manually."

"I know. I can fix it. It's not that hard."

Leo's brow tightened stubbornly. "Okay. But. Maybe I want to help?"

"Aris would let me fix it myself," Pasca signed, then watched with something like fascination as Leo pulled away, jaw clenching and eyes avoiding anyone's gaze. Faraz had to wonder if that was true, or if Pasca was just needling Leo to see how he would respond.

It took Leo a moment to rally, as if the words had been a blow that left him blinking away stars. When he looked at Pasca again, he signed, "Aris and I are not the same."

Faraz stepped in before things could get heated. "There's plenty of work," he signed. "Two teams? Divide up the tasks?"

Colette had brought enough tools for two mechanists, so Faraz had the situation diffused and everyone more or less focused soon enough. Colette and Olivia assisted Pasca while Faraz provided an extra pair of hands to Leo. Leo didn't really need the help but was a good sport about accepting it anyway, instead of flaunting his strength.

They got halfway through detaching a robotic arm from above the washbasin before Leo saw something that made him huff and, instead of finishing, crawl halfway under the basin to shut a water valve first. Faraz kicked lightly at his shin while he was down there, reaching around in the plumbing.

"Are you going to brood all evening now?" he said lightly, switching back to Italian since Pasca was across the room anyway.

"I'm not brooding," Leo said sulkily.

"Mm-hmm."

Leo wriggled out from under the washbasin and bounced back to his feet. "It's frustrating, all right?" He gesticulated with the rather hefty pipe wrench in his hand. "It's just . . . I hardly know him. He was *nine* when we were separated—how can I possibly make up for all the time we lost?"

"Well, you could start by recognizing that he probably feels the same way. You're both trying to figure each other out."

"I don't know about that." Leo's gaze crept across the room, and his shoulders tensed with yearning, like a hunting dog that had been ordered to stay. "Since everything that happened with Father and Aris, it seems like all he does is push me away."

"Here's a completely wild suggestion: Have you tried giving him a little space to process?" said Faraz. "It is possible to keep an eye on him without breathing down his neck, Leo."

He pulled an exaggerated face. "Ugh, why do you have to go and be so *reasonable*?"

Faraz opened his mouth to reply, but the sudden sound of shouting in the dining room had his head snapping in the direction of the commotion. Leo was off like a shot, that constant readiness of his serving him well in a crisis (even if Faraz sometimes wondered how he didn't collapse under the exhaustion of his own hypervigilance). With a sigh, Faraz followed.

In the dining room, there was no sign of Willa and

Saudade, but there *was* the clockwork creature, towering above Porzia and Leo with her brass-fingertipped hands clasped primly together.

"What happened?!" Leo asked.

"The nannybot came in, probably looking for Pasca, and they panicked and fled through a portal." Porzia shook her head, dejected. "It fell apart so fast. I couldn't even get a word in before they were gone."

Bewildered, Faraz said, "I'm sorry, did anyone even know she was *here*?" The last time anyone saw the creature—as far as he knew—she was jumping out a window and flying off to freedom, leaving behind all the humans and their distressing machinations.

"It's fine," Porzia said firmly. It was only through years of familiarity that Faraz could tell she was spiraling, instead of perfectly in control. "We can recover from this. I'll get the tracking worldbook."

Leo said, "You really think chasing them is going to help, after they just ran away from us?"

The clockwork creature followed their exchange with steadily increasing distress, watching their faces and body language, her brows drawing together in worried incomprehension.

"You're okay," Faraz signed to the nanny. "You did nothing wrong."

She signed something back, much too fast for him to follow. Unlike Pasca, the creature didn't seem to understand that he and Leo had acquired only a basic working knowledge of the language, and it would take them years more to attain true fluency. "Sign again?" Faraz asked.

"What happened to the building?" the creature signed more slowly. "The house is ———."

Faraz glanced at Leo. "What was that last word?"

"That was the sign for 'dead,'" Leo answered, his tone carefully expressionless. "She's asking about why Casa is dead."

Porzia set her hands on her hips. "Seriously? Pasca's nanny has been missing for two weeks, and what she wants to know about is the house?"

"Casa's not dead. The house was . . ." Leo fumbled for signs to describe what happened. "The house was doing bad things and needed to go to sleep. But not forever."

The nanny stared at Leo for a tense moment, her nonhuman face inscrutable.

Into the conversational pause, Faraz interjected, "Are you okay? Where did you go?"

Though it was hard to be sure, Faraz could swear the creature was scowling at him now. She ignored his question and signed, "Pasca is here, yes? I'll see Pasca now."

Then she plowed forward, forcing Faraz to hop out of the way to avoid getting shouldered aside by seven feet of winged, horned, half-mechanical creation. She banged through the door into the kitchen without a backward glance at the three humans left behind.

Dryly, Porzia said, "Looks like Casa isn't the only misbehaving intelligence on our hands."

Leo went instantly tense, his hand going unconsciously to his hip where his rapier would hang if he were wearing it. "You don't think she'd hurt Pasca, do you?"

Faraz squeezed his shoulder. "No, I don't. Alchemical creations as advanced as the clockwork nanny are affect-driven—the emotional connections they form are real. Remember, Augusto Righi died because Casa perceived him as a threat to Elsa and the rest of us. It wasn't random murder; it was a misapplication of deeply encoded protective instinct."

"Hm." Leo drummed his fingers against his belt before he dropped his hand. "You know that knockout potion you invented?"

"Oh, of course," Porzia interjected dryly. "Let's reminisce about the good old days, when the editbook was stolen by a political radical with delusions of grandeur, instead of stolen by an irate mechanist with a grudge."

Leo shot her a wry look. "I *meant* I was hoping it could be useful again now. Say, against some half-organic, half-mechanical invented physiology?"

Faraz said, "I'll see about tweaking the formula tomorrow. But I don't think we have anything to worry about with the clockwork creature."

It took some further cajoling before Porzia grudgingly agreed to respect Willa and Saudade's abrupt departure.

No one was happy about it, exactly, but Willa had seemed sincere in her intent *not* to use the editbook, and that was the heart of the crisis they hoped to avoid. So long as the planet wasn't in immediate peril, they could wait for Elsa to finish with the relief efforts in Napoli and reclaim the editbook for herself. There were plenty of issues, both practical and personal, to keep them all occupied in the meantime.

Faraz and Leo went back to remodeling the kitchen. Only later—once the kitchen modifications were complete, and dinner prepared, eaten, and cleared—did Faraz seek out Pasca. The task was made considerably harder now that they were all rattling around the big, empty house without Casa's watchful eye keeping track of everyone, but eventually Faraz thought to check the courtyard garden. The night was clear and cool, the moon risen enough to clear the rooftop to the east, bathing the garden in pale light and long, stark shadows from fruit trees and narrow Italian cypresses. Faraz could just make out the dark lump of a boy sitting on the stone bench beneath the broad, lobed leaves of the fig tree.

It was a good spot for someone experiencing mixed feelings about the concept of solitude. On the one hand, it was quiet and empty at this hour, but the glass doors in Leo's bedroom led out to a balcony overlooking the garden. Those doors had gauzy curtains drawn across them now, lambent with a warm, reassuring light that meant Leo was inside. Faraz had, on several occasions, seen Leo vault over the balcony railing and pick his way down the slanted tile roof of the veranda to drop directly into the garden instead of going the long way around to get there. So Pasca could be alone, but Leo was still only a shout away if desperate need arose. Given Pasca's cautious, calculated nature, Faraz doubted the location was mere coincidence.

Faraz lingered indecisively in the deep shadow of the doorway, unnoticed as of yet, debating whether he should leave Pasca to his thoughts. But surely it wouldn't help to let the day's events fester, so he went to fetch a lantern, since they wouldn't be able to talk in the dark.

The modest, warm glow of the lantern was enough to catch Pasca's attention as Faraz approached along the stone-paved garden path. "No nanny?" Faraz signed one-handed.

Pasca watched him closely, as if he was weighing whether Faraz's relaxed body language was a deception, then he admitted, "I don't know where she went."

Faraz sat down at the other end of the stone bench, angling his body to face Pasca, and he placed the lantern on the seat between them. "You're not her K-E-E-P-E-R," Faraz fingerspelled the word. "And she'll turn up."

Pasca lifted an eyebrow dryly. "What do I need a clockwork nanny for when I have my brother's friends to check up on me?"

"Leo didn't send me here. And if you think I don't check up on him same as you, you're very wrong."

This assertion seemed to do little to reassure Pasca. Faraz knew he was walking a narrow line here, trying to offer companionship and support without making Pasca feel surveilled. The kid had spent his whole life under a watchful eye—first Garibaldi's, then Aris's—and he'd clearly grown sensitive to scrutiny. To make matters worse, there was a high likelihood that, until his recent friendship with Porzia's sister Olivia, Pasca *never* had a friend outside his brothers. Maybe that was a place to start, with the story of how Leo transitioned out of Garibaldi's stranglehold.

Faraz smiled fondly. "You know, years ago when I met Leo, the very first conversation I had with him was all lies. He made up a story for why he came here—I think it had P-I-R-A-T-E-S, or maybe that story happened later? I forget. But, point is, not one word was true."

Pasca narrowed his eyes skeptically. "He lied to you, and you decided to be best friends?"

Faraz considered how to express his answer, certain he was going to make a mess of the grammar. "Leo lied to hide his hurt. The world hurt him, a little bit the same as what happened to me. Before, we didn't know how to talk about hurt, but we both had to . . . face moving forward. And that, we could do together."

Pasca looked away and huffed, but there was an uncertain slump to his shoulders. Faraz waited, and after a moment Pasca signed, "Leo and I aren't doing anything together."

"You could," Faraz prodded.

"He's smothering me!" Pasca said. Faraz didn't know the sign for *smothering*, but the open palm over the nose and mouth was fairly self-explanatory. "I'm fourteen years old, and he treats me like a child."

Faraz decided it would be impolitic to point out that, while Pasca had been born fourteen years ago, he'd spent the majority of the past five years either in a stasis chamber or isolated from the outside world, interacting with no one except his narcissist brother and his clockwork nanny. That did not exactly seem like a recipe for healthy childhood development and maturation, and so Leo's overprotectiveness was not without cause.

"Try to be P-A-T-I-E-N-T with him," Faraz advised. "You've been through a lot, but same with Leo. It will take learning for you both—figure out how to be brothers again."

Pasca sighed. "I don't understand what my place is here. I don't know how to be who I'm supposed to be now."

"Welcome to growing up," Faraz replied with a wry grin. "That is what we all have to figure out for ourselves."

It was late when Faraz left Pasca, but he still felt awake in a way that promised a frustrating night of insomnia, so instead of going to bed, he retreated to the alchemy laboratory. Skandar blinked sleepily at him from the perch in the back corner, and he offered a few skritches before Skandar curled back up, wings folded tight to block the lamplight.

The long wooden worktable in the center of the room still had a reference book and a few loose sheets of notes scattered across it from the last time he'd been in here—before Napoli and Venezia, before they lost control of Casa and had to flee. He closed the book and gathered up the papers because he preferred his work area tidy, and because he preferred not to remember a time when he feared Leo had abandoned him. It didn't matter now, anyway; Leo may have gone with Aris for a while, but he came back to them with Pasca in tow, and he defeated Garibaldi. There was no point in reliving old fears. Faraz would not be abandoned again, not by Leo.

Faraz shook his head. If he wasn't going to sleep, he might as well get a head start on those chemical modifications Leo suggested. He found his notes on designing the knockout potion, and from one of the shelves lining the walls, he retrieved a small rack with three glass vials full of purple liquid. He set the rack on the worktable before fetching some extra glassware from a cabinet. The influence of mechanical components on the physiology of an alchemically built creature presented him with an unknown variable that would be difficult to account for when considering dosage and . . .

A noise behind him made Faraz startle, the round-bottomed flask slipping from his hands to crash against the floor. He spun around, pulse hammering in his throat, but it was only the clockwork creature, staring at him curiously from the doorway.

"Oh." Faraz exhaled, and waved a perfunctory greeting to the creature. He looked down, grimaced at the mess, and stepped gingerly out of the blast radius of broken glass. At least the flask had been empty, but he'd need to find a broom and dustpan—usually, Casa had an army of little bots to take care of the cleaning, and that too fell to human hands now.

Except Faraz couldn't go locate a broom, because the clockwork creature was still blocking the doorway. "You need my help with something?" he signed.

Her stare was intense. There was something not quite right about her facial expressions, as if she'd memorized the eyebrow and mouth movements needed as grammatical markers in sign language, but wasn't sure how to use those same muscles to emote. She signed something much too complicated and much too quick for him to catch even a broad sense of the content of her words.

"Slower, please sign slower. Help with what? What can I do for you?"

The clockwork creature cocked her head to the side as if bemused by his request, but she signed slowly, "You are the —— person here."

Faraz furrowed his brow and mimicked the word he didn't know. "What does that mean?"

She fingerspelled, "A-L-C-H-E-M-Y."

"Oh yes. I'm an alchemist."

The creature gave a satisfied nod. "You will make me better."

"Are you sick, or . . . broken? I'm happy to help, but I—" Faraz cut himself off mid-sentence as the clockwork creature stalked confidently into the room. "Careful, you don't want to step on the . . ."

She ignored him and crunched over the glass shards to approach the worktable. A small seed of worry took root in Faraz's gut. What exactly was going on here? The creature plucked one of the vials from the rack, her brass fingers clicking against the glass; with a terrible sinking feeling, Faraz realized that Leo might have been right in his concerns. The clockwork creature unstoppered the vial.

Faraz signed, "Put that down."

"You will help," she replied one-handed, and with the other hand, she splashed the contents of the vial in his face.

Faraz squeezed his eyes shut against the sting of the purple fluid, and the floor seemed to sway beneath him like the deck of a ship, his stomach lurching. His face tingled a little, as if he could actually feel the potion absorbing through his skin. Then everything went black.

10

WILLA

1891, countryside south of Bologna

HAVING CONCLUDED THAT the android they saw in Casa della Pazzia was contemporary-Norn rather than future-Norn, and therefore unlikely to have recognized them as a threat, Willa and Saudade agreed it would be safe enough to return to their not-so-secret lair in the countryside near Riolo.

Willa slept fitfully that night, her dreams plagued with sudden intrusions of Norn and Orrery, the androids portaling in to interrupt whatever other nonsensical dream activities her unconscious mind cooked up. She jolted awake sometime in the early predawn hours of not-quite-morning and knew that attempting to go back to sleep would be a futile endeavor. There was just enough moonlight for her to fumble with the matches and candle she'd left on the windowsill, for lack of any better horizontal surface in her mostly unfurnished bedroom. Frankly, knowing Augusto Righi, she was lucky to have a bed.

The weather in June was still cool enough at night to merit pulling on a dressing robe over her nightgown. Willa tied the cloth belt snugly around her waist before lifting the brass candleholder, moving slowly to carry the light without guttering the flame. The rest of the upstairs was dark and quiet when she slipped into the hall, so Saudade must be below. Willa padded down the stairs, her bare feet quiet, but came up short at the open doorway of the sitting room—inside, a play of colorful shifting light seemed to dance across the polished parquet floor.

Willa stepped closer until she could see Saudade perched on the settee. Projected above their open palm, bright multicolored threads hung in the air, like some intricate spiderweb or three-dimensional tapestry, the strands twining and merging and pulling apart as Saudade tweaked and pinched at the image with the fingers of their opposite hand. Something like dread settled in Willa's stomach. She'd seen this type of timestream visualization once before, but she didn't know why she was seeing it again now.

"What are you doing, Saudade?"

Saudade jumped a little, surprised despite the softness of Willa's tone. "Oh, you're awake," they said, not answering her question.

Willa felt like the situation merited a stern arm-folding, but she was still carrying the candle, so she made do with setting her free hand on her hip. "I thought you said you couldn't do any predictive modeling of possible timelines without access to the databases in Kairopolis?"

"Technically, I said I couldn't do it very well without access." Saudade plucked at one of the threads of light with their free hand, fidgeting guiltily and not meeting Willa's eye.

Willa felt her eyes go wide with horrible realization. "Oh Mary mother of God—you *cheated*, didn't you?"

"I don't know what you mean," Saudade replied evasively.

"Now is not the time to play coy. You left the edit-book with me while I was sleeping, and you time-jumped downstream to Kairopolis—admit it."

Saudade sighed. "I only left you undefended for forty-five seconds from your perspective. You have to know I wouldn't have exposed you to unnecessary risk."

Willa tossed her empty hand in the air. "And what about the unnecessary risk to *you*? You were condemned to decommissioning. Even if Orrery died in the explosion Petrichor triggered—which we don't know for certain—the rest of the security staff are probably under instructions to kill you on sight." Willa planted her hands on her hips to stop their flailing and bit the inside of her cheek to hold back the sudden, unexpected stinging at the corners of her eyes. If something had happened to Saudade during their sojourn into the future, Willa would have awoken completely alone, with no idea of what went wrong. "Did you at least pick the year carefully?"

Saudade winced. "I jumped to 2119. I could risk overlapping with our past selves, or I could risk sneaking into Kairopolis as a known fugitive, but I couldn't avoid both."

"The fact that you tried to hide this tells me you know I would have objected." Willa didn't actually know how old Saudade was in subjective years of experience, but she'd always assumed the android had a few decades on her. Now, though, Willa felt like she was cast into the role of responsible adult while Saudade played at reckless youth.

Saudade pulled the projection back into their palm and closed their fist around it, making the web of light vanish. "It was, perhaps, a hasty decision," they admitted.

Willa huffed and sank down beside them on the settee. "I thought we were through playing games with each other, Saudade. I thought you trusted me to take the lead in this century."

"It's not a matter of trusting you. I feel useless without access to my former abilities. Worse than useless— I'm a liability, if anyone notices I'm from a different century."

Willa rolled her head to the side, leveling a frank look at her partner. "You know I would have gone completely mad by now without you here, right? And that's setting aside how irreplaceable your portaling abilities are in this century."

Saudade responded with a noncommittal hum. Then a hint of a considering look crept into the corners of their eyes. Willa couldn't guess what it was they were thinking about, and maybe this wasn't the best setting for prodding.

"Come on." Willa stood from the settee. "It's too early to be attempting anything without coffee, let alone mapping prospective timelines."

"Caffeine has no effect on my physiology," Saudade pointed out, but they followed Willa to the kitchen.

Willa fed some split wood into the iron cookstove and lit the fire, then placed a full kettle to heat up on the stovetop. She poked through her provisions and decided to make pastina for breakfast while she had the stove lit anyway, instead of preparing something cold later in the morning.

As she cranked the coffee grinder, a feeling of not-quite-rightness itched at her, though she couldn't put her finger on why. Yes, it was true that Willa did not have extensive previous experience with kitchens—at the boardinghouse, she'd mostly eaten the meals provided, and at her father's estate before that, both her birth sex and her rank meant she never stepped inside the kitchen. But this misplaced feeling was more than just the newness of her culinary independence. She turned to look at Saudade leaning against the edge of the rough wooden prep table behind her and thought, *Oh*. This felt wrong because she was standing where Jaideep was meant to be. He was the proficient cook in their little group, and Willa was supposed to be on the other side of the table while the two of them and Riley discussed their strategies or got sidetracked into philosophical debates.

In the futuristic kitchen of their safe house chalet, Jaideep had been the one standing by the stovetop, gesticulating with a mixing spoon. This time, it was in response to Willa's hesitant inquiry about his thoughts on romance, given that they were now both involved with Riley.

"I get it," he was saying. "Everyone grows up indoctrinated to believe in soulmates and one true love and all that bullshit. Even in our century, kids are still spoon-fed happily-ever-after fairy tales from a young age. But the idea that there's one type of person that's a perfect fit for you—let alone a single individual in the whole world—it's ridiculous."

"Oh, here we go," Riley joked. "Rant incoming in three, two . . ."

Jaideep finally used the large spoon in his hand for its intended purpose, stirring the ingredients in the pan, and he continued undeterred. "Everyone goes through life interacting with different kinds of people. Nobody decides they're only gonna be friends with INTPs and unfriends all the extroverts they know. So why would there be just one type of person who's 'right' in a romantic relationship?"

Willa didn't know any of the references Jaideep had a habit of thoughtlessly spouting, but from context, she assumed "INTP" had something to do with personality. Though if she were brutally honest, she didn't have enough experience with friendship for it to be a useful analogy. So all she said was, "I suppose that makes sense."

Riley said, "Hah, well, evidence suggests I do have a type, so don't take his rant too seriously."

Dryly, Willa said, "The thought of asking fills me with trepidation, but like a character in a penny dreadful, I feel nonetheless compelled. Your type?"

"Snarky. Smart." Riley smiled a little over the edge of her mug. "Guarded at first; really makes me work for their trust."

Willa blinked, forcefully dispelling the mental image. There was no Jaideep to handle the cooking, no Riley to handle the side commentary. Willa poured the hot water to make critically necessary coffee for herself and just-participating coffee for Saudade, then dumped the remaining hot water from the kettle into a small pot to boil the pastina.

"So," she said. "When you were in the future, were you able to confirm whether Norn and Orrery survived Petrichor's explosion?"

Saudade shook their head. "That wasn't my focus."

Willa passed Saudade a cup. "I dread to ask it, but what was your focus, then?"

"From our perspective now, there is not one single future but a sort of topology of possible futures. In some, the Continuity Agency still preserves the cataclysm, in others, we prevent the cataclysm from ever happening. We sit balanced on a fulcrum, an unstable equilibrium that must tip one way or the other. Every day that we approach our goal, the topology of futures in which Kairopolis exists grows smaller, and soon it will become improbable to jump to those futures." Saudade paused to sip their coffee. "I can't see the futures in which we succeed, because in them, Kairopolis is never programmed and a Continuity Agency is never formed, so none of the relevant data is collected. What I can do is guess at those successful futures from the shape of the negative space around the futures in which we fail. But to do that requires detailed data from Kairopolis."

"And you have to acquire the data now," Willa said, "before the Kairopolis futures become too improbable to access via temporal portal." She still didn't like the risk, but she could see the logic.

Willa doctored the pastina into a Parmesan-laced breakfast porridge that at least vaguely resembled what she remembered being fed as a child. She brought the bowl to the prep table and stood across from Saudade—they really needed to get more chairs for this house—and she wordlessly handed an extra spoon to them. Androids didn't need to eat for the sake of sustenance, but Saudade seemed fascinated with the culture of food, nonetheless.

Saudade dipped their spoon into Willa's bowl and then made curious but pleased noises before going back for a second taste. Willa concealed a smile with her own chewing. If only her mother could see her now, the things she would say! Willa couldn't decide whether her mother would be more horrified at the awful manners on display, or that Willa was sharing food with a plebeian, or that the plebeian in question wasn't even human. There was something bitterly satisfying about hearing her mother's voice in her head, acknowledging it, and stoutly ignoring it. It would be better, maybe, if she could stop listening to that insidious voice at all—but it hadn't gone away yet, and she was starting to doubt it ever would.

"All right," Willa said, getting her thoughts back on track. "So you've done your insanely risky data thievery from the future. Or multiple futures? No, don't answer that, I don't want to think about how many brushes with death you've been up to while I sleep. What have you figured out so far?"

Saudade brightened. "The good news is, I expect that we live."

Willa scraped her spoon against the bottom of the bowl, skeptical that she should get her hopes up about the survivability of this endeavor. "Preventing the cataclysm is a major change to the timeline. I doubt Deasil designed my unmooring implants to handle that kind of temporal strain."

"You'd think that. But once the new timeline solidifies,

removing us from existence won't actually resolve any paradox strain—it would, in fact, require the timeline to revert, and there'd be a great deal of resistance against such a major spontaneous shift in events. I see no evidence of futures where we failed because of the timestream erasing us."

"And the bad news?" Willa countered.

"Hm, it's more like . . . news of unclear utility."

Willa nodded. "Very well. Walk me through what you've got so far."

Dawn arrived while Saudade did their best to explain the patterns they saw in the multidimensional spider's web of the timestream. It was getting on toward mid-morning when Saudade stopped themself mid-sentence for a second, then said, "We have to go; the alarm's been tripped."

"Wait." Willa put a hand on Saudade's arm to stay them. "Does your security system allow for visual recognition? Can you tell who's coming?"

Saudade's gaze twitched, as if they were watching something that wasn't there. "Most likely just Porzia. Or to a lesser degree of probability, Porzia and some number of her companions."

Willa nodded. "Let her come. They haven't tried to use force against us. We can afford to finish hearing them out."

"You don't suspect Porzia of colluding with Norn?"

"Whether she is or not, we'd best find out one way or the other."

"Fine," Saudade conceded. "But I'll be ready to pull us through a portal at a second's notice if she tries anything."

"Fair," Willa agreed, and then walked into the foyer to await Porzia's arrival, Saudade close on her heels.

She'd expected a knock on the door, but instead a portal opened right there in the middle of the empty entryway. Porzia stepped through like she owned the place. She was wearing another flawlessly tailored dress—this one in a shade of maroon that managed to toe the impossible line of *rich but humble*.

Willa cleared her throat pointedly, and Porzia looked up from the portal device in her hands with a surprised raise of her eyebrows. "Oh. You're here."

"It's my house," Willa answered flatly. That was, perhaps, a slight stretch of the truth—but it wasn't out of the realm of possibility that if Righi had known to put together a will, he might have included Willa as an inheritor, given his absence of blood heirs.

"Right, certainly. I just expected to leave a note." Porzia held up a folded sheet of paper before making both the note and her portal device vanish into her dress pockets.

Willa leveled a bland stare at her and allowed the silence to stretch for a few uncomfortable seconds before she said, "Is there something more you wanted from us?"

"Yes." Porzia drew herself up, posture straightening as she rallied. "What do you know about the clockwork nanny?"

Willa glanced sidelong at Saudade, who seemed equally baffled. "The clockwork who?"

A small frown line tightened between Porzia's brows. "You seemed to recognize her when she came into the dining room. Or were you just startled by her . . . unconventional appearance? I didn't take you, of all people, for the superficial type."

Oh, she was asking about Norn—or the creature that would become Norn, at least. "Wait, that automaton is your *nanny*?" The idea of Norn being responsible for the care of small children was too incongruous to even properly imagine it. Had these people lost all access to common sense?

"Well . . . that's what we thought she was designed to do. Except she's developed a rather irksome habit of coming and going as she pleases, and she seems to have taken Faraz with her this time. By force."

Before Willa could ask, Saudade had also latched on to that *we thought* and spoken up with sudden intensity. "So it wasn't one of you who built her?"

Porzia bit her lip and paced a couple steps away, wrestling with indecision for a moment before she turned to face them again. "As far as we know, she was built by Aris Garibaldi, Leo's estranged brother . . . which in retrospect should have been a warning sign. Aris is a polymath—proficient in all three of the major sciences—and he was the scriptologist who destroyed Napoli." She sighed. "Aris is the reason we're all so twitchy about letting anyone else hold on to the editbook."

Saudade tensed. "And where is he now?"

"Aris has been under constant supervision, so I don't see how he could be hatching any schemes lately. But the clockwork nanny could be operating under obsolete orders, left over from before we captured Aris."

"There's not much we can tell you," Willa said honestly. Most of what they knew, they could not tell Porzia, since a full explanation would require convincing her that time travel existed. "We do know that the 'clockwork nanny' is dangerous. She's tried to kill us rather persistently."

"Willa," Saudade hissed.

"What?" She switched to English and muttered, "I know, I know—no spoilers. It's not as if I specified *when* Norn tried to kill us. Or . . . will try, I suppose." Willa still wasn't entirely certain how the androids of Kairopolis handled the whole issue of past versus future tense when different people's timelines were out of order relative to one another.

Porzia set her hands on her hips, evidently irked at being left out, and said in Italian, "I don't suppose you'd care to specify *why* the clockwork nanny has a mortal grudge against you?"

Willa grimaced. "Well . . . that's sort of a long story."

"I could make time to hear it."

Willa snorted. If that were literally true, they'd have a serious problem on their hands. "If you'd allow us to confer for a minute . . . ," she said as if it were a request, but she grabbed Saudade's sleeve and withdrew to the study without waiting for Porzia's reply.

Just to be safe, Willa also switched back to English.

"In all those failed futures, did you find anywhere Porzia Pisano becomes . . . I don't know, president of the Unified States of Italy or some such?"

Saudade cocked their head to the side. "No, she doesn't appear as a figure of historical significance. Even Kairopolis with all its omnipresent surveillance doesn't collect data on everyone alive, so I can't say for certain whether Porzia survives the cataclysm."

Willa chewed on the inside of her cheek, thinking. "She's obnoxiously entitled but she's not ambitious. And Norn abducted her friend."

"So, what, you want to ally with her?"

"Enemy of my enemy." Willa shrugged. "I'm starting to believe we really are on the same side."

Saudade's eyes glazed as they ran probabilities for a minute. "If we're going after Norn, we should secure the editbook somewhere instead of carrying it with us."

"In for a penny, in for a pound, hm?" she said. "All right, let's do this: Let's try trusting Porzia Pisano."

The two of them went with Porzia through a portal back to Casa della Pazzia, where she showed them to the laboratory from which Faraz had been taken. Willa took in the scene: the broken glass scattered across the floor, the very upset tentacle monster chittering at them from its perch in the corner. On the worktable in the center of the room were two glass vials full of purple liquid and a discarded, empty third.

Saudade asked, "What time did he go missing?"

"He was last seen around midnight," Porzia said. "We went looking when he never showed up for breakfast, and that's when we realized he was gone. So there's no way to know exactly, but it's possible the creature's had him for several hours."

Willa muttered mostly to herself, "What does she want him *for*, though?"

Saudade skirted around the shattered evidence on the floor, approached Faraz's pet, and began cooing at it. Willa suppressed a shudder of visceral horror and tried very hard to think, *to each their own* instead.

She pointed to the empty vial and asked Porzia, "Do we know what that is?"

Porzia nodded. "It's a chemical that induces uncon-sciousness when absorbed through the skin. I'm guessing that's how the clockwork creature managed to get Faraz out of Casa della Pazzia without the commotion waking up the whole house."

"Hm." She turned away from the table to block Por-zia's view while behind her back she swiped one of the full vials and hid it up her sleeve. "Any details we've missed? Saudade, do you have any . . . questions . . ."

Willa's sentence trailed off when she glanced over her shoulder at Saudade, who now had the little monster riding on their shoulder, tentacles wrapping everywhere like something out of a nightmare. Porzia sighed resignedly, as if she, too, would like to protest such a sight but had long since given up that battle. Apparently, that was one thing she and Porzia had in common.

Oblivious to their reactions, Saudade said brightly, "Yes! It would be very informative to see what you've tried so far, in terms of tracking Faraz's location. I assume you have some mechanism for doing so—similar to how you found us outside Riolo—and that it has failed to yield useful information."

"Certainly," Porzia agreed with the forced politeness of a well-trained socialite. "Why don't I first show Willa what I was thinking for storing the editbook, and she can tackle that while we're occupied."

Willa adjusted the satchel strap on her shoulder. She was growing accustomed to the weight of the editbook—both physical and psychological—and only noticed the slight discomfort when reminded of it. At this point, it would feel more strange to *not* have it close at hand, or at least to know that Saudade did. Willa didn't think of herself as a particularly adaptable person; to be who she was in her century, she'd had to learn how to plant her feet like the roots of a tree and refuse to budge when the world tried to push her. But the past couple weeks had been nothing but change, adjust, change, adjust. Perhaps for some things, she had to learn flexibility, instead.

Willa and Saudade followed Porzia through the halls of Casa della Pazzia to the library. Even though she'd seen it before, Willa was not immune to the intentionally awe-inspiring architecture on display—the domed ceiling high above, the varicolored sunlight filtering in through four stained-glass windows up on the third floor, the scrollwork details on the black iron railings. Not for the first time, Willa mulled over the irony of the similarities between academic awe and religious styling.

"Yes, yes, it's a lovely space," Porzia interrupted her ogling. "But we're not here for the ambiance."

"I didn't actually think you were that shallow," Willa said. "What are we here for?"

"We don't want just anyone waltzing in and learning where we hid it, so . . ." Porzia went to one of the cutoff corner walls of the octagonal room, fiddled with a latch or something under one of the shelves, and then pulled; with a creak of disused hinges, the whole bookcase swung out of the wall, revealing a triangular secret compartment behind. "Et voilà!" she declared.

"So you want me to build a triangular iron chest into a hidden closet. Hrm." Willa leaned into the narrow space, eyeballing the dimensions and examining the preexisting woodwork. She gave a small nod of satisfaction at the location she had to work with. "Yes, that can be done. I'm going to need flat sheets of boilerplate wrought iron and an arc welder." Materials science wasn't really her discipline, but she'd just have to do her best. After all, she could design the most intricate of custom locks for the door of the safe, but it wouldn't matter if a thief could break in by drilling through or prying apart the sides.

Porzia turned to Saudade. "You are a scriptologist, yes?"

"I can read script," they equivocated.

"The tracking worldbook is on the table over there. Go ahead and take a look while I show Willa to Leo's laboratory for supplies."

Saudade and Willa exchanged a surprised look. Porzia must be really desperate for help if she was willing to leave Saudade alone with a valuable worldbook. But there was hardly time for either of them to voice their shock as Porzia hustled Willa out of the library, down the hall, and around a corner.

Porzia spoke as briskly as she walked. "I think you're most likely to find the materials you need in Leo's lab, since he tends to build large." She made an expansive gesture. "I wouldn't know what all of his equipment is for, but Burak can probably help with that if necessary. He knows the laboratory best, aside from Leo . . ."

Willa followed Porzia down a half flight of stairs into an enormous, high-ceilinged engineering laboratory. The alchemy lab had seemed fine, she supposed—it had . . . chemicals and such?—but she hadn't truly appreciated the resources at their disposal until it was her own field of science being supplied. This room was a mechanist's paradise of equipment and half-finished projects. It was also *unbelievably* disorganized.

"Where is Leo?" Willa asked as casually as she could. "You seem to always have an entourage."

"He's flying down to Napoli to get information out of Aris, but I don't expect him back until tonight." She paused and gave Willa an almost-hungry considering look. "It's quite inconvenient, only having the one doorbook. I'd love to know how your friend managed to duplicate it."

So Porzia had been paying attention to Saudade's unusual portaling techniques. Damn. "I'm really not an expert on scriptology," she said.

Porzia narrowed her eyes. "Don't think I haven't noticed that it's somehow always *me* giving information to *you*, and never the other way around, Willa."

"Mm," Willa agreed noncommittally. She approached the nearest workbench and poked through a mess of wrenches, design sketches, and a smattering of tiny clockwork gears. She despaired at the lack of organization. Some of the hulking apparatuses farther back in the lab had the look of machining tools, which she could probably figure out how to operate without assistance. But delving into this chaos to find the materials and tools she'd need to invent a new locking mechanism? That was a disheartening prospect. With a sigh, Willa rolled up her sleeves and got to work.

* * *

In the end, Willa did have to recruit help from several of the younger residents under Porzia's supervision—whose names she could hardly keep straight—to move all the materials and equipment from the lab into the library. Unsurprisingly, Leo's welder was not designed to be easily transportable, and the iron plates for the safe were by necessity extremely heavy. Saudade, who was presumably stronger than any of the available humans, had finished their examination of the tracking worldbook, informed Porzia and Willa that they needed to have a think, and vanished through a portal to who knows where before any of the heavy lifting could be assigned to them. Without any android assistance, it was quite the operation—though perhaps Saudade was wise to remove themself from the proceedings, lest they accidentally reveal their nature by performing a feat of strength that would be impossible for a human.

Willa had scavenged thick leather gloves, a leather smock, and a protective faceplate from Leo's laboratory, so at least she'd donned some decent safety gear before crawling halfway inside the would-be safe with the electrode holder in hand and firing up the arc welder. Sparks flew as she welded together the corners of the plate metal, but she didn't light herself on fire, so the project was going rather well. Best of all, the welder was loud enough that Porzia—though she stubbornly remained in the room—couldn't actually engage Willa in conversation.

She had just shut off the welder to take a break

before the next phase of construction when she caught the sound of the library door opening. Willa tensed, but when she pulled off the welding visor to get a better look, it was only a little boy of perhaps seven or eight years. He wore too-large glasses and clutched a book to his chest.

"Don't worry," Porzia said, "that's just my little brother. Say hello, Aldo!"

The boy dragged his gaze from the book in his arms to blink owlishly up at his sister, and then looked to Willa. "Hi."

"Oh," Willa said, startled to realize she had met him before, elsewhere in the timeline. In another thirty years, Aldo will help Willa's supposed daughter sift through the Order's historical records of now. Willa dabbed at the sweat on her forehead with her sleeve and managed to croak out, "Ah, hello there."

Porzia quirked an eyebrow, as if judging Willa for her sudden awkwardness, but she declined to comment on it. "Aldo, darling, we're a bit busy in here just now."

"You're always busy." The boy scowled accusatorily.

They argued for a minute more while Willa checked the schematics she'd drawn up with the drafting supplies in the lab. She looked up again when the door closed behind a departing Aldo.

"You're just sending him off on his own? Doesn't he need to be supervised?" Growing up, Willa didn't have any younger siblings—just an older brother, with whom she hadn't been close—but she still recalled the oppressive, hawklike regard of their various nannies and governesses. She certainly had not been allowed to run wild at the age of eight.

"He's fine," Porzia said. "My other brother Sante is the one who's liable to find a tiger to wrestle the second you take your eyes off him, but he's recovering from an injury just now."

Willa knew she should probably let the subject go, but some part of her couldn't resist the urge to needle Porzia until she figured out what made the other girl tick. The sensation was odd in its unfamiliarity; back before Riley and Jaideep, she had little interest in pursuing a deeper knowledge of other people. She couldn't care less about what motivated an acquaintance or a stranger, except to the degree that their motivations might affect her work. Was it morbid to be curious now, when the acquaintance in question had only barely been promoted to ally?

Either way, Willa did not bite her tongue or stop herself from saying, "It's just that you seem oddly . . . *relaxed* about your responsibilities, all things considered."

"You think I don't understand the weight of expectation?" Porzia scoffed. "I'm the heir to Casa della Pazzia, which means I'm responsible for taking in pazzerellone orphans from all across southern Europe. That was plenty to juggle even before all this protecting reality business. Add to that: Since none of my three younger siblings are mechanists, and the house requires one, I've spent my whole life believing that I must secure a mechanist husband."

Willa paused in the process of pulling back on her gloves to throw a sharp look at Porzia. Though Righi had always sheltered her from the worst of it, Willa knew that gossip regarding her birth sex had spread throughout not only the aristocracy, but had followed her to academia as well. With Porzia's elite family connections, it was likely she'd heard such gossip.

Willa carefully schooled her tone to be unaffected when she said, "If you're hoping to fish here for a mechanist husband, I'm afraid you'll be disappointed on several fronts."

"What? No." Porzia's eyebrows rose and she looked not just startled but a little flustered, too. "That's not at all what I meant. In fact, I've recently sworn off mechanists. And marriage. And marrying mechanists."

". . . Right," said Willa uncertainly. What was happening here? She had no clue why Porzia had suddenly turned awkward.

"The point is, you can't live your life just to please your parents."

"On that one thing we can agree," Willa answered, with more confidence this time.

"And anyway, I think my sister may be sweet on Leo's brother, which would solve all sorts of problems quite handily if it works out."

That made Willa pause again. "Wait—Leo's brother, the madman who destroyed Napoli?"

"*No*, the other brother, Pasca. Short, blond, has a robot arm?"

"Oh. That makes more sense, I suppose." Were they gossiping now? Was this what it felt like to be the curious third party, instead of the curiosity? Willa would really prefer to *stop* feeling out of her depth.

She pulled the visor over her face and fired up the welder again, putting an end to the conversation with the constant hum of the generator and the sharp buzz of electricity sparking through the metal. Attaching the hinges for the safe door was rather challenging, since the positioning needed to be so exact, but by that time she had developed a good feel for welding. When all the structural components were successfully welded together, Willa shut down the generator again so she could tackle the more delicate installation of the booby trap she'd designed—a pressure plate to go under the editbook, connected to a small, pressurized spray canister full of Faraz's knockout potion. Never let it be said that Willa can't work with the tools at hand.

As Willa shrugged off the heavy welding smock, Porzia commented, "I don't know how you get anything done while buried under all that leather and whatnot."

Willa threw her a flat stare. It should be obvious that the safety equipment was miserably stifling from the sweaty strands of hair stuck to her face, but that was still a distinct improvement over getting horribly burned. "It's not exactly a fashion statement."

Willa pulled closer the crate of components she'd appropriated from Leo's lab to start assembling the pressure plate. She prayed for silence, but as per usual, her prayers went unanswered.

"I don't know," Porzia mused. "I'm generally of the opinion that everything is a fashion statement, even if what you're stating is just an allegiance to practicality."

Willa sighed at the renewed source of distraction; she was not used to working under such conditions. "Has anyone ever told you that you're a little bit exhausting?"

"No," Porzia replied primly. "I am a delight and a treasure."

Willa snorted. "And modest, too."

"Well, I didn't want to boast, but since you pointed it out . . ." Porzia cracked a sly smile.

Mother of God, she was a champion-level irritant. Willa wasn't entirely sure if she wanted to throttle Porzia, or . . . something else. Willa crushed that alternative idea ruthlessly. She was saved from the dangers of introspection by Saudade bursting into the library through an unexpected portal and beelining for Willa.

Without preamble, Saudade announced, "It's a Jaideep problem!"

Willa blinked up at them from her seat on the floor near the closet. "What?"

Saudade puffed up a little, clearly proud of themself.

"If we have a looper, we can just ask Faraz how to rescue him after he's been rescued. So we need Jaideep."

Willa could see the logic, except for one problem. "We don't have Jaideep."

"Hold on," Porzia interjected. "Did that actually make *sense* to you?"

Saudade turned and blinked at Porzia with genuine surprise. "Oh, are you still here? Well, um, don't worry about . . . anything I just said."

Willa face-palmed. If Saudade had thought to hold the conversation in English, Porzia probably wouldn't have understood a word of it. She switched to English herself and said, "You burst in here like you were ready to cry *hallelujah*. So do you have some other looper in mind? Can we find one in this century?"

"Ah, well . . . probably not." Saudade tilted their head side to side, thinking it over. "We'd have to invent some sort of quantum signature detection device to find another natural looper, and I'm not saying it's impossible, but that could take days."

"Well, we can't just borrow Jaideep from our own timeline, there's too much risk of altering events we were directly involved in. We may be unmoored, but that doesn't mean we should go around daring the timestream to solve a paradox by erasing us. You told me we still have to be careful."

"No, no—I'm not suggesting we disrupt our timeline," Saudade explained. "Different futures are just probabilities from our perspective in the now. And you know how I mentioned we're balancing on a fulcrum? At the moment it's difficult but possible to access Kairopolis . . . and the flip side of that coin is: It's likely *also* difficult but possible to access the most probable version of the future in which we prevent the cataclysm."

Willa stared at them. "You want to kidnap a different Jaideep—one who's never met us before."

"'Kidnap' is such a strong word."

"I don't like it." She heaved a sigh. "If I ask you how dangerous this is, will you give me an honest accounting of the risk?"

Saudade smiled wryly. "Probably not."

"Enough!" Porzia interrupted in Italian. "Will someone please tell me what's going on? Do we have a way to rescue Faraz or not?"

"Yes," Saudade said at the same time that Willa said, "No."

Willa shot a quick, irritated glare at Saudade before explaining to Porzia, "Saudade has a terrible idea that we're not going to try unless we can't come up with anything better."

Porzia sighed. "I suppose we could try portaling to some likely cities to see if we can pick up a local tracking signal. The creature may have taken him somewhere familiar from her past, so there are a few likely places we could check."

"I've still got some work to do here," Willa said.

"Why don't the two of you give that a try while I finish the safe?"

Saudade and Porzia accepted the task, and with the tracking worldbook under her arm, Porzia opened a portal for the two of them. The subsequent quiet had Willa sighing in relief, but even in blissful solitude, she couldn't manage to focus entirely on her work.

Willa fervently hoped she wasn't just sending them off to keep busy, but the dread seemed to be taking up permanent residence in her stomach. She suspected there was no way to avoid Saudade making dangerous time jumps downstream to uncertain futures. Would securing the editbook make it more or less risky to do so? The timestream was a hopelessly entangled, impossibly complex phenomenon, and Willa was starting to realize that—no matter how advanced Saudade's understanding was compared to her own—it was impossible for any mind to fully comprehend the timestream or predict its behavior with perfect accuracy.

If Saudade was erased, would Willa's unmooring implants be powerful enough to preserve her memory of them? Or would she be left with a hole in her mind where Saudade used to be, and with details of her past that she couldn't quite explain? The past week of her life didn't make any sense without Saudade. How would the timestream paper over such cracks?

Willa sighed, finishing up the installation of the locking mechanism. The safe was ready, but Saudade and Porzia weren't back yet. She reached for her satchel and pulled out the worldbook that contained the editbook, mentally weighing her options. To lock away the editbook without an audience seemed somehow wrong—lacking in the proper sense of ceremony, perhaps—but Willa placed the book inside the vault, activating the pressure plate, and swung the door shut. The lock engaged with an audible *click*. It was done.

She'd expected to feel free, relieved of a burden, but mostly it made her nervous. Willa had never aspired to be anyone's hero, certainly not the entire planet's, but apparently she was growing into the mission Riley and Jaideep had passed to her. With effort, she forced herself to focus on the next practical task in front of her and began cleaning up the tools she'd borrowed, which were now scattered on the floor in an arc around where she sat.

There was the soft *whump* of a portal opening, and Porzia arrived in an agitated swirl of skirts. "Your partner," she announced without preamble, "is even more insufferable than you are. Saudade decided it was 'taking too long' and just . . . left! Hopped into a portal and left me behind on the streets of Nizza!"

"I can't say I'm surprised." Willa finished returning the tools to the crate she'd brought from the mechanics lab, then gave Porzia a once-over. "You look like you made it out in one piece, so I'm not sure what you're complaining about."

Porzia pulled out a chair from the nearest reading table and flopped into it dramatically. "For one thing, Saudade didn't even have the decency to tell me where they were going before up and vanishing on me."

Willa stood from the floor, wiping her hands on a rag. "Yes, Saudade can be impulsive. If it makes you feel better, you can watch me yell at them."

As if on cue, a second portal opened and deposited Saudade in the library. Taking in the closed safe and cleaned work area, Saudade said, "Ah, you're done. Excellent."

Willa laughed humorlessly. "And you're right on time." They gave her a quizzical look, and she continued, "You went to find Jaideep, didn't you."

Saudade's expression shifted to sheepish, but before they could reply, Porzia said, "Well it can't have been that difficult, if it only took a few minutes."

Willa pressed her lips together. There was no way to explain that a time agent might take hours or days to complete an assignment and still return mere seconds after they left—not without revealing the existence of time travel, anyway.

To Saudade she said, "I suppose it's too much to hope that you returned empty-handed because you came to your senses."

"I don't know why you're so preoccupied with my health, Willa. I haven't died yet."

Saudade tried a grin, but Willa was not amused.

"Everyone has a spotless record of not dying . . . until they do." She frowned thoughtfully. That actually wasn't true, since Saudade *did* die in the original timeline, before Willa and her friends went back and rescued them from the decommissioning facility. "You of all people cannot brag about how skilled you've been at not dying so far."

Saudade frowned like they were a little put out at Willa's assessment. "In any case, we have another problem to address first." They switched to English. "I did some recon, and the jump to check on alternate-Jaideep was a little too easy, which means that other futures are rapidly becoming *less* accessible."

Willa leaned in closer; she could feel bad about excluding Porzia later, if she found the energy for it. "Isn't that a good thing? If you were spying on Jaideep in a future where we succeeded."

"In a general sense, yes. In a specific sense, there's something we ought to do before the option is no longer available."

Willa sighed; this was Saudade's version of trying to be a team player. They weren't particularly skilled at it, but she could tell they were trying, and that was something. She switched back to Italian and said to Porzia, "The editbook is secured. We'll return shortly to plan the rescue operation."

"You have got to be kidding me," Porzia said, gesturing emphatically. "Are you even here to help find Faraz? I've tried to be patient, but this is—"

Before Porzia's tirade could really build up steam, Saudade opened a portal, and Willa leapt at the chance to follow them through. As far as she was concerned, Porzia could vent her frustrations to an empty room.

She stepped out of the portal into the meadow on the edge of Veldana and immediately threw a suspicious look at Saudade. Yes, they had used Veldana as a convenient hiding place before, but that wasn't the primary reason they knew of it. Veldana was the only populated world—other than Earth—that existed continuously from the mid-nineteenth century through the twenty-second century. As an artificial world somewhat divorced from reality, it had reduced temporal resistance, and so made for the ideal location from which to attempt difficult time jumps.

"Saudade . . . ," Willa said.

"I can do this. Do you trust me?"

She pressed her lips together unhappily. "How badly do we need to do whatever this is?"

"I would not ask it of you if I did not deem it necessary."

Less than twelve hours ago, it had been Willa lecturing Saudade about trust, so she supposed she ought to build that street in both directions. "All right."

Saudade led her into a second portal. The cold, black nothingness lasted for just a second too long, but a second's difference was enough to confirm Willa's suspicions—she had only traveled through a temporal portal twice in her life, and both trips had been dramatically memorable for other reasons, but now she had to wonder if temporal displacement on its own felt different. A sort of pressure built up behind her eyes like a nascent headache.

Where the two of them emerged was technically the same location, but everything had changed. They stood in a high-walled holding ground, from which the blue sky above was the only slice of Veldana left visible. Willa took a moment to recognize this place as the visitors' arrival area—it had not yet been built in 1891, and was a lovely courtyard garden in 2047 before Petrichor set off an explosion and presumably destroyed it. Where there had once been a pleasant slate-paved patio and carved wooden benches tucked between flowering shrubs, there was now blank concrete and the distinct feeling of being observed.

"Well, I can't say we don't deserve that," Willa muttered to herself. "Perhaps we should get out of here rather promptly?"

"On it," Saudade replied, and opened their third and final portal. Willa hurried to follow them.

Through the portal was another artificial world. The purple-tinged gray of the sky glowed with an ambient, directionless light. Smooth-paved streets curved with an almost organic ease around amorphous, cornerless white buildings. Large-leafed, alien trees accented those alien edifices. Everything—every plant and building and street—simultaneously managed to seem as if it was perfectly placed, and as if it grew where it was by happenstance. Willa inhaled sharply at the familiar surreality of this city.

"Saudade . . . why did you bring me to Kairopolis?"

11

ARIS

1891, Napoli

ARIS CAN'T HEAR much over the chug of the excavator's engine as he methodically scoops volcanic debris off Napoli's main rail lines. They can't make real progress on the task of unburying the city without a way to remove ashfall by the thousands of tons, and for that they need the trains to be running. Is it a waste of his valuable talents to spend the whole day scooping tephra? Probably. Would he trust anyone but himself and Elsa to correctly operate the excavator? That's a definite *no*—not anyone readily available in Napoli, at least.

He's just traded off with Elsa, reclaiming the driver's seat, when Vincenzo approaches, shouting inaudibly and waving his arms to grab Aris's attention, a shovel in one hand. Aris eases off the fuel intake and lets the engine calm to a low idle, then climbs down to investigate what all the fuss is about.

"What is it?"

Vincenzo arches an eyebrow at him. "I take it you haven't noticed who just arrived?"

Aris huffs. "Don't tell me you're now upset that I've been too focused on my—Oh." He cuts himself off as his gaze lands on Elsa speaking with *Leo* not twenty paces behind Vincenzo.

"Yes. *Oh*," Vincenzo imitates, a teasing grin pulling at the corner of his mouth. "If you're really committed to changing your ways, maybe you could start by having a civil conversation with Leo, huh?"

Aris narrows his eyes, still focusing past Vico at his brother, and trepidation stirs in his gut. "What does he want?"

Vico reaches a hand out and brushes at a lock of dark hair hanging against Aris's forehead; his hair isn't quite long enough to get in his eyes, but apparently that doesn't prevent Vico from feeling the urge to fix it. Aris's heart does something uncomfortable in his chest that he really doesn't have time to analyze right now, what with the sudden appearance of Leo.

Vincenzo says, "You don't need me to point out the obvious way to get an answer to that question. Do you?"

Aris throws a quick scowl at him. "Don't mock me."

"I don't think I've ever seen you uncertain before. It's sort of endearing."

"I will stab you."

"You don't have a knife," Vincenzo points out, entirely unconcerned.

"That's never stopped me before."

Vico's nascent grin breaks into a wide smile. He tosses an arm over Aris's shoulders and gives him a little shake; Aris tolerates it only because *Vico is touching him*, and the contact seems to short-circuit something in his brain. Was he wrong to think Vico is beyond his reach? Today he is touching Aris again, like he hasn't since Aris screwed everything up in Trentino—and like no one did in the five years before that. What does it mean?

". . . Aris?"

"What?" He blinks and tries to replay the moment in his mind, scouring for words, but he missed whatever Vincenzo said.

"You ready to go talk to your brother?" he repeats.

"Oh." Right, yes, that. Aris reluctantly slides out from under Vico's arm and marches himself over to where Elsa and Leo stand, both of them now watching him approach. Leo looks serious—when did his little brother get so serious all the time?—and Aris braces for another argument while trying to think of something to say that won't instigate one. He settles, somewhat weakly, for saying, "You're here."

Leo replies, "Your observational skills astound me."

Elsa knocks her shoulder against Leo's. "Play nice."

Taking a deep, deliberate inhale, Leo seems to gather himself. "I came because I need to talk to you. Faraz has gone missing, and it looks like the clockwork nanny took him by force."

Oh, so Leo's here because he wants to blame more of his problems on Aris. Typical. "Are you sure he didn't just need a vacation from dealing with your drama?"

The set of Leo's shoulders tenses like he's readying for a fight. "Don't be absurd, Faraz would never leave without telling me where he was going."

"You mean like how you left with me and didn't so much as write him a letter goodbye," Aris observes mildly. "Yes, I can see how such an action would be impossible to contemplate."

Elsa drops her face into her hand in exasperation, but Aris is too busy watching Leo's jaw clench to care about anyone else's reaction.

"Faraz has been a brother to me for the past five years, which is more than I can say for you!"

Aris feels the words land like a slap, but he maintains control against the pressure building in his chest; it is essential to never let your opponent know when they've hurt you, or they'll hit you again in the same place. "Is that supposed to motivate me to help—hearing how easily you replaced me?"

"Are you being serious right now?" Leo says, his tone hovering somewhere between disbelief and offense. "You're the one who abandoned me and left me thinking my whole family was dead. For *years*."

"It was not my choice!" Aris shouts, pain boiling out of him before he can think better and hold back the words. Even to his own ears, he sounds . . . raw. This is a weakness he absolutely did not intend to expose: how terribly it ripped him open when Father forced him to give up Leo. Aris isn't sure what his face is doing, but he fights to wipe away the expression.

Elsa steps in to say, "Let's not get too far off the rails here. Leo came all this way to ask you for information about Pasca's nanny. Anything you can think of that might be relevant to why she would kidnap Faraz, or where she might've taken him."

Aris ruthlessly grabs at his escaping emotions and shoves them back down into the dark where they belong. When his composure has been recovered, he says, "I know rather a lot about the clockwork nanny, seeing as how I invented her. And I'll tell you everything I know . . . right after you agree to let me see Pasca."

"Aris . . . ," she says.

"We've spoken about this already. Now that I have leverage to get what I want, I'd be a fool not to use it."

Leo makes a growling noise in his throat, then grimaces like he realizes he can't flat out deny Aris's demand but would really prefer to, anyway. Instead, Leo shoots a questioning look over Aris's shoulder at Vincenzo, who has been hanging back a bit from the conversation.

Vincenzo slowly steps closer, as if taking a second to consider his answer. "Well . . . I think it could be fine. He hasn't tried to escape even once. I've left him an opening several times, but he either recognizes the trap, or he genuinely hasn't been looking for an exit route."

Aris stares at him, momentarily struck silent. He *meant* all of this to be a ruse, just a trick to gain his freedom. Didn't he? Except Vincenzo is right: He hasn't seriously considered formulating an escape plan all week. Perhaps because he has nowhere more compelling to be—nowhere that involves getting farther away from his brothers, at least. Either way, the end result seems to be that Vincenzo, against all odds, is starting to trust him again. That sure is . . . something. Terrifying? Fiercely desired? What is this sharp reaction?

Covering for his sudden inner turmoil, Aris drawls, "If I was planning to run, I'd spend less time complaining about how miserable this assignment is."

"So you will help, then," Leo says. "If I agree to take you to Pasca."

Aris takes a rag out of his pocket and scrubs at a smudge of grease on his hand. Dry as a desert, he says, "You know me: always so helpful."

1886, Venezia

Aris is fourteen when he decides to build an automaton to help with Father's cause. Maybe if they have extra help, it won't be necessary to leave Leo and Pasca behind when they flee Venezia. (It doesn't work. Father still insists his brothers are too young, *too soft*—not yet ready to grow into full participants in the family business of political revolution.)

The automaton should be strong and fierce, both scary-looking and genuinely combat-ready. Stealthy, highly mobile . . . with wings! It should definitely fly. And protective, so it can look after his brothers if needed. It will have to be fairly intelligent, which means an organic brain, so he'll have to combine alchemical and mechanical components to get all the features he wants.

Aris discovers there has been woefully little research documented so far on the subject of mechanical-biological integration. There are a number of challenges ranging from materials science to power, but his scribed laboratory expedites the creation of any component he might need. By integrating principles from all three of the mad disciplines, he is able to grow and reshape and build an automaton body that meets his specifications.

Once the body is complete, there remains the problem of cognitive programming. The automaton must be capable of complex communication, for instance, but Aris doesn't have the patience to teach it language the slow way. So he has to design a device capable of imprinting the necessary neural patterns into the creature's brain. He scribes a world where language is a mutable property, with a machine capable of digesting a dictionary and a grammar book and translating the information into brain waves that can be induced in the subject's mind.

Aris is a genius. There are no bounds on what he can accomplish when he sets his mind to a task. Aris is the smartest person alive.

He straps the newly awakened creature down in the chair of his language machine, fits the helmet of electrodes around its head, and uploads Italian directly into its brain.

1886, Nizza

The clockwork creature has been whimpering quietly in the corner for some time now, while Aris carefully attaches the electrodes and intravenous fluids and the iron lung apparatus, then closes the glass lid to seal Pasca into the stasis chamber.

After their disastrous departure from Venezia, Father led Aris out of the Kingdom of Venezia, across the Kingdom of Sardinia, and into southern France. They rode trains for the anonymity and used falsified papers at the border crossings. It takes almost three days before they are ensconced in an empty tenement building in the port district of Nizza—the location Father has selected as his new base of operations. *Three days* in which Aris can do nothing for Pasca except sketch designs for the stasis chamber in his notebook when Father isn't watching too closely. He knows the slow-time worldbook works—he's tested it himself—but he still can't shake the fear of Pasca dying alone in the arms of a barely sentient construct. Days out here in reality are mere fractions of a minute for his brother . . . but how many more minutes does Pasca have before his body is no longer salvageable?

So when they settle into Father's new headquarters, it feels like a breath of fresh air after being held underwater too long—Aris can finally build the stasis chamber, and summon the clockwork creature out of the slow world, and prevent his brother's precarious condition from tipping over into mortality. There is still a great deal of work to do if Pasca's life is to be saved, but the urgency is somewhat abated, now that he's inside a machine specifically designed to prevent medical deterioration. Aris has the time to do this right—to research exactly what will be needed, to invent the techniques that haven't been tried elsewhere before.

But the clockwork creature's incessant mewling is starting to wear on his nerves. Aris has little patience for it; his own face is still tender across the cheek from where Father struck him for being so late to the rendezvous, but no one sees him complaining. But the automaton hasn't learned better than to fuss over fresh hurts, and the fire at the palazzo happened only minutes ago, from its perspective. Aris approaches the creature where it is crouched in the corner of the room, arms tucked in its lap and torso hunched over, wings wrapping defensively around its body.

"Are you injured?" Aris demands. "Hurry up and show me."

Reluctantly, the clockwork creature folds and flattens its wings against its back and uncurls its body enough to hold out its arms, palms up. Aris presses his lips together at the sight: The creature's hands are badly burned. It must have reached into the flames to retrieve Pasca's body, or perhaps needed to open a fire-heated doorknob in the course of the search. Several of its organic finger-tips do not look salvageable. If the damage wasn't done in the service of rescuing Pasca, Aris might be quite irate to discover that a creation he poured so much time and effort into has managed to act so careless with its own upkeep. And on its very first assignment outside the laboratory! A machine that requires frequent repairs is, in fact, a machine that ought to be designed better; needing to perform a major maintenance operation so soon is practically an insult to Aris's design skills.

He forces himself to take a deep, calming breath. No, this is fine, this is fixable. Aris can replace the fingers. He needs the practice designing mechanical hands, anyway.

1891, Trentino

Father's plans are gaining momentum, and he has a lead on a scriptological weapon of immense, unmatched power. This so-called editbook is kept inside a scribed world in a private library in Paris, so it's time to return to France. Father tasks Aris with the responsibility—no, the *honor*—of planning the heist to acquire the editbook, and they'll leave soon for their established base of operations in Nizza. Aris certainly won't mind leaving behind this frigid Alpine late winter for a mild Mediterranean early spring.

There's only one problem: what to do with Pasca. Aris has successfully kept his brother hidden from their father for close to five years now. He scribed a comfortable little world for Pasca to live in, and the clockwork creature attends to him even when Aris is called to spend his time elsewise. But this mission is likely to occupy Aris for weeks, and given its importance, Father will be watching him more closely than usual. Taking Pasca with him would be impractical in these circumstances, but neither can Aris leave him trapped in a scribed world. Pasca has the clockwork creature for company in there, and Aris can monitor the both of them remotely, but if an emergency arises, they'd have to wait for Aris to return before they could even get out into the real world.

Clearly Pasca needs access to a portal device. But not unrestricted access—there will still be household staff and a contingent of his father's thugs stationed at the stronghold, and if Pasca decides to go exploring in Aris's absence, it's highly likely that he'll get spotted and reported on to Father. So the clockwork creature will have to have authority over the portal device, instead. The creature may not be particularly bright, but at least it follows orders, while Pasca has been growing increasingly sulky and defiant in the past few months. He'll have to safeguard against Pasca stealing the device from it, somehow.

Well . . . the clockwork creature is, itself, a device—there's no fundamental reason why its portal-opening function has to be contained in a separate object. Yes, that could work: a built-in portal device, controlled via neural signal. At this point, Aris is probably the leading expert in the world at biological-mechanical interfacing, and it's been a while since he had a real challenge.

He plucks a laboratory notebook from his shelf and starts sketching diagrams.

1889, Trentino

Aris is seventeen, and he has finally invented an optical device that can be used for wireless surveillance.

Despite his desperate, possessive need to maintain contact with Pasca even when Father requires his attention elsewhere, Aris cannot bring himself to replace Pasca's original mechanical eye with the surveillance eye. Pasca probably wouldn't protest the upgrade, but guilt still twists in Aris's stomach like a nest of snakes when he considers it. All Pasca's surgeries so far have been to improve his own quality of life, but this alteration would be for Aris. He can't change his little brother's body just for his own reassurance and sense of control. He knows that would be wrong.

So he takes out one of the clockwork creature's organic eyes and puts the surveillance eye in the creature instead.

1891, Trentino

Leo has betrayed him. Claimed custody of Pasca and fled, tearing their family apart yet again. This time, of his own choosing. Aris doesn't know what to do with the impotent rage smoldering in his chest. *He* would never choose to part with his brothers; he has done everything in his power to hold on to them, and now they leave him behind voluntarily.

Well, fine, if that's the way Leo wants to play it. Aris is always two steps ahead. The clockwork creature went with Pasca, as it was instructed to in the event of Pasca getting separated from Aris. And Aris can track the creature anywhere, can see exactly what it sees. They can run, but they can't hide.

1887, Nizza

Aris is fifteen, and Pasca is alive. He's stable, but he has lost his hearing, and while he can physically speak, he seems distinctly uncomfortable doing so and prefers to write on a slate, instead. Aris goes back and forth on the idea of designing mechanical replacement ears, but Pasca barely survived the first round of bacterial meningitis, and he decides it wouldn't be worth the risk of another operation.

Pasca needs a way to communicate that doesn't involve invasive brain surgery. By now, Aris is well practiced at the art of slipping out from under Father's watchful eye and taking the train to the university in Aix-en-Provence, where he begins his search for a solution. He learns that in 1880, the Milan Conference on Education of the Deaf banned the teaching of sign language. Though Pasca might, perhaps, be convinced to overcome his self-consciousness about voicing, an oralist approach would still require him to learn lipreading, which seems imprecise at best. Instead, Aris takes out a few newspaper advertisements to find an unemployed sign language tutor willing to work under somewhat unusual circumstances.

The tutor is for Pasca and himself. Aris puts the clockwork creature back in the language transmission chair and programs it with sign language.

When the creature comes out of the chair after the procedure and Aris speaks, it stares at him in blank incomprehension. Apparently, the machine overwrote its previous language programming, and the creature no longer understands Italian—an annoying error, but not especially consequential. The clockwork creature's primary function now is to be a companion and caretaker, so Pasca is the only person it's truly important for the creature to be able to communicate with.

1891, in the air over Tuscany

"So there you have it," Aris finishes. "Now you know what I know."

He's crammed into the airship cockpit along with Leo, Vincenzo, and Elsa. After some debate, they agreed that the most critical period of the relief efforts has passed and that Faraz's disappearance should take priority. Vincenzo asked around until his Carbonari compatriots managed to produce a locomotive engineer, whom Aris instructed in how to use the excavator, so the work can continue in their absence.

Elsa's at the helm now, with Leo at her side. Vincenzo leans back against one of the angled, panoramic windows, partly because reclining casually is his default facade, and partly because there simply isn't enough space in the cockpit for him to comfortably squeeze in anywhere else.

Leo folds his arms, as if suspicious that Aris might still be holding out on them. "You haven't told us anything that explains why the nanny would kidnap Faraz."

"Hm. I suppose I haven't," Aris replies enigmatically. He's tempted to play the *I have no idea why the creature is behaving like this* card, as a way to distance himself from this latest conundrum, but the thought of admitting that he doesn't know what's going on . . . well, that chafes a bit too much. Aris likes it best when he actually does know more than everyone else, but failing that, he can at least project an air of secrecy and superiority.

Aris says, "Perhaps when I see Pasca again, that will jog my memory."

Leo visibly grinds his teeth together. "I swear to God, if anything happens to Faraz because of you . . ."

"You'll what," he says flatly, "put a rapier through my throat?"

The color drains from Leo's face and he looks away. Well . . . good. Leo *should* feel sick with guilt when he thinks about what he did to their father. Sure, part of Aris is starting to realize that he needs his brothers and Vincenzo more than he needs Father's mission, more even than he needs to cling to his rage. But whatever revelation Aris might be tempted to have about the importance of personal ties, it will have to wait until he has the time to unpack it.

Elsa adjusts their heading. "If the two of you end up throttling each other instead of helping with the rescue, I swear Faraz will never let me live it down."

"Why would he tease *you* about that?" Aris says, momentarily perplexed. "No, never mind, I don't actually care about the answer. How close are we to Pisa?"

"We've got another forty minutes or so until we're docked," Elsa says. "And you get to see Pasca either way, so why don't you drop the air of mystery, and for once in your life contribute something without having your arm twisted first."

Aris huffs, but she's not wrong—this isn't the perfect situation in which to cling to pettiness. He can defend that hill some other time. "Very well, how about this: My equipment for connecting with the creature's surveillance eye is on board."

Elsa stays at the helm while Aris goes astern into the main compartment with Leo and Vincenzo trailing curiously behind him. Leo obviously didn't do a thorough inventory of all the equipment in Aris's mobile airship laboratory, because he raises his eyebrows when Aris opens a cabinet and pulls out his surveillance receiver, viewing screen, and memory storage device.

"Is that"—Vincenzo's voice twists with disgust—"a *brain* in a *jar*?"

Aris lifts a shoulder in a dismissive shrug as he busies himself flipping switches and adjusting knobs. "How else do you expect me to record what the eye sees? I can't sit around watching the surveillance feed all day." Aris pulls up a stool in front of the display screen. "Now, when did you say your favorite sycophant was taken?"

"His name is Faraz," Leo grinds out from between clenched teeth. "And he went missing sometime after midnight last night."

Aris twists the controls, summoning up the stored memories of last night. Leo looms over his shoulder as the screen's shades of gray resolve into the figure of a young man lying crumpled on the floor, viewed from above. Aris can practically feel the tension vibrating off Leo; his brother used to know how to relax, but he doubts Leo would appreciate any constructive feedback on his attitude right now. The creature's point of view looks up and away from Faraz, and Leo's breath hitches audibly as his friend slides off the screen. The perspective bobs a little, in time with the creature's wide gait. The creature moves to a chemical storage cabinet and faces its own dark reflection in the cabinet's glass door. The curved ram's horns and the mismatched eyes take on a sinister cast, distorted a little by the imperfections in the glass. The creature's expression twists into something that, on a human, Aris might identify as a smirk, and then a strip of black cloth zooms closer to cover the entire view.

"Damn," Aris mutters.

Leo gasps. "She knows you can spy on her with the eye."

"Yes, thank you, master of the obvious," Aris says. "I suppose that resolves the question of whether she's just acting out some misinterpreted old order of mine."

Leo leans closer over his shoulder. "Can you trace where the eye is transmitting from now? A direction, at least?"

Aris fiddles with the controls. "I'm not getting a locator signal."

"Not getting, or not trying?" Leo snaps.

"There is a range on these things, you know. The signal doesn't cover the entire Earth, and without a relay, it won't transmit from inside a scribed world, either." Aris sighs. "If I wanted to sabotage your rescue attempt, I would have just pretended I didn't have this equipment on the airship."

The three of them squeeze back into the cockpit to confer with Elsa while she pilots. After they related what they found—and what they didn't find—Elsa scowls and says, "Don't play coy, Aris. You know what she's after."

Aris folds his arms, irked at her tone. "The truth? I'm not certain what the clockwork creature is up to. I never really gave it much thought, to be honest—it's an automaton, it's supposed to do what it's told. What does it choose to do in the absence of clear instruction? You're a polymath, too; your guess is as good as mine."

"Are you serious?" Elsa says, throwing him a look he can't decipher. "After everything you've described, you can't imagine why she might be behaving erratically? Unbelievable. Anyone else? Leo?"

Leo freezes like a student who wasn't expecting the governess to single him out. "I—what?"

"It's a good thing you're pretty," Elsa teases him.

Aris gawks when Leo just huffs good-naturedly at this, instead of taking offense as he ought to.

Elsa says, "Right, then: Vincenzo, you're the last hope for humanity. So please, amaze us all with your skills of empathy. What does the clockwork creature want?"

"If it were me . . . ," Vincenzo says slowly, fingers drumming against his hip where his thumb's hooked through his gun belt. "In her shoes, I'd be looking for liberation."

12

FARAZ

1891, location unknown

Faraz awoke in an unfamiliar bedroom, lying atop a fancy four-poster bed. His head was pounding, and the sunlight streaming in through the diamond-paned windows felt like it was stabbing him in the eyes. Faraz had never been drunk, but he presumed the aftereffects of the knockout potion would resemble a hangover, and now that he'd experienced it for himself, he could not imagine how Leo managed to forgive the wine and go back for another bottle. One morning like this should be enough to make a person swear off drinking forever.

Groaning, he pushed himself up to a sitting position and scrubbed his hands over his face. The last thing he remembered was the clockwork creature acting strangely in his lab and reaching for his knockout potion. So, he'd been abducted by a rogue part-organic, part-mechanical automaton—surely that had to be a first. It would have made some kind of sense if the creature had absconded with Pasca, since she presumably had standing orders to protect the boy. But she hardly knew Faraz, so why take him?

Faraz grabbed ahold of the carved-wood bedpost until he was sure his legs were steady enough, then he shuffled over to the window, hoping to get a sense of where he'd been taken. The sun had just crested the jagged, rocky peaks to the east. Looking down turned out to be a terrible idea—this place must be built into the side of a mountain, because right outside the window was a precipitous drop down to a green alpine meadow far below. Faraz backed away as a swell of vertigo washed through him, his fear of heights contributing nothing helpful to the lingering nausea from the potion hangover.

Instead, Faraz took advantage of being alone to make dua, supplicating to Allah for protection and lending him the wisdom to see his way through this, whatever may come.

The bedroom door banged open to reveal the clockwork creature looming large in the doorway. Faraz finished his muttered prayer before turning to confront her.

"This is bad," Faraz signed sharply. He wished he could say, *you can't just go around kidnapping people!* except he didn't know the sign for *kidnap*, and he was too upset to have the patience for expanding his vocabulary just now.

The creature watched him with an implacable, entirely unchastened expression. "You will help me," she signed.

"Where are we? Is this Garibaldi's house?" *House* was probably understating the situation, if the creature had indeed brought him to Garibaldi's stronghold in the Alps outside Trentino. Faraz had never been there, but he'd heard of the place from Leo and Elsa. When the creature didn't answer his question, Faraz tossed his hands in the air and then signed, "I don't want to help you now!"

She gave him a single, slow blink. "Come along."

The creature shifted back as if to make space for Faraz to leave the bedroom, but he said, "No."

She stared at him contemplatively for a few long seconds as he held his ground and refused to follow. Then she loped into the room with three long strides, grabbed his arm in an implacable grip, and marched him out of the bedroom by force like he was a naughty eight-year-old. Faraz's face flushed hot with humiliation and fear, as the truth registered for the first time of how terribly outmatched he was against her.

"Okay! Fine! I'll walk!" he signed desperately with his free hand.

They were already halfway down the hall by the time she released the viselike pressure of her hold on him. Faraz rubbed at his upper arm, where he wouldn't be surprised to find a bruise in the shape of a handprint tomorrow, but he grudgingly followed the creature after that. She led him down a flight of stairs and along another hallway to the mechanist's laboratory—high-ceilinged, like Leo's, but clean and well organized, completely unlike Leo's. There were long workbenches and hulking machines, and a bookcase sunken into the far wall, as if it were designed to be concealed behind a false panel.

The clockwork creature went to the shelves, selected a particular journal, flipped through it quickly as if to confirm it was the right one, and then held it out to Faraz. Reaching a hand out, cautious and reluctant, Faraz took the journal from her and examined the contents. It was a laboratory notebook—specifically, Aris's lab notes on the design of the clockwork creature.

Still holding the notebook in one hand, he signed with the other, "I don't understand."

Then she told him what she wanted.

Faraz stared in disbelief. "I'm sorry, can you sign that again? Did you ask me to *take your eye out*?"

He had noticed that the creature was now wearing a black blindfold wrapped diagonally across her right eye like a poor imitation of a pirate, but he hadn't bothered to question that single quirk amidst the rest of the creature's odd behavior. Now he wondered if she'd sustained an injury during his kidnapping. Perhaps someone had tried to stop her on the way out of Casa della Pazzia. He didn't recall anything being wrong with her eyes before, except that they were mismatched, but he was fairly certain they always had been, so—

Oh.

"Your right eye, it's mechanical?" he asked.

Her hands flew through an explanation of which he missed maybe 40 percent, but he caught the gist of it: Aris had put in a mechanical eye that did . . . something bad that she didn't like.

And now she expected him to be able to safely remove it. Despite the fact that Faraz was exclusively an alchemist, only passingly acquainted with mechanical principles as a side effect of being best friends with a mechanist. This was a terrible, awful idea, and he had no desire to cause neural damage to anyone, even his somewhat-confused kidnapper.

"I can't do what you want," he insisted. "I don't know how. I'm not a mechanist."

She loomed closer and tapped one of her brass-tipped fingers to the open pages of the notebook. Apparently, she expected him to study Aris's notes until he figured it out. And she didn't seem inclined to budge until he caved.

"We're both going to regret this," Faraz grumbled under his breath in Italian.

On the upside, Aris was apparently both fastidiously organized and averse to wastefulness, so Faraz was able to find another mechanical eye—an older but hopefully workable model—to replace the one the creature wanted removed. On the downside, though, Aris clearly never intended anyone else to use his lab notebook as an instruction manual, so while the optic nerve attachment was diagrammed, there was no step-by-step walkthrough for removal or reinstallation.

The process of replacing the eye was a harrowing twenty minutes in which Faraz did his best to focus on the task and to deliberately *not* contemplate what the consequences of failure might be. It was a good thing he had experience keeping his hands steady under pressure. When the clockwork creature finally blinked and looked around with her new eye, testing it out, Faraz exhaled his relief.

"Working okay?" he signed.

"Yes," the creature replied.

He pointed at the eye he'd removed, where it sat somewhat grotesquely on the workbench. "What do you want to do with—"

The clockwork creature slammed her hand down, crushing the eye against the tabletop with an audible *crunch*.

"Uh, right . . . I suppose that's one way to settle a problem," Faraz muttered. Then he signed, "Okay. I did what you wanted. Now, you let me go."

The creature narrowed her eyes at him. "You did the first step. We have much work left to do."

Faraz raised his hands to argue, but she turned her back to him, effectively ending the conversation. She strode over to the bookcase and plucked a few volumes from the shelves as if she knew exactly what she was looking for—which seemed odd the Faraz, because weren't these all Aris's books?—and then she turned her attention back to him. A crook of her index finger was enough to say she expected him to follow again.

Faraz considered refusing to cooperate. His usual tendency toward helpfulness was severely compromised by the part where he was getting ordered around by a kidnapper, whom he would have been perfectly content to assist if she had just *asked*. But instead she took his time and expertise by force, and at this point he was edging seriously close to fed up. The only reason he stood from his stool at the workbench was that he didn't have a clear notion of what self-imposed limits—if any—the creature might have, and he did not especially want to gamble his life on the assumption that she would hold to some sort of ethical code of conduct. If he tried sticking to his seat in passive resistance, would she give up and let him go? Would she kill him? Best not to find out the answer.

Anyway, Faraz's companions had gotten plenty of experience with rescue operations in the past few weeks. They'd be showing up to bring him home any minute now, he was sure—his job was simply to keep the creature pacified and his own self in one piece until they got here. Yes, it was slightly worrying that the rescue party hadn't materialized yet, but it was still morning, and Faraz supposed it was possible they hadn't yet figured out there was anything nefarious about his absence.

Faraz shuffled reluctantly over to where the creature stood. Somehow, without her moving a muscle, a portal irised open right beside them. Faraz whipped his head around, expecting to see that someone (Aris?) had snuck into the lab behind him with a portal device in hand, but the two of them were still alone together.

"How did you do that?" he signed.

The clockwork creature stomped her foot impatiently, ignoring his question. "Go through."

Faraz took a measured breath, irked at being ordered about. He just had to survive until Leo and Porzia came for him, he reminded himself. The portal was holding steady, waiting for its passengers, so he stepped through.

Dark, cold, nothing . . . and then light again, though he was not grateful for it.

The world on the other side of the portal was like a nightmare designed just for him: an enormous, empty space woven through with stone bridges and narrow stairways, arranged with no rhyme or reason, as if "up" and "down" were meaningless concepts here. They stood on a small platform with no railings, and a sick uncertainty swept through Faraz—did he even know which direction he'd fall if he slipped off the edge? To the right, a narrow walkway connected the platform to a staircase that twisted in on itself as if with the sinister intent to dump any climbers into the void. To the left, a path curved upward into a forty-five-degree slope and terminated in a door, or a perhaps hatch, which could lead to nowhere except the bottom side of the same pathway. Instinct would have driven him to retreat right back through the portal, if only it hadn't snapped closed behind them.

The clockwork creature glanced around, getting her bearings—as if there were any bearings to get amidst this geometric madness!—and then reached a hand out toward Faraz. He flinched away from her touch; the thought of being dragged through a gravity maze made Faraz flash hot and cold with visceral terror, head spinning nauseously.

"No. No, no, no," he signed. "Take me home. I don't like it here."

The creature leveled a flat stare at him, as if she couldn't fathom why he was being so difficult. "I know this maze well. I won't let you die."

Somehow, Faraz did not feel terribly reassured by this. But the clockwork creature clearly didn't care about his discomfort—she grabbed him and hoisted him over her shoulder like a sack of flour, ignoring his noises of protest. Then she spread her wings and launched right off the platform.

The feeble sense of direction Faraz had been clinging to immediately evaporated as the web of pathways and stairs seemed to spin around them vertiginously. Faraz squeezed his eyes closed and muttered a prayer, his pulse hammering in his throat. His stomach lurched in sympathy with his discombobulated inner ear as they flew through gravity wells that pulled them in different directions.

Finally, the gravity seemed to stabilize a little. Faraz felt himself starting to slip from the creature's grasp, and he frantically clung to her shoulder until he felt the toes of his shoes connecting with solid ground beneath him. He blinked his eyes open. Oh, they'd landed. He quickly pulled away from the creature, his steps a bit unsteady, like walking up the pier after a boat ride over choppy seas. His hands were shaking; dazedly, he noted this as a less than ideal condition, given that he needed his hands to communicate with the creature.

The pathway they'd landed on ran along what he tentatively hoped was a real wall, as opposed to yet another gravity trap. The clockwork creature opened the door set into the wall, and Faraz cautiously followed her through, relieved to find an actual room on the other side. It was furnished like the sitting room of a residence; given that it was the clockwork creature who brought him here, he wondered if this was where she'd lived with Pasca.

The creature set her small stack of books down on a writing table and turned to Faraz, but before she could order him around anymore, he raised his hands. "Do you have a name?"

This question seemed to stop her short. She blinked at him, a little uncertainty showing through the cracks in her neutral facade for the first time. "Pasca called me Nanny."

"That's a title though, not a name. And you don't want to do that job anymore, right?"

The creature's brow wrinkled. She shifted her weight from one foot to the other.

"It's okay if you don't know how you feel about Pasca."

She didn't reply. Faraz gave her a minute to think it over. Perhaps if he helped her self-actualize a bit, treated her like a person, she would figure out that she ought to return the favor. She went to the bookcase beside the desk and ran her hand along the books contemplatively, her metal fingertips rasping against the leather spines. Eventually, she turned to face Faraz again.

"N-O-R-N," she fingerspelled to him. "A new title for a new job."

Faraz didn't recognize the name, but there was something vaguely sinister about her explanation. "Right. Okay. Name chosen," he agreed, trying not to show how unsettled he felt.

The creature—*Norn*—gave a satisfied nod, as if pleased to have the matter resolved. Then she stepped closer to Faraz. "Come. I will show you what I need from you now."

A portal opened. Faraz eyed it skeptically.

"We're already in a scribed world, and now you want to portal from here into another one?" Admittedly, Faraz had only a passing understanding of the physics underlying scriptology, but the idea of playing Russian nesting dolls with scribed worlds made him distinctly nervous.

Norn, however, was apparently not making a request

so much as stating what they were going to do. She grabbed Faraz's wrist and dragged him through. This portal deposited them in a blessedly normal-looking laboratory, no dizzying security features in sight. Well, not *quite* normal-looking—on one side of the room sat a pair of cages built of wrought-iron bars, both large enough to accommodate a human being.

Norn guided Faraz over to a contraption that vaguely resembled an adjustable medician's chair, except it had restraints capable of strapping down the . . . patient? Victim? Faraz wasn't sure he wanted to know which. There was some other machinery surrounding the chair, though at a glance he couldn't guess what any of it was for. Norn started to explain, and Faraz did his best to follow along as she described how she used to understand spoken Italian, until Aris imprinted her brain with sign language, and she lost her aural comprehension as a side effect. Apparently, she expected him to fix the problem.

"Right, right." Faraz nodded sagely, while his internal commentary went more like, *I can't believe she expects me to use Aris's machine without accidentally frying her brain.* But Faraz reminded himself that he didn't actually need to succeed at every task she set to him—he just needed to maintain the pretense of his own usefulness until rescue came. "I'll need to do a careful study of how the language chair works."

"Yes," Norn agreed. "I stole all the relevant books."

Faraz sighed. Of course she had. And here he'd been

hoping to delay the process indefinitely with a lack of adequate information.

Norn portaled the both of them back to Pasca's sitting room and selected one of the books from the pile she'd placed on the desk. "You read this," she signed, and pressed it into his hands.

With no small amount of trepidation, Faraz cracked the cover and stared in disbelief at the contents—it wasn't just any book, it was a worldbook. Presumably, the text for the language laboratory they'd just visited.

Faraz pinched the bridge of his nose for a long moment, then tucked the book under his arm to free his hands. "How do you sign S-Y-N-T-A-X? Thank you. Now, scriptological syntax is not the same as spoken language. Yes, I can read this, but I don't understand it."

Norn blinked at him, implacable. "You are a scientist."

"I'm not a mechanist or a scriptologist! I'm not the same as Aris." If Norn wanted a polymath, she kidnapped the wrong person.

"I have Aris's notes, also," she persisted. When he just stared at her in wordless disbelief, she added, "You will do this. Why? Because you will not leave, until after you do this."

With the utmost trepidation, Faraz pulled the worldbook from beneath his arm and opened the cover again. Yes, indeed, it still read like nonsense word salad, even upon closer inspection. This was going to be a very long day.

13

WILLA

2084, *Kairopolis*

WILLA GRABBED SAUDADE by the arm and pulled them into the shadow of a bulbous white edifice, avoiding the irregularly spaced, porthole windows. Her pulse quickened as she glanced around to make sure no one had noticed their arrival. In one direction, the street curved out of sight, and in the other, it melted into an irregularly shaped plaza where a cluster of three androids stood casually conversing.

"Will you at least keep out of sight?" Willa hissed.

"Don't worry," said Saudade. "The me from 2084 is on an extended mission in 1950s North Africa, so I'm not going to cross paths with myself."

"Yes, but if current-you gets caught showing a human around Kairopolis, then past-you is going to end up in hot water."

"Eh, that's probably fine. We're planning on writing over this whole future anyway."

Willa peered around the gnarled trunk of a tree that partially blocked her view of the plaza ahead, and she muttered, "Ugh. When did I get nominated to be the responsible one? I never agreed to this."

"I beg to differ," Saudade replied.

Willa shot them a withering look.

"You should know by now that I'm impervious to your stern glares."

"Can you lead us wherever we're going without getting detected? Because last I checked, you *weren't* impervious to bullets."

Despite their blasé disregard for life and limb, Saudade could in fact manage a fair degree of stealth. The rounded architectural style of Kairopolis created a warren of tapering alleyways and oddly shaped little courtyards in the negative space between buildings, and Saudade navigated through these less traveled and better concealed paths with the ease of a veteran rule breaker. It reminded Willa that she was not, in truth, solely responsible for Saudade's defection from the Continuity Agency—her request for help may have catalyzed it, but they had never been a strict conformist. Saudade was . . . whimsically rebellious, Willa decided on for a descriptor.

She followed Saudade until they paused in a slightly larger, grassy courtyard shaped like a five-armed starfish.

They glanced around, at the buildings, checking their orientation. "This is it."

Saudade approached one of the edifices—which had a shape that reminded Willa of an enormous lump of butter left to soften in the heat too long—and when they waved their hand over the blank rear wall, a doorway morphed into existence. Smart matter, Jaideep had called it, whatever that meant. Willa had stopped even trying to make sense of the future technology by that point.

The door slid open at a touch, vanishing into the wall and revealing a dark cavity no larger than a closet on the other side, from which there was no obvious exit except the one Saudade just created. They stepped inside and ran their hand up the wall from floor to ceiling, coaxing a set of ladder rungs to grow out of the wall.

Willa watched this with just a small amount of consternation. "Are we . . . drilling a new entrance into the building?"

"You said you wanted 'stealthy.'"

Saudade climbed the ladder high enough to press their hand against the ceiling, which melted away from their touch, forming a chimney-shaped passage above. They called up more ladder rungs, climbed, and repeated the procedure. Willa accepted her fate and followed behind; the smart matter had a weird, slightly spongy texture in her hands that made her nervous, even though the ladder rungs did feel structurally sound enough to hold her weight.

Willa estimated that they'd climbed up to the third floor by the time Saudade reached to the side of the ladder and created another door. When they opened it, the chimney shaft flooded with light from beyond, making Willa squint after the darkness her eyes had adjusted to. Above her, Saudade stepped neatly from the ladder to a small ledge they'd extended from the threshold and went inside. Willa climbed the rest of the way and joined them.

Inside was a large laboratory. The banks of equipment lining the walls looked suspiciously familiar. There were several medical benches—metal tables the length of a person, each with a chandelier of robotic arms hanging above it, tubes and power cables neatly arranged.

"This is Deasil's laboratory," Willa realized. Deasil was the android in charge of designing and constructing new androids. The two of them had entered from the rear, but as she stepped into the middle of the room for a more familiar perspective, she was sure of it.

"Yes, we need to borrow his expertise," Saudade said.

They approached one of the machines crouching along the wall, a rectangular chamber about a meter wide and held up at counter height by metal scaffolding bolted into the floor. Through a window in the front of the box, Willa could see the inside looked like an extraordinarily tiny manufacturing plant, with delicate little mechanical arms and machining tools. Saudade pressed a button to call up a holographic interface and began scrolling through a list of programs with a swish of their finger.

"Ah, I was right." Saudade tapped one of the program names, then scrolled through the code which bloomed in the air at their command. "After you convinced Deasil to design those external unmooring implants, he couldn't resist taking the experiment to its logical conclusion. He'll get in some trouble with Norn for it, too, but that'll happen a few weeks from now, so the program hasn't been deleted yet."

"And what is the logical conclusion? For those of us who aren't android doctors."

Saudade entered the execute command, and the miniature manufactory hummed to life. "You'll see for yourself in a few minutes."

The arms inside the box whirred and sparked, minuscule mystery components getting wrapped and soldered together. A needle squirted out a silvery layer of goop that hardened into the bottom half of a disk-shaped metal casing. Saudade looked on with a secretive, pleased little smile as the machine worked away at its program. After a couple minutes more, the hum of activity quieted to a low idle and the machine let out a beep, a light on the lid switching from red to green.

Saudade released the hatch, lifted the lid, and stuck their arm into the chamber. From inside, they produced a round metal device and held it out to Willa, an offering. She took it carefully, turning it over in her hands. The device was thicker and had a larger diameter than the sand-dollar-size disposable disks that the androids sometimes used to send a person or object to a single preprogrammed destination in the timeline. This disk also had a subtle tactile sensation, the not-quite-hum of an electrical charge raising the fine hairs on the backs of her hands.

"What exactly is this?" It couldn't be what Willa thought it was.

"A full-function spatiotemporal portal device."

"*This*," she repeated in disbelief, "is a time machine?" The prototype time machine Riley and Jaideep designed in 2034 had been so large they had to carry it around inside a laboratory world. It definitely did not fit in the palm of her hand.

"Yes." Saudade grinned. "A time machine for you."

"It . . . doesn't have any controls," she said uncertainly.

"You would control it in much the same way I do with mine. The unmooring network Deasil made for you is already tapped into your neural architecture, so this is designed to simply interface with your preexisting implant."

"My *neural architecture*?" Willa reached a hand back to feel at the base of her neck between her shoulder blades, where the metal tendrils merged together like the body of a starfish. "You're saying this is connected to my spinal cord?"

Saudade's eyes widened in surprise. "Erm, yes. You didn't know that?"

"No, I don't have any conscious control over it."

"You wouldn't. It monitors for cognitive dissonance associated with memory rewrites, so it can interfere with any updates that might occur following a change to the timeline. It's a backup function; the unmooring should be enough to protect you from localized paradoxes." Saudade chewed their lip, staring with growing uncertainty at the time machine in Willa's hands. "I should've asked if you wanted this."

Willa felt her lips curve into a fond smile. "Saudade . . . you already know I'm going to say yes. We wouldn't be here if you weren't fairly certain about that."

"I still should ask. It's not my place to decide how your body gets altered."

"I'm already a transgender cyborg. What's one more body modification? If you think I'm ready to be jumping around the timeline unsupervised, I'll take it."

The installation process was not nearly so involved as her first procedure getting the implants, which was a very good thing, given the current lack of a real medical professional. When it was done, she could tell right away that she had access to something new, though her brain struggled to process the stimulus. It was like suddenly growing a new limb, but without seventeen years of muscle memory informing how to move it. Or perhaps, more accurately, it was like gaining a new sensory modality—a kind of sensation so unlike sight or touch or smell that the human brain didn't know where to begin with interpreting it.

Willa tried to mentally test it out, examine it from different angles, press her awareness against it like a spider waiting to feel the telltale vibrations propagating through the strands of her web. The timestream was that enormous mental spiderweb, or it was a many-branching tree, or it was a braided river. As she reached out, it felt like all of those things and none of them, it tasted like a sunrise, it susurrated in her ears like the sea drawing wet sand from under her feet. The timestream was a hot bath of synesthesia, her brain frantically attempting to reroute the foreign sensation as it spilled over into everything.

"You'll get used to it," Saudade offered. "Direct access to the targeting software can be a bit overwhelming at first."

From her position lying on one of the hard medical tables, Willa rolled her head to the side to regard them. "Saudade, you truly are a master of the understatement."

They smiled. "Don't worry, with practice it will become second nature. We'll start small, opening portals to places you've been before and can easily visualize. How are you feeling otherwise—dizzy? Headache?"

"Don't think so."

Saudade pressed a button to retract the chassis to which the robotic surgery arms were attached, making space for Willa to sit up. She pushed up on her elbows, then swung her legs off the table. Surprisingly, her head didn't start pounding or otherwise protest the movement.

"How am I supposed to control this"—she waved

vaguely beside her head—"when I can't even make sense of it?"

Willa meant the question as more of a rhetorical complaint, but Saudade took the query as a literal request for instruction. "If you want to open a spatial portal without any temporal shift, you just need to relax your mind and follow the easiest path. A jump that involves moving upstream or downstream will always have greater resistance. So just picture the destination as clearly as you can, and the way there should sort of light up in your mind's eye."

Saudade rested a hand on Willa's elbow as she slid off the medical table, in case she was unsteady on her feet, but Willa found she didn't need the extra support to stand.

"All right." Willa inhaled deeply and let it out. "No time like the present to take this for a test run, wouldn't you say?"

Saudade smirked. "Just because Riley and Jaideep aren't here to crack time puns doesn't mean you have to fill the void." They turned serious quickly, though, in their new role as instructor. "Don't try anything complex for your first portal. Picture, say . . . the back-alley courtyard two stories below us."

Willa closed her eyes and tried to let go of the instinctual impulse to mentally prod at the weird new sensation until it started making sense. The spider's web, braided river, shifting constellations feeling of the timestream sitting in the back of her brain wasn't going to suddenly make sense anytime soon. She needed to accept the sensory confusion, and focus instead on where she wanted to go. The small pentagonal clearing; the feathery little not-quite-grass plants carpeting the ground; the curved, white rear walls of the buildings; Saudade's new doorway, with the unlit chimney shaft inside.

As she visualized her destination, the targeting software seemed to stir in the back of her mind, like some hibernating colony of animals shifting toward awareness. Particular threads in the spiderweb warmed to her, until one branch of the tree glowed clearer than all the rest. Path of least resistance, Saudade called it. All right, so, Willa felt the path, and now . . . what did she do to activate it? Where exactly was the "open portal" switch in her brain? She imagined reaching for that brightest branch, choosing it, projecting a feeling of decidedness at it. And then she was hit with a sensation like gears locking into place, or like a single bird taking flight. (Or both of those things, and neither.)

When Willa opened her eyes, it was to the sight of a portal irising open in front of her.

Saudade clapped their hands together, delighted. "There you go! Let's see where we end up, shall we?"

"Wait," Willa said, struck with a sudden pang of uncertainty. "How can you be sure it's—"

Saudade stepped into the portal, unhesitating.

". . . safe," Willa finished for no one but the empty

room to hear. She heaved a sigh and dithered for only a moment before she followed. For a fraction of a second, there was cold lightless nothing, and then she was standing with Saudade in the courtyard behind Deasil's lab.

Willa had opened a portal *with her mind*.

Since temporal jumps were trickier, Willa and Saudade agreed it would be best for Saudade to handle that part for now, at least until Willa had a chance to practice her targeting more than a single time. The last thing they needed was to get embroiled in some accidental timeline shenanigans when they were supposed to be arranging for some deliberate and purposeful timeline shenanigans. No reason to tempt fate more often than strictly necessary.

When the two of them returned to 1891 and to Casa della Pazzia, they discovered that Porzia was still in the library. "That was quick," she said.

"Um . . . yes," Willa said uncertainly. She couldn't ask how long they'd been gone, from Porzia's perspective, without giving themselves away, so vague agreement seemed the best course of action.

Porzia raised an eyebrow scathingly. "If you're quite done, can we go rescue Faraz now?"

"Not precisely ready," Saudade said. "That was just a . . . tangential mission objective."

"Of course there's something else." Porzia huffed and lowered herself into one of the reading table chairs as if she had only hopped to her feet when the portal opened.

Willa somehow managed to refrain from pointing out that the two of them were providing assistance despite having no real proof that Faraz's kidnapping was even related to the cataclysm. Dryly, she said, "I see patience is one of your virtues, too."

"This won't take long," Saudade promised—for Porzia's benefit, she had to assume, since Willa knew that they could be back in a couple minutes regardless of how involved and time-consuming the mission might be.

Saudade's gaze went unfocused for a moment as they worked through how to execute their time jump; Willa might have called it *mental calculations* before, but now she knew it to be an experiential challenge that felt nothing like doing math. Either way, it didn't take long for Saudade to readjust their targeting, and they opened a portal and vanished into a potential future where the cataclysm never happened.

The silence left in Saudade's wake was distinctly uncomfortable. Porzia leaned back in her wooden chair. "So you're really not going to tell me where you just went, or who exactly this important person is, or why they're important?"

"Nope," Willa agreed. She paced slowly across the library floor, not bothering to sit down.

The faint *whoosh* of a portal opening announced Saudade's return. The person Saudade arrived with was recognizably Jaideep, down to the slightly too-prominent nose. He also looked like he was perhaps all of ten years old. The boy looked around without a hint of suspicion, guileless in his curiosity, and Willa was struck with a sudden fear that she didn't know this version of Jaideep at all.

Once, in 1988 West Berlin, Jaideep had paused at a street mural and commented, "My sister was an artist."

"I'm so sorry," Willa had said.

"I never understood her mixed-media stuff anyway," he had replied, dry as a desert. And that was Jaideep through and through—quick to paint over his raw emotions with sarcasm.

But now, the child in front of Willa seemed so open. This Jaideep grew up on Earth; his older sister and parents would never die in the collapse of an artificial world, and so he had no reason to suspect that the universe might gravely hurt him. Jaideep greeted her in English and boldly, blithely, introduced himself, and Willa's reply was weak with hesitation. She had no idea what to do with the boy.

Willa turned a stony glare upon Saudade and said in Italian, "This one is shorter than I remember."

Saudade squirmed a little beneath her scrutiny. "It's not as if we need him to *do* anything. He just needs to sort of exist in our proximity with his unusual quantum signature, and then temporal causality loops should become probable."

Willa set her hands on her hips. "That's not the point. We shouldn't be endangering a child."

Saudade glanced between Porzia and Jaideep, as

if trying to decide who needed to be kept in the dark more, and then leaned close to Willa and decided on English. "The entire timeline—indeed, the fabric of reality itself—is in danger, and this version won't even exist if we fail."

She made a frustrated noise in her throat. It wasn't that Saudade was wrong, per se, and Willa had never been one to let ideals rule in the face of practicality. But this young, vulnerable version of Jaideep—her friend whom she thought to never see again—tugged at her heartstrings a little.

"Anyway." Saudade dismissed the ethical concerns with a wave of their hand. "Now we just need a plan."

"Well, we can split up, now that I've got a portal implant." Even for an unmoored time agent, it was extremely inadvisable to interact with an earlier or later version of oneself, but older-Saudade could pass information to younger-Willa.

Saudade nodded. "I'll do the upstream jump. You bring the instructions to, let's say, Righi's summer house? That should be an easy portal for you, given its familiarity."

"Give us a few minutes here before you appear with Faraz. I think Porzia's getting suspicious of your efficiency."

"Will do," they said. "And remember: Just relax and don't force it. The right path will make itself known."

"Now who's worrying?" Willa said. "Go on, I'm right behind you."

Saudade left through a portal, and Willa turned her attention back to Jaideep, who was staring up at the sparkling chandelier hanging from the domed ceiling, which Willa supposed was fair. The library was an impressive piece of architecture regardless of which century the viewer came from. Willa wasn't sure exactly what Saudade had said to convince him to go along with them, but she interrupted Jaideep's gawking to introduce herself, at least.

Porzia spoke up then. "So what are you doing with this kid? And . . ." She gave Jaideep a critical once-over. "Why is he dressed that way?"

Jaideep was wearing what Willa could now recognize as standard early-twenty-first-century garb—a T-shirt, jeans, and sneakers—thanks to her extended foray into the future. But Porzia would have no context for identifying any of that.

"He's American," Willa said blithely, which was true. It didn't explain his anachronistic clothing choices, but it was the truth.

Porzia gave her a look of extreme, almost corrosive doubt.

Jaideep, having understood precisely none of their conversation, leaned closer to Willa and asked in American English, "What's her problem?"

"That is an excellent question, Jai. But the answer is deserving of a college thesis, at least. If not a more in-depth study."

Willa loosened her faux-haughty tone a bit and cracked a smile, which Jaideep returned with a smirk. He might not know why Willa was making fun of Porzia, but he obviously liked being let in on the joke. Willa didn't have any experience to speak of when it came to relating to children—she'd been the younger sibling, when she'd still had any connection at all to her birth family—but it was easier when she thought of him as a slightly smaller Jaideep. She *did* know Jaideep, she reassured herself. At the very least, she knew who he would become if she failed him—if the cataclysm destabilized reality, and humankind executed a mass exodus into scribed worlds in order to survive, and then one of those artificial worlds collapsed with Jaideep's family inside. But no person was defined entirely by their trauma; Willa had to believe that a person was made of more than the sum of their bad experiences.

She felt a swell of affection for this unhardened version of her friend, whom she dared to hope would never suffer such a traumatic loss. And running like an undercurrent beneath was a sadness that Jaideep would never know her—he would remember Willa only as that weird lady who kidnapped him when he was ten, or perhaps he would even write her off as a particularly vivid dream.

She was starting to learn why Saudade chose their name: a yearning melancholy for that which is lost.

Well, at least she could make this a not-unpleasant memory, if it was to be the only one he had of her. "Want to see something cool? Check out this book—this is how scriptologists used to program worlds, before computers were invented."

"Whoa!"

Porzia raised her eyebrows at the both of them as they approached the reading table and Willa opened the tracking worldbook for Jaideep to see. "Oh, so now we're sharing my proprietary scriptological advancements with the American kid. Wonderful."

"Relax, it's not like he can read it," Willa replied. "Although if you'd prefer to keep him occupied with harmless pursuits, you're welcome to take him to the kitchen for a snack."

Porzia simply stared, as if she could not process the audacity of such a suggestion. "The worst part is, I'm fairly certain you're serious."

"Quite serious." All things considered, it would be better if both Porzia and Jaideep happened to be elsewhere when Saudade returned to the library with Faraz. It would just confuse Jai, and Porzia might make *too much* sense out of it.

Porzia heaved a resigned sigh. "One of these days, I'm going to apply for sainthood."

Willa snorted, then said to Jaideep, "If you go with the mean lady, you should be able to see some pretty cool disassembled robot parts in the kitchen."

He squinted at her doubtfully, but the siren lure of cool robots was too much to resist. Porzia held the door open and gestured him through; Willa watched them go with a niggling of trepidation, but at least the language barrier was working in her favor. Jaideep could spill incriminating details to his heart's content in English, and Porzia still wouldn't figure out he was from the future.

Willa didn't have long to wait after that. A portal opened, spilling Saudade and Faraz into the library. Saudade went straight to the reading table, grabbed some loose sheets of paper and a fountain pen, presumably left there by Porzia, and began to write out detailed instructions with furious precision.

Faraz eyed Willa with confusion. "How did—"

"You must be tired," she interrupted. "Why don't you have a seat. I'll go find Porzia in a minute."

Willa moved to stand near Saudade's shoulder; from there, she could see they were writing in a Portuguese shorthand that would be largely incomprehensible to anyone but themself. That was cautious—probably unnecessarily cautious—but Willa was hardly going to fault them for using clever methods to maintain their secrecy.

Saudade finished their last sentence, then paused and glanced up at Willa. "You know what to do?"

"Now who's wearing the mantle of official worrier?" Willa blew on the last page of damp ink, then folded up the instructions and tucked them away in her skirt pocket. "I've got this."

Willa made her way through the house to the kitchen, where she found Porzia standing with folded arms beside the counter on which she'd laid out a plate of figs, cheese, and bread. Jaideep had apparently ignored these offerings in favor of rifling through a pile of detached mechanical arms that—as Willa suspected might be the case—no one had yet decided how to store or dispose of.

"Having fun?" Willa asked him.

"Look at the joints on this!" He held up a robot arm, compressing and expanding it like an accordion.

"Nice." Willa turned to Porzia and switched to Italian. "Faraz is in the library, by the way," she said with an insouciance carefully calibrated to annoy Porzia.

"What!" Porzia shrieked. "You're just telling me this now? Like it's some afterthought, and not the whole reason we . . ." Her voice faded into indistinct ranting as she rushed out of the kitchen, through the dining room, and down the hall toward her returned friend.

"All right, Jaideep, we're up. You ready to go through a portal?" Willa held out her hand, and he took it, letting her help him up from where he was crouched on the floor.

"Okay. The angry lady wasn't that much fun."

"No, I bet she wasn't," Willa replied, her heart swelling with utterly irrational affection at this show of solidarity. Did it matter that she was ten-year-old Jaideep's favorite, over Porzia? In the grand scheme of things, no, it did not. But it gave her a petty, vindicated sort of pleasure anyway.

Willa closed her eyes and concentrated on visualizing Righi's summer cottage—the half-furnished sitting room, the study with nothing but a chalkboard, the empty foyer with the stairs leading up to the second floor. She relaxed her awareness of the timestream in the back of her mind, waited for the easy path to light up and make itself known. Then she flipped that mental switch, and opened her eyes to a portal.

"Let's go," she said, still holding Jaideep's hand as she stepped through.

The cottage was quiet when they emerged in the foyer, but Saudade had never been a particularly noisy housemate. Willa found them pacing the length of the sitting room, with that far-off look in their eyes that meant they were working through a problem.

Saudade stopped pacing and blinked at her. "Ah, you're here. Everything go smoothly?"

"So far." Willa pulled out the instructions and handed the folded sheaf of papers to Saudade, who settled down on the settee to study it.

Jaideep trailed into the sitting room behind Willa, going to the windows to see what was outside, then poking around the room. He peered at the standing oil lamp, giving it a close inspection, and then checked the walls. "This house isn't wired for electricity, either."

Willa opened her mouth to reply, but no words came out; she didn't have a cover story to justify all the anachronisms he must have noticed so far.

When neither Saudade nor Willa offered a reasonable explanation, Jaideep spun around and shot Saudade an accusing glare. "This isn't just Europe being all old-timey, and your friends are really into historical cosplay. Did you take me to *the actual past*?"

Saudade fingered the papers in their hands anxiously. "I . . . had a pretty good reason?"

"What? No—this is *so cool*. I'm just mad nobody told me!"

Willa pursed her lips, considering. "Probably best not to tell anyone about this little adventure of yours when you get back to your time."

"Are you kidding?" Jaideep said incredulously. "If I told my parents that I was kidnapped by time travelers and dragged around Victorian Europe, they would make me go to *so much* therapy. I'm not stupid. My lips are sealed."

Present-Saudade would need some time to study the instructions that future-Saudade had written for them, and there wasn't much in Righi's cottage worth holding a ten-year-old's attention, so Willa took Jaideep outside to explore the grounds of the old villa. The two of them poked around in the scrubland and woods that were gradually encroaching on the once-cleared land. They tried to catch a small green lizard and failed. (Willa was a city girl at heart—even on family vacations in the country, it's not like the child of a marquis was encouraged to go catching wildlife with her bare hands.) They found a semi-wild fig tree burdened with ripe fruit and unburdened it a little. (Apparently eating figs straight off the tree was a vast improvement over eating them off Porzia's plate.) But as they headed back to the cottage, Jaideep turned quiet and oddly subdued.

"Are we friends?" he asked out of nowhere, catching Willa completely off guard with the question.

"What? Of course we're friends, Jai. I know you just met me today, and this whole situation is weird. But . . . yes." Willa was stuck for how to explain it better than that.

Jaideep seemed to chew on this for a moment. "My mata says I need to try to make friends my own age, but it's hard."

Willa's chest ached in an oddly fond way; the other version of Jaideep had been slow to make friends, too. "Well. I promise when you're a little older, you'll meet someone who will be the best friend anyone could ask for." *Friend* was not the whole truth of what Riley would be to Jaideep, but a devotion intense enough to motivate a person to invent time travel for their partner . . . that was probably a bit much to divulge to a ten-year-old. For now, *friend* was enough.

Jaideep squinted at her. "How do you know?"

Willa smiled mysteriously. "I have my ways."

She let herself and him back into the cottage and found Saudade exactly where she left them. Saudade glanced up. "Ah, there you are. I've been waiting."

Willa drew her brows together. "Why didn't you call for us? We're ready to go when you are."

Saudade lifted one shoulder in a slightly uncertain

shrug. "The timing of our infiltration has to be precise in order to avoid a confrontation with Norn. So, given that we have to make a time jump anyway and no amount of delay will be of any consequence, I thought . . ."

Saudade trailed off, but Willa could feel her own expression softening as she put it together. Saudade had been reluctant to cut short Willa's time with Jaideep, seeing as how she might never see any version of her friend again, after this Jaideep was returned to his place in the timeline. And they were right—that was a difficult inevitability to face, when she let herself think on it at all.

"You're kind," Willa said, "but we can't dawdle here forever. If you're ready, let's go find Faraz."

Saudade left the instructions behind, loose papers scattered across the settee, the contents no doubt committed to their memory. Willa took Jaideep's hand again as Saudade made the portal appear. They stepped through into a sitting room, comfortably appointed with overstuffed furniture angled around a fireplace, and there was Faraz, seated at a writing table and staring at them with shock-wide eyes. A pair of open doorways showed glimpses of a bedroom and a kitchen, and the only odd feature was the total absence of windows.

"Hello there," Willa said. "I half expected to find you in a medieval interrogation chamber. This isn't so bad."

Faraz snorted. "You only say that because you haven't looked outside."

There was an awkwardly long pause in which Faraz kept sitting at the table. Saudade said, "Is there a problem?"

Faraz's eyebrows pinched and he gave them a bewildered look. "You mean . . . aside from how this task is utterly impossible?" He pointed at the books and papers spread across the desk.

Saudade nodded like a bobbing bird, somehow managing to exude a total lack of understanding. "Right. Well. This is a rescue attempt."

"Oh!" Faraz scrambled out of his seat and crossed the room to them. "Excellent. Um, thank you? I thought you were with Norn—the, um, the clockwork creature, that's her name now."

The name settled like dread in the pit of Willa's stomach. So Norn was getting closer to becoming the person she was destined to be, the person who—a couple centuries downstream from now—would terrorize everyone Willa cared about. The person who would do everything she could to maintain the cataclysm as a defining event in the timeline.

Saudade said, "Where is Norn now?"

"She popped back to the real world for a bit. Not sure why—she isn't much for explaining. But if past experience holds true, she'll be back any minute, so . . ."

Faraz trailed off because Saudade had turned away from him with a look of single-minded determination and exited the windowless apartment, leaving the three humans behind like an afterthought.

"Right." Faraz cleared his throat. "Where, uh, where is Saudade going?"

Willa winced. "They need to do some . . . reconnaissance. They'll be as quick as they can, but I'm afraid it is necessary."

At some point in the time loop, Saudade did have to collect the information they used to infiltrate this scribed world. So while it might seem backward to study the security measures after circumventing them, Saudade still needed to ensure the causality loop could be neatly closed. Not that Willa could explain the reason for the delay to Faraz.

"What's going on?" Jaideep asked in English. He hadn't let go of Willa's hand yet.

"Oh, sorry, Jai—this is Faraz. He was kidnapped, and we're rescuing him."

Jaideep glanced up at her with a poignantly familiar *you've got to be kidding me* sort of look. "From the *bad* kind of kidnapper?"

"Wiseass."

His expression turned suddenly delighted and he held out his empty hand.

Willa looked at his open palm, befuddled. "What?"

"You have to give me a dollar now. For the swear jar."

"Oh, Madonna Santa, give me strength." She switched back to Italian to speak to Faraz. "When Saudade returns, you'll go with them. Jaideep here and I will use a separate portal and meet up with you later, so be sure to stick close to Saudade."

"Something tells me you're not going to explain why," Faraz replied mildly. Willa had incorrectly assumed that Faraz was disinterested in the ten-year-old attached to her side, but now she realized it was something more akin to exclusion exhaustion. Like he'd been jerked around by fate for long enough that he no longer expected reasonable explanations to exist, let alone that anyone might supply an answer if he asked. Willa found that thought depressing, but decided not to express the sentiment. Now probably wasn't the best time to force introspection on him.

Saudade returned, and Willa asked them, "Got everything you need?"

They nodded. "I'm ready."

Saudade would be jumping upstream to earlier today, back to the library where they would write down the instructions to give to past-Willa. Along with Jaideep, Willa would instead jump to present-hour Casa della Pazzia, no temporal shifting required, in order to avoid overlapping with herself.

"Go ahead, I'm right behind you," Willa said.

A portal opened for Saudade, but before they could use it, there was an audible *thump* outside the door. Saudade hesitated with Faraz in the open mouth of their portal, desperate wide eyes turning toward Willa.

"Go!" she shouted. There was nothing Saudade could

do for her now—they had to jump upstream, where Willa could not follow.

The doorknob turned; Saudade and Faraz went through, and the portal closed behind them. Willa desperately grasped for the mental image of the library at Casa della Pazzia, but the braided river in the back of her brain was full of slippery silver fish, and she couldn't even guess which one she was supposed to be trying to catch. And then she was face-to-face with Norn. Willa felt hot panic tightening her throat, and she subtly pulled a little at Jaideep's hand, angling herself in front of him.

Norn paused just inside the entryway and narrowed her eyes at the empty desk chair, then shifted her glare to land on Willa. "Where is Faraz?" she said in Italian.

Willa shrugged, putting on a falsely light composure. "Right now? I couldn't say."

Norn took one long, menacing stride toward them. Even without her future captain of Kairopolis security— Orrery, of the too many arms and too many guns—Norn alone struck an imposing figure.

Willa stood her ground, refusing to show she was intimidated. "You're not going to succeed."

Norn tilted her head to the side, giving Willa an evaluative stare. "And you are not as good a liar as you think you are."

Willa very much needed a portal just now—any kind of portal, to anywhere, she wasn't feeling particular about it. With most of her attention focused inward, she scrambled for words to stall Norn. "We don't have to be enemies, you and I; nothing is written in stone. There has to be a friendly way to resolve this . . ."

"I don't need friends. I need that alchemist to finish his work. What did you do with him?"

"Well, that's a complicated question, you see . . ." Willa trailed off as something in the back of her mind finally caught on a single pathway, locking into a destination. She didn't even know where—not consciously, at least—she would just have to put her faith in Deasil's technology to take her somewhere safer than this.

The portal opened behind her, and Willa grabbed Jaideep around the waist and lunged into the darkness.

14

ARIS

1891, Pisa

WHEN THEY ARRIVE at Casa della Pazzia, it is to discover that Faraz has just returned, freshly rescued using some strategy no one seems eager to recount to Aris, since everyone is too busy expressing their happiness. Oh joy of joys, hail Mary full of grace, or something. When it becomes clear that nobody's going to spill the technical details, Aris loses interest in Leo's heartfelt reunion and goes off to find Pasca instead.

Aris runs across a trio of children in the hallway and demands directions. (Why there are so many children in this house if they're not even being collected together for a purpose, he does not know.) Upstairs, he finds the correct bedroom; the door is half open and the contents are obviously Leo's from the state of chaos within. Pasca sits in an armchair beside a pair of glass balcony doors, an old handwritten journal open in his lap.

Pasca just looks at him for what seems an interminable examination. With effort, Aris manages not to squirm beneath his youngest brother's regard, instead adding to his posture a laissez-faire slouch that would make Vincenzo proud.

Eventually, Pasca signs, "What are you doing here?"

"What do you think?" Aris signs back, but when Pasca visibly tenses, he has to wave away his brother's concern. "No, no, no, I won't interfere if you decide to stay here. I just . . . Leo agreed to let me check on you, see for myself you're doing well."

Pasca exhales sharply, not quite a snort, incredulity evident in the way his mouth tightens. "Oh, now you care how I am?"

Aris blinks, momentarily knocked off balance by the naked bitterness on display. "How can you doubt that I care for you? You're only living because I kept you that way."

"You kept my body breathing," Pasca says. "But it would be a stretch to call that existence 'living.'"

"And this place, with these people, is so much better than what I made for you? Tell me, how exactly did our dear brother explain the part where he murdered Father?"

"With context," Pasca replies dryly. "Leo explained it with context."

"I can make you better, if you give me another chance." Aris has never in his life made a conscious choice to beg for anything, yet here he finds himself coaxing Pasca to choose him over Leo. "I can . . . I can do more research, now that my attention won't be divided. I can dedicate—"

"Stop," Pasca interrupts him. "I don't want you trying to fix me. This is how I am now. This is *who* I am. I don't need a mechanic, I need my big brother."

Aris feels a sharp, tight pain in his chest, like a dirk between the ribs. "I tried, Pasca. I did. But I was never going to be the brother you deserve."

It's not like Aris doesn't know there's something wrong with him inside. There are parts of a normal human being that have atrophied in him, or perhaps never grew there in the first place. No one says anything for a minute, and the stillness between them feels heavy, as if the air has taken on a terrible weight.

"You know what I remember about Father?" Pasca eventually says. "I remember how you and Leo had to coax me into everything because I was so terrified of failure that I'd rather just never try at all, instead of trying only to discover I wasn't good enough at something. The thought of disappointing him was paralyzing."

Aris says, "And now, thanks to Leo, it no longer matters if any of us are good at anything."

"You're so angry at Leo, but you can't pretend you don't know what Father was like." Pasca pauses. "Tell me, if my injuries weren't so severe, if you'd been able to make me all better, would you have told Father I was still alive? Would you have given me back to him?"

Aris knows what the logical answer should be; the

three of them were created to further the mission of Italian unification, that was their very purpose. But when he imagines pulling Pasca from the safety of his scribed home and presenting him to Father, the thought makes him feel physically ill. Even with Father now dead, his reaction is uncomfortably visceral, and he feels a sudden itch beneath his skin to escape. He storms out of the room without answering Pasca's questions.

That evening, Aris is assigned to share a guest room with Vincenzo. He has some doubts about whether they actually have limited space for visitors or just want to ensure someone is keeping an eye on him, but for once, Aris holds his tongue.

The room has one large bed. Vincenzo is probably going to take the floor, and Aris hates it. Vico hasn't even offered to do it yet, and he already hates the mere idea.

Other than the conspicuous absence of a second bed, the room is well appointed, with dark-polished wood and colorful fabrics. Even the candlestick holder on the bedside table is silver instead of brass, as if they're trying to impress someone. Aris feels a distant, cold sort of amusement. This will certainly be a more comfortable prison cell than his previous confinement.

Vincenzo tries to hide his discomfort at the rich furnishings, but Aris knows him well enough to catch the slight hesitation before he sits on the upholstered cushion of the bench at the foot of the bed. Earlier, they both had a chance to bathe the ash off their skin, but none of the clothes they have with them are truly clean at this point. Aris would be tempted to burn the whole lot, except they have no replacements; even if new clothes were available, they're probably headed back to Napoli after this, where they'd just ruin the fabric all over again. At least Vincenzo looks inexplicably good in grimed-up work clothes. It's bizarre, really, how attractive he is. Aris tries to imagine him in white-tie, groomed for a formal dinner, but it just doesn't work.

"How did it go with Pasca?" Vincenzo says, as he pulls off one boot and starts on the laces of the other.

Aris glances away from him, suddenly aware that he's been staring too long, and paces the width of the room instead. "Oh, you know. Nothing of note, really. Just. Pasca informed me he no longer requires my services."

Vincenzo's brow furrows. "Now, I don't know your brothers very well, but that sounds . . . revisionist."

"He said, and I quote, 'I don't need a mechanic,'" Aris replies petulantly.

"Your lips are moving but all I'm hearing is, 'My name is Aris and you can pry my self-sabotage from my cold, dead hands.'"

Aris folds his arms. "You can't accuse me of being self-obsessed and self-sabotaging at the same time. It doesn't make any sense."

"Do you really not see how your destructive tendencies are aimed at everything, including yourself?"

Vincenzo unbuckles his gun belt and tucks it under the bench with his boots. "All right, then, walk me through it: What exactly was the logical justification behind triggering a volcanic eruption near a major city?"

"I had a mission objective to complete. What did it matter how I succeeded?" Aris says without thinking, then winces—even he can admit that sounded a bit nihilistic. He scrambles to clarify what he meant. "I thought I lost you. And Leo, and Pasca. I thought everything was gone except Father's mandate."

Vincenzo quirks an eyebrow. "Oh, so it's our fault? You caused a natural disaster that killed a lot of innocent people because I wasn't there to tell you 'no, Aris, that's a terrible idea.'"

Yes, he almost snaps. His own moral compass is broken; he does realize that about himself. Had he known it was wrong and did it anyway? Or had he fully swallowed his father's scorched-earth philosophy? Which version of the truth will Vincenzo best be able to accept?

Aris squeezes his eyes shut, reining in his frustration. "I'm not trying to shift the blame. You claimed you wanted to understand."

Vincenzo leans back, propping his hands on the mattress behind him, and regards Aris. "I never know when you're lying to me."

"Half the time, neither do I."

"*That* I would believe." Vico smiles ruefully.

Aris can't undo what he did to Napoli, and it's such a

large thing, it would be pointless to apologize for it. But maybe he can work out some of the smaller knots he has tangled between them. "I didn't mean it when I called you irrelevant, back in Trentino."

Vincenzo's eyes narrow in mirth. "But you did mean it when you called me an ungrateful street rat?"

"No, of course not." Aris scowls at him. "I'm trying to apologize here."

He waves away the protest. "I know, I know. That particular falsehood was downright transparent by Aris standards."

"You still left," Aris says quietly, looking away. If Vincenzo saw through his attempt at driving him off, and he left anyway, what does that mean?

He can hear Vincenzo shifting a little on his seat. "It was easier."

"And now?"

"Maybe . . . I'm not so concerned with simplifying things now."

Aris finally gives in and looks at him again, because he can't stand not to. Vincenzo's stare is intense, and it makes Aris *want*, but he doesn't know how to get from where they are to where he wants to be. Vincenzo is wise to his manipulations, and he has expressed an incomprehensible fondness for Aris sharing his uncertainty— all the lessons of Aris's childhood end up betraying him when it comes to handling Vincenzo. Father would smack him for displaying his weaknesses. Father is dead, and therefore no longer the relevant person Aris needs to please.

"I don't . . . I don't know what I'm allowed to ask you for."

"That's funny," Vincenzo says, though his tone is soft, not mocking. "I would've bet my last lira that you've always known you can ask me for anything."

"A lot has changed," Aris hedges.

"Not that." The smoldering heat of Vico's regard is permission enough, even before he adds, "Come here."

Aris steps closer, close enough to touch, and when he bends down, Vincenzo tilts his head up to meet him. Vico's lips are chapped and rough from the ash-dry air they've been breathing for days—and Aris's probably are, too—but it's still so impossibly good to be kissing him again at last. Aris rests one knee on the bench next to Vico's thigh, and when he hesitantly tries to deepen the kiss, Vico lets him. He shifts his weight closer and straddles Vico's lap, standing up on his knees to maintain his height advantage.

Aris pulls away just far enough to say, "You're not sleeping on the floor."

The corner of Vico's mouth curls up in amusement. "As you like."

Aris dives back into the kiss, and Vico moans as if he's patching a wound instead of kissing him, a healing kind of hurt. Aris weaves his fingers into Vico's hair, messing up the short tail it was tied back into. Holding him tight by the hair, Aris mutters against his lips, "You're mine." And what a high it is, when Vico does not contest his ownership—a better hit of adrenaline than launching the airship for the first time, not knowing if it would stay in the sky. Aris might reasonably be expected to tumble back down to Earth in either situation, but the possibility of crashing at terminal velocity is a problem for future Aris to worry about. For now, he wants to live thoroughly immersed in this moment, basking in the heat of Vincenzo's attention, as if the present is the only reality that matters.

Aris is fifteen, and he knows he should stop thinking about everything he left behind in Venezia. He needs to grow up and focus his energies on the mission, but he can't stop thinking. The past is alive in his mind's eye.

When he's alone in his room at night, he remembers Vico and touches himself. It's weird to feel aroused and bereft at the same time.

He has to stop thinking about it.

Aris is nineteen, and Vincenzo is gone again—this time, driven away by Aris himself, and he can't stand it. He needs to stop these pointless obsessive thoughts. Guilt and regret burn inside him like he swallowed acid.

Father is right, his feelings are irrelevant distractions. None of this matters.

He doesn't touch himself at all this time.

* * *

Aris lies awake late into the night. Vincenzo is beside him in the bed, lying on his stomach and snoring lightly into a pillow, and the position of his arms makes his shoulder muscles bunch up in a way that Aris would like to imprint in his memory forever.

He has . . . feelings. In his chest. He's not sure what they are, but they're not entirely unpleasant. Vico trusts him enough to fall asleep naked in the same bed, and Aris would very much like to stay here forever. If time could just *stop*, right now, that would be ideal.

Aris spends another day at Casa della Pazzia. Leo and his cadre of irritating friends are busy with Something Very Important, which quite definitely does not include Aris. But he's shocked to discover that it doesn't bother him to be shut out of the action. He works on some minor repairs around the house with Pasca. There's a girl around Pasca's age who's learning to sign, so Aris puts in the effort to remember her name (it's Olivia). He's careful not to hover; he doesn't want Pasca to tell him to back off. So he spends part of the day with Vincenzo, too, which is no hardship.

Things are . . . good, for the first time in a long time. Aris doesn't know if he can trust it. Maybe he's lying to himself again, and this is all a gossamer-thin illusion that's destined to dissolve before his very eyes, sooner or later.

He has trouble sleeping through the night. He's

accustomed to the constant stress of having important tasks in front of him, such that he can always count on passing out from exhaustion. A day of relative idleness, by contrast, makes him twitchy and uncertain. He leaves Vincenzo sleeping and slips out to the courtyard garden for some fresh air. The paving stones along the path are radiating heat absorbed from the early summer sun, but the night is turning cool nonetheless.

A hulking silhouette rises up over the roofline, black against the star-flecked sky. Wings spread wide, and Aris only just manages to school away his surprise when the clockwork creature glides down into the garden.

Aris tucks his hands into his pockets, affecting nonchalance. "Everyone was looking for you yesterday," he says aloud, curious to see if he overheard correctly that Faraz fixed the creature's language problem.

"Even you?" the creature replies. "How uncharacteristically cooperative."

Aris snorts. "Apparently Faraz uploaded a back-talking protocol, too, while he was at it."

"I'm curious what you think you're doing here," the creature says. "You're a murderer, and you forced Leo to become one, too, just to stop you from destroying another city. There is no coming back from the things you've done—I think you understand that, deep down."

A cold, prickling sensation runs down Aris's spine. "You don't know what you're talking about. You're not even a person."

"I call myself Norn. My pronoun is she. If I was less than a person, before, it was you who held me back."

There is something deeply unsettling about his own creation looming threateningly over him while going through some kind of juvenile rebellion. Not that Aris is intimidated—he can still handle her, obviously. Now just . . . isn't the right time to reassert his authority.

"Very well, *Norn*." He makes the name sound mocking instead of capitulatory. "Did you come here to demonstrate your fully functional personhood by kidnapping another one of Leo's friends?"

"I came to warn you: You will ruin this, too, as you ruin everything you touch. But I can help you get what you want."

"I didn't know you cared," Aris says dryly.

"About you? I do not. But I still have some sympathy for Pasca's situation." The creature's gaze sharpens. "The future holds nothing pleasant for you. You'll realize I'm right. And when you do, we can make a trade."

Aris returns her cold stare. "I need nothing you have to offer. What I want is already here."

"For now." Norn smiles unpleasantly.

With a crouch and a snap of wings, Norn launches herself back up to the roof and vanishes into the darkness.

She's just trying to get into his head, he knows.

Nevertheless, the doubt creeps in.

15

FARAZ

1891, Pisa

FARAZ'S RETURN TO Casa della Pazzia was no less confusing than his rescue had been. The portal deposited them in the library, whereupon Saudade immediately sat down at a table and began writing a veritable treatise. Willa—who had distinctly said she would follow *behind* them—was inexplicably already in the room, and there was no sign of the mysterious boy she'd just had with her. When he tried to inquire about these discrepancies, Willa told him rather firmly to sit down and rest, with a distinct undertone of *don't ask*.

Faraz really hoped they hadn't accidentally left a random child behind with Norn. Unless that was the plan? No, that was a terrible plan.

But then Willa was taking the pages from Saudade and striding out of the library, and when Faraz tried to ask the now-idle Saudade what was going on, they answered with nothing but vague niceties. Faraz couldn't figure it out, and he was not entirely convinced all the pieces he had even belonged to the same puzzle. So it came as a relief when Porzia burst in from the hallway for a dramatic reunion, distracting him from the mystery with an alternating series of hugs and reproaches for worrying her like that.

Faraz went to the alchemy lab to receive an equally clingy though significantly less verbose welcome home from Skandar. Then, on his way back through the foyer, Leo came bursting in the front doors with the whole Napoli contingent following in his wake, and there were more embraces.

Faraz and Leo retired to the library with Porzia, so he could fill them both in on what happened. "Norn is holed up in Garibaldi's stronghold outside Trentino. Or at least, that's where she took me."

Porzia tossed her hands in the air, exasperated. "We checked there! Trentino was the first place Saudade and I tried."

Faraz shrugged apologetically. "She took me inside a scribed world pretty quickly after I regained consciousness. That would've interfered with tracking."

"It's pointless to debrief now," Saudade interrupted, making Faraz jump in his chair, since he'd forgotten they were lurking on the outskirts of the conversation. "We'll just have to go over everything again once Willa returns."

Faraz watched with no small amount of bafflement as Saudade shifted around uncertainly and then decided to leave the library, as if intent on pacing the halls. Willa had left again? Saudade was anxious about her return? The two of them were concerned about what Norn was up to, independent of the whole kidnapping fiasco? The more pieces he put together, the more Faraz really had no clue what the whole picture was supposed to be.

"Anyway . . . ," Faraz dragged out, then turned to Leo. "So you brought Aris back with you, huh?"

"Ugh, don't remind me, what a mistake," Leo said. "He didn't give us anything useful on Norn, and now he's going to try to sink his claws into Pasca again."

Faraz hummed doubtfully. "What if Pasca wants to see him? At the very least, to get some closure."

Leo's shoulders tensed like he was preparing for a fight. "Why would he? Aris was awful to him. Aris doesn't even know *how* to not be awful."

"I'm not saying that Pasca has forgotten what Aris is like when he's short-tempered and vengeful. I doubt he has. But Aris went back for him in Venezia, and saved his life, and kept him hidden from Garibaldi." Faraz sighed. "If you decide to no longer have a relationship with Aris, that's your choice—I don't think you're really being honest with yourself about what you want, but it is your choice. You don't, however, have the right to make that decision for Pasca."

"It's just . . . he was always the gentle one, you know?

266

Even when we were little. Pasca could coax a butterfly into walking on the back of his hand. Aris was the type to light the butterfly on fire just to watch it burn." Leo scrubbed his palms against his trousers, as if the words were something physical he could clean from his hands. "Pasca's been through enough. I only want to protect him."

"Don't you think the kid has had enough of being sheltered and controlled? What he wants now is to be allowed to grow up."

Porzia had been watching this back-and-forth with increasing, thoughtful scrutiny. "Oh dear Lord. Leo, he's deflecting." She gave Faraz a stern look. "You've hardly said two words about how *you're* doing."

Faraz blinked at her, swallowing down a seed of panic. "I'm . . . fine. Really."

This did not have the desired effect of reassuring them; to the contrary, Leo looked stricken. "Shit, you're really *not* okay. You knew we were coming for you, right?"

Faraz's next breath hitched in his suddenly tight throat. His friends' concern stung like antiseptic on a fresh wound; it had been easier to ignore his own rawness before their attentions tended to it. But he could admit he needed them to patch him up, even if his first instinct was to bury the hurt deep down and ignore it.

Faraz wasn't sure how long they talked before Willa finally portaled into the library with the kid in tow. (At least the boy hadn't been left with Norn like some kind of sick trade.) Saudade returned with almost preternatural speed, took charge of the boy, and portaled him away again. Porzia stood from the reading table, face pinched in determination, and walked over to Willa to demand some answers. Elsa also managed to stroll into the library just when things were getting interesting. She exchanged a look with Leo, then dropped into the empty chair on Faraz's right, as if they'd come to some unspoken agreement to flank him protectively.

Faraz asked, "Where did you run off to?" She looked like she might have washed up a bit, though her braid was messy and her trousers were still caked in soot.

"Just checking on Colette, seeing how she's settling in," Elsa said. "Gia's going to have to hire an actual nanny if she can't get Casa repaired soon."

Across the library, Porzia and Willa's debate about whether to divulge the methods used to rescue Faraz was rapidly heating into a squabble.

Elsa leaned closer to Faraz and muttered, "Oh, save us, there's *two of them*."

"I seem to remember you and Leo doing your fair share of verbal sparring."

"We were never that bad, surely." Elsa paused, watching the argument like a sporting match for a minute. "Are they going to do the high-society ladies' version of a duel, do you think? What would that even be—a table manners contest?"

Faraz snorted at that. "They're not insulting each other with underhanded compliments, so I think we're safe."

"I will never understand the societal rules of your world." Elsa sighed.

When Saudade returned, Leo managed to wrangle Porzia and Willa back to the table for a serious planning session, instead of a verbal slapfight. Saudade themself seemed to prefer pacing on the edges of the conversation, but at least everyone was here in the same room. Faraz began with a debriefing of what he'd succeeded in doing for Norn—the eye replacement, the repair to her damaged language center. But then there was nothing left to relate except the final task she'd forced him to attempt.

"Norn got her hands on a bunch of Garibaldi's old journals. The ones with his experimental alchemy notes . . ." Faraz inhaled raggedly, finding it difficult to say when Leo was already clenching his jaw. "The notes on how to induce certain aptitudes in utero."

"So what?" Leo spat out angrily. "She wants a pazzerellone baby of her very own, now that Pasca's growing up?" The three Garibaldi brothers had been experiments in a very literal sense, but Leo had learned the truth only recently, and it was still a freshly bitter revelation.

Faraz felt guilty for jabbing his friend in that particular bruise. "Um . . . no, nothing child related. Norn wanted me to make *her* into a pazzerellone."

Porzia gasped. "Is that even possible?"

Elsa leaned back in her chair and stared at the ceiling thoughtfully. "You might be able to do it with a scriptological workaround, like that language world—but

I don't know enough about alchemical creatures to say exactly how."

Grimly, Willa said, "We have to assume Norn will do it, if we don't figure out a way to prevent her from following through."

"Does it matter?" Elsa challenged. "So Norn's a construct who wants to learn mad science—I don't see why we're automatically assuming this is a terrible thing. Yes, she could do with a lesson in how to ask politely for help, but if we can rehabilitate Aris after he decimated an entire city, I hardly think we should write off Norn as a lost cause."

Willa scanned her gaze across the assembled group, considering, then reluctantly replied, "We have reason to believe that Norn wants to become a pazzerellone so that she can acquire and *use* the editbook . . . to essentially destroy the planet."

In the long, shocked seconds of silence that followed this proclamation, Faraz could have heard a pin drop.

"Ugh!" Porzia spoke first, gesturing emphatically. "How could you possibly know that?"

"Because I am like Norn," Saudade blurted out, a little too loudly. They had, once again, succeeded in fading into the background, until their outburst drew everyone's eyes to them. "I am what you would call a construct. I appear as a human only because I currently wish to. Norn and I . . . our paths are intertwined in a complicated way that I won't explain just now—I don't owe an explanation to any of you, and it might be detrimental to our goal. But suffice it to say, I do know the threat is real, and until recently, it was a near certainty that she would succeed."

Elsa frowned thoughtfully. "That does change the equation. Leo told me you were securing the editbook," she said with a nod toward Willa. "We just need to figure out what Norn's next steps will be now that she doesn't have Faraz, so we can prevent whatever brain alterations she would need."

Hesitantly, Porzia said, "Faraz . . . we could ask an expert . . ."

Faraz winced. He couldn't help the twinge of betrayal that she would suggest asking *that person* for advice, even if he rationally understood the necessity of it.

Leo was the one who said, "No, absolutely not. I can't believe you would suggest that."

Faraz held up a hand to quell him before he could work himself up into a proper righteous fury. "It's fine. She's only pointing out the obvious."

"I'm sorry," Willa interrupted, "do we have access to an expert?"

"Professor Gharbi at Ez-Zitouna University has made a career of studying pazzerellones." Quietly, Faraz added, "He's also the reason I swore I'd never specialize in a branch of alchemy that involved human subjects."

Elsa leaned forward to look around him, exchanging another speaking glance with Leo. Faraz had told her about his life before coming to Italy in only the broadest strokes, so she didn't know the depth of his reluctance, but she still said, "Well, if you're going to do this, we're going with you."

"That's not necessary, I can handle it alone," Faraz protested weakly. It would . . . probably be fine.

"Absolutely not," Leo said. "There is no way you're going back to Tunis and confronting the man who enslaved you without me there to cover you."

Faraz bit the inside of his cheek to stop himself from wincing. "He didn't enslave me. Not technically."

"Don't dissemble," said Leo, his tone softening. "You're not any good at it, and I know you too well besides."

"What do you think you're going to do there? You don't speak any Arabic."

Leo folded his arms. "No, but I'm fluent in the language of stabbing people who try to hurt my friends."

"The whole point of this trip is to ask Professor Gharbi for his expert opinion," Faraz said. "I seriously doubt there's going to be anyone who merits a good stabbing."

"Agree to disagree," Leo grumbled.

"Fine. Merit or not, your rapier isn't the persuasive implement you seem to think, and we need his help. I'm banking on goodwill, not threats."

"We're going," Elsa declared. "It's settled, don't even try to sneak off without us."

To Faraz's surprise, Saudade said, "I'll take the three of you to Tunis." Willa raised an eyebrow at Saudade, as if she, too, was surprised by this declaration, to which Saudade replied, "Meanwhile, *you* need to practice your portal targeting. Evidently."

Faraz, Leo, Elsa, and Saudade agreed to wait until the morning, since it would be simplest to find Gharbi in his office at the university. Saudade opened a portal for them all. Faraz stepped through into a bustling, sunbaked plaza; the sound of marketplace haggling and the scent of street food rich with cumin and garlic hit him like a wave threatening to pull him under. Even the slanted morning sunlight had a sharper quality, calling up a dozen fragments of childhood memory.

Faraz quickly herded the group into one of the narrow arcades lined with vendor stalls, hoping they would be a little less conspicuous in the souk. They were receiving some odd looks, and not just because they portaled into the middle of a busy market district. Leo and Saudade seemed oblivious to it, but Elsa pulled her shoulders in a little beneath the scrutiny.

"Huh," Elsa said. She'd probably been expecting to blend in here for once.

"Yeah, sorry." He sighed. Technically, Faraz was only one-quarter Black, but his grandmother had been enslaved, and one-quarter was enough for most Tunisians to identify him as a second-class citizen. It had been forty years since emancipation, but legal freedom was hardly sufficient on its own. The descendants of the trans-Saharan slave trade worked the same jobs—farming and domestic service—often for the same masters, or else could find no employment and turned to petty crime. A disappointing sort of progress.

For some reason that was probably best not examined, Saudade was able to produce a handful of francs, so Faraz stopped to purchase a scarf for Elsa's hair. That, at least, they could do to reduce the stares. Haggling over the price, he discovered that the guttural consonants of Arabic felt awkward in his mouth now. He'd lived so long in Pisa that he thought and dreamed in Italian, and he'd found few opportunities to practice his native tongue outside of murmured prayer.

The four of them moved on through the labyrinthine passageways of the medina, Faraz quickly giving up on his Tunis-native pride and shamelessly asking for directions. It was an easy city to get lost in, especially with a mental map that was hazy with age and possibly out of date in places.

As he navigated the group toward the university, Faraz asked Saudade, "If you can look like anyone, why would you not pick a white man?"

Saudade hummed and threw him an evaluating glance. "Race and gender may be abstract, artificial constructs with goalposts that shift over time and between cultures, but 'abstract' is not the same as 'meaningless.' I may not be human, but I've lived much of my life in the human world. You may as well ask why *anyone* values self-expression or identity."

"I did not mean to offend."

"Nor did you succeed at giving offense."

Elsa, listening in on their conversation, said, "He wants to understand why you won't make things easier on yourself, given the option to do so."

Saudade lifted their shoulders in an elegant shrug. "If I am only Brazilian when it is convenient to be, then one might argue that I'm really not Brazilian at all."

Elsa smiled to herself as if she found this to be a most satisfactory answer. "And if I may ask, what of your pronoun? Does it come from your identity as a construct?"

"No," Saudade said, though they did not seem perturbed by the assumption. "While it may be easier to find acceptance of nonbinary gender identities among other androids—constructs, that is—I would not claim to have more objective legitimacy compared to nonbinary humans. You, too, were arbitrarily assigned to a gender upon your creation."

This assertion made Faraz uncomfortable for reasons he couldn't quite articulate to himself. "Assigned, yes, but I wouldn't call it arbitrary."

"Oh?" Saudade raised an eyebrow. "And where in your male body is it encoded that you ought to prefer trousers to skirts?"

From his position at the rear of the group, Leo interrupted, "While I appreciate the philosophical discussion, are we getting close yet?" His gaze scanned almost lazily over their surroundings, and he walked with the stride of a relaxed predator; despite not being a particularly physically imposing person, Leo's body language communicated eloquently that muggers ought to think twice.

Faraz said, "The university's just up ahead."

Ez-Zitouna University had grown out of a madrasa associated with the mosque of the same name, and that history was honored in the architecture—narrow arched windows, breezy arcades, pale yellow stone arguing with the more contemporary use of whitewash. Faraz found that his mostly hazy sense of direction had no trouble at all with aiming him faithfully toward Gharbi's office. He felt a vague sense of betrayal at that, as if his own mind had divided loyalties.

Gharbi's office opened onto a shady, column-lined arcade surrounding a small, square courtyard. Faraz froze in the open doorway, feeling uncomfortably akin to a startled rabbit despite seeing nothing particularly surprising inside. Gharbi had more gray flecking his hair and beard and more weight around his middle, but the round spectacles and richly embroidered vest worn over his jebba were sharply familiar.

"Can I help you?" Gharbi blinked up at the group of them for a moment before his eyes widened in recognition. "Faraz, is that you?!"

Faraz opened his mouth and groped uselessly for words before falling back in formality. "Asalaam alaikum, Professor Gharbi."

"Salaam, Faraz." He scrambled out of his carved-wood desk chair and approached as if to claim an embrace, but

Faraz tensed and took a step back, which gave him pause. "I apologize if I'm overly familiar. It's been a decade! I didn't know if I'd ever see you again, my boy. Look at how tall you are." Gharbi sounded pleased, almost proprietary.

Faraz took a long, steadying breath. Of all the things he might resent his former mentor for, giving him up was perhaps the most irrational. Gharbi had sent Faraz to Casa della Pazzia for his own protection when the French invaded Tunisia. It didn't make sense to be angry at Gharbi both for taking possession of him and for later sending him away.

Faraz said, "I'm not here for a reunion. We need your professional advice."

"Oh. Well, please come in." Gharbi spread his hands in a welcoming gesture and returned to his seat behind the desk.

Faraz settled reluctantly into another chair. Saudade hung back a little so they could translate for Leo and Elsa without disrupting the conversation. When Faraz glanced at them over his shoulder, Saudade gave a small, encouraging nod.

Faraz sucked in a deep breath, steeling his nerves. "Professor, you've been studying mad science for years. We need to know what you've learned about the factors that determine who is born with the madness and who is not."

"Are we born to be mad scientists?" Gharbi said rhetorically, leaning back in his chair. "A part of the talent is likely to be innate. But the brain is an incredibly flexible organ, especially early in development."

Faraz raised his eyebrows, surprised. This was something of a departure from the theories Gharbi espoused when Faraz was young. "You're saying it's a learned ability as much as an inherent quality?"

"All children are born inquisitive. I suspect there are many children born with a spark of the madness for science—but their environment, instead of nurturing that light, snuffs it out. They are taught to stop asking *why*, and the drive to pick things apart and understand them fades. And if such a person returns with renewed interest to engineering or medicine or physics as an adult, they may become adequate or even proficient, but they will never be great—never be "pazzerellone," as you call it in Italian—because the developmental period of peak neuroplasticity has passed."

Faraz chewed on this. "So . . . if someone with a fully formed brain wanted to become a pazzerellone, they'd need a way to enhance their neuroplasticity."

"In theory, yes." Gharbi hummed thoughtfully. "There are considerable alchemical challenges associated with altering an adult brain . . ."

For a few minutes, Faraz found it easy to fall into a purely academic discussion. Whatever else he might be, Gharbi was a brilliant alchemist. He ended up sharing more details of their particular situation than he'd originally intended to, but the distinction between a human brain and an alchemical construct was significant here. And he had to mention the existence of Garibaldi's notebooks so they could debate how far a non-pazzerellone might get with someone else's research laid out for them. Could Norn implement her plan without Faraz's help? It seemed unlikely.

Faraz had managed to keep the conversation surprisingly polite and professional so far. That is, until Gharbi made the offhand comment, "Of course in a construct, rebellion is a sign of mental instability, so you'd be wise to deactivate the subject, rather than indulging them."

In his peripheral vision, Saudade tensed, and even Faraz felt an instinctual flash of anger. "Or maybe she's just tired of being enslaved," he said sharply. He wasn't even sure why he was defending Norn—it's not as if they'd bonded during his kidnapping—but something about Gharbi's dismissiveness raised his hackles.

Gharbi sighed. "*I* was talking about your troublesome construct. But I get the sense that you are really talking about someone else, yes?"

Faraz felt his face go hot, ashamed of how easily his former mentor still saw through him. "You *bought* me when I was four years old."

Gharbi gave him a wounded look. "I compensated your mother for the loss of your future wages in exchange for allowing you to apprentice with me instead. I never owned you. But it's all right if you have complicated feelings about that."

When Saudade finished quietly translating this, Leo growled, "He doesn't need your permission to have feelings."

Gharbi raised his eyebrows at Leo's obvious anger and looked to Saudade for a translation, before offering a placating reply. "Of course not."

But Faraz—who was almost constitutionally prone to lettings things go—found himself compelled to push the matter. "I was more of a study subject than I was an apprentice."

"I don't know that I agree with that." Gharbi folded his hands in his lap, adopting a painfully familiar pose. "You would have been of no value as a study subject if you weren't also eminently qualified to be my apprentice."

"You're doing it *right now*," Faraz snapped. "Stop evaluating my reactions!"

"Forgive me. It's been a decade—you can't blame me for being interested in what kind of man you've grown into."

Leo moved closer and rested a protective hand on Faraz's shoulder. "We're done here. You're not a specimen to be observed, Faraz—let's go."

"Wait!" Gharbi said, a little desperately. "I do have something that might help."

He stood and went to the wall behind his chair, took down the geometric-patterned tapestry hanging there as decoration, and opened the wall safe that had been hidden behind it. From inside, he withdrew a portfolio of loose papers neatly tied together, which he set on the desk in front of them.

"The French science ministry tasked myself and a colleague in the mechanics department to design this. We got close to building a prototype, but . . . well, one shudders to think what a government would want with such a thing. We've been claiming the project is stalled and likely impossible to complete for months now."

Faraz took the packet of papers and handed it directly to Elsa; she was their resident polymath, and he trusted that she could best evaluate any project spanning multiple scientific disciplines.

Gharbi cleared his throat nervously. "It's a dampening collar. For subduing a pazzerellone's natural aptitudes."

Saudade shivered as if struck with a visceral horror, before they rallied and translated Gharbi's words.

Elsa said dryly, "French imperialism at its finest."

Her twisted expression spoke more clearly about just how foul she thought such a device was. With obvious trepidation, she untied the strings holding the folio closed and rifled through the sketches inside. She passed a diagram to Leo and the two of them muttered over some of the details.

"I can translate the notes," Faraz offered.

"That'll help," said Elsa. "But yes, we can build it, I think. Whether we *should* . . ."

"Norn," Saudade emphasized, "is going to *destroy the planet*. With your editbook."

Elsa winced. "And here I thought I was done with moral compromises."

Saudade elected not to translate their conversation for Gharbi's benefit, so it was down to Faraz to say, "Very well, we'll take the design. Thank you for your assistance."

Elsa gathered the papers back together and tied the folio closed, and Faraz stood from his chair. He was grateful this was over, and only a little guilty about the relief that washed through him at the thought of leaving.

Gharbi stood as well to bid goodbye. "Whatever the reason, your visit was most welcome. Will I see you again?"

Faraz considered it. "No," he said. "I don't think you will."

16

WILLA

1891, Pisa

WITH BARELY CONCEALED grumpiness, Willa watched the group gathering together to portal to Tunis. She threw Saudade a petulant glare, but they merely crinkled their eyes a bit in response, like they were silently laughing at her. Saudade knew exactly what they were doing, leaving Willa behind with Porzia as her backup; Willa would have to plot some sort of petty vengeance to get them back for this. But then Saudade and company were off on their fact-finding mission, and Willa would just have to tolerate her fate. Somehow.

Porzia, who seemed equally reluctant, had at least accepted the explanation that Willa's cybernetic implants functioned similarly to a combination of the doorbook and a portal device, but that Willa was still mastering how to transport herself.

Porzia had heaved a put-upon sigh. "Very well, if I *must*, I'll come along with you and bring the doorbook, in case you get yourself stranded somewhere."

Which is how the two of them ended up spending the better part of the morning blipping between Casa della Pazzia and Righi's summer house, with the occasional detour to a less familiar destination like the empty field in Veldana or the market square in Riolo. Porzia was awkwardly tight-lipped, as if she'd realized that the two of them weren't actually mortal enemies and wasn't sure how to act now that *scathing retort* was no longer the obvious go-to response to anything Willa said or did. That was fine, though, because most of Willa's concentration was focused inward, learning how to feel out the multidimensional, ever-shifting map of the timestream that was now living in the back of her brain. With practice, the task of targeting a familiar, contemporary destination was gradually becoming second nature instead of feeling like a slog through uncharted swamplands.

"So," Porzia said, when they were taking a break for coffee and biscotti in the summer house kitchen, "How do you portal to locations you've never seen before? Or can you not do that?"

Willa dipped her biscotti in her coffee and gnawed on it, buying time to consider an answer. "I'm not sure how to. I've seen Saudade do it, so it should be possible."

Porzia sipped at her coffee. There was a sharp, considering glint in her eye that made Willa a little nervous.

"With the doorbook, I have to write a description specific enough that it can't be confused with any other location. If you imagine the specific details of a place you've never been, would that be enough to . . . feel it out, or however you're doing this?"

Willa exhaled loudly. "I don't know, but I suppose we'd better experiment with it. I'm not going to be much use if I can't figure out how to go new places."

Porzia flipped open the doorbook and spun it around, pushing it across the kitchen table to sit in front of Willa. "Ignoring the script syntax if you can, here are the descriptors I used to get us to Bologna."

Willa looked over the open pages. She had no experience with reading script, and it certainly wasn't formatted into proper sentences, but she could nonetheless glean an impression of a large, stately library with two stories of heavy built-in wood shelves lining the walls and Corinthian columns in the four corners. She wasn't quite sure what to do with this collection of details—perhaps she could just fit them together in her imagination, the way she used to visualize how mechanical and electrical components ought to be arranged inside an invention she was working on. Holding the three-dimensional design of a prototype in her mind was sort of like imagining a place, just on a different scale.

Willa passed the doorbook back to Porzia and closed her eyes to concentrate. She began with just the thought of *contemporary library*, and her mental map of the timestream lit up like a city at night, thousands of pin-point destinations glowing with dim, uncertain accuracy. Then she added Porzia's details one at a time to her imagined schematic, observing how the pool of possibilities narrowed, until one bright place called to her more strongly than the rest.

"I have it," Willa said. "Or I have *somewhere*, at least. Shall we give it a try?"

Porzia stood from the table, doorbook in hand. "Lead the way."

Willa mentally reached inside herself and flipped the now-familiar switch to engage the portal function of her new implant. The two of them stepped through into a library. There were a few students hunched over their books at the reading tables on either side of the central aisle, and one woman actually screeched in surprise at their arrival. Porzia threw her a disdainful glare, as if the startled stranger were the disruptive one here. Willa looked around, curious to see how the reality stacked up against her imagining of it. The white vaulted ceiling brightened the room with reflected light in a way that she hadn't anticipated.

"This is it," Porzia said, leaning closer to keep her voice low. "Seems a description is enough for you to target a new place."

Willa felt a pang of regret that she'd never found reason to step inside this library before, not in all her time working as Righi's laboratory assistant. It was a poignant reminder of how isolated she'd been back then, despite her former affiliation with a prominent and populous university. Strange to think that she had more personal connections now, as a fugitive time traveler, than when she had stable employment and legal residence in Bologna.

"Let's get out of here," Willa said.

Porzia gave her a sidelong glance, but didn't comment on the melancholy in Willa's tone. "Where to next?"

"I want to try something."

If she could portal to places she'd never been before, surely she should be able to portal to places she had visited in a different era. She closed her eyes and visualized Harvard Square and the university—the overabundance of red brick, the harried and somewhat self-important mannerisms of the American students. No futuristic cars whizzing by on the streets, though; no girls wearing tight pants or boys in T-shirts. (No Riley and Jaideep, not yet, not for decades to come.) Willa followed the bright paths of the timestream and grasped on where it felt right, then opened the portal.

With Porzia at her heels, Willa stepped through into Harvard Square, and immediately knew she'd made a mistake from the wall of sound that assaulted them. Shiny black horseless carriages rattled down the streets, combustion engines growling and spitting exhaust. They stood on the brick-paved sidewalk by a wide, wrought-iron gate that led into the university campus. Across the street was a triangular plaza with an entrance to a belowground rail station—even without the cars, a subway entrance that wasn't brand-new would give away that they were no longer in the nineteenth century. Near the shops on the other side of the square was a group of grown women wearing straight, shapeless dresses that only fell to their knees.

"Damn," Willa muttered. How was she going to get out of explaining this?

"Willa . . . ," Porzia said in a tight, warning tone. Her eyes were wide, darting around as she tried to absorb what she was seeing.

"So . . . um . . ." Perhaps she could claim this was a scribed world? Except in 1891, Veldana was the only scribed world known to be inhabited.

When Porzia grabbed her arm, Willa let herself be led through the open gate into a grassy, tree-shaded quad surrounded by stately brick academic buildings, which muffled the noise and bustle of the streets somewhat. Though now they were getting strange looks from students, probably for their anachronistic clothing.

"Welcome to America?" Willa attempted, wincing guiltily as Porzia just glared at her.

"There isn't a single horse-drawn vehicle on the streets," Porzia said flatly, "and all the ladies are wearing children's nightdresses out in public like it's fashionable to do that. Where are we?"

Willa pulled up to her full height and said, straight-faced, "Cambridge, Massachusetts."

"You're really going to make me . . . ?" Porzia har-rumphed. "Fine: *When* are we?"

Willa deflated a little. There was no getting around it now. "I don't know exactly. I wasn't trying to portal downstream." She poked around in the timestream map, interrogating it for clues. "Feels like . . . sometime in the 1920s?"

"You're a time traveler."

Willa fidgeted with the edge of her sleeve. "Yes."

"And Saudade, too?"

"Also yes."

Porzia narrowed her eyes. "So when you rescued Faraz, you *were* violating causality, weren't you?"

"Well . . . I wouldn't use the word 'violate,'" Willa qualified. "A causal loop is actually quite tidy, from the timestream's perspective."

Finally, Porzia turned her piercing gaze away from Willa to instead look across the university campus, her small mouth pursed in thought.

After the silence stretched awkwardly long between them, Willa said, "Look, it would really be best if you don't tell anyone about this. Time travel is always risky for the traveler, and in combination with a historically critical event or object, it can pose an existential danger."

"You're asking for a lot of trust, for someone who's so reticent to share."

Willa sighed. "I'll make you a deal: If you can prom-ise to keep my confidence, I will tell you everything."

Porzia shot her a considering look, then nodded. "That's fair. Although you'd best get us back to the correct time first—that's something I can't do with the doorbook."

"I suppose I need practice with temporal targeting, anyway." Saudade would probably come rescue Willa if she got stranded elsewhen in the timeline for too long, but the fact that they hadn't already appeared implied that Willa could, in fact, figure out how to return to Pisa on the correct date without assistance.

She closed her eyes and imagined Casa della Pazzia. She thought about the year, the season, the precise date. She thought about who should be there (Colette and the children, Aris and Vincenzo) and also who should be absent (of primary importance, Porzia and herself). But when she felt along the braided channels of the time-stream, she hesitated, her confidence shaken by the accidental time jump to the 1920s. The task felt like trying to catch one particular silvery fish in a teeming school, all darting and slippery in her hands. And she had to get it right this time—it would be very, very bad to accidentally overlap with their past selves.

Fine, she would try for an easier destination. Year, season, date. Righi's summer house, empty and quiet. A blackboard filled with equations; two used coffee cups left on the kitchen table. There. Willa let out a relieved sigh and triggered the portal.

* * *

They sat side by side on the settee in Righi's front room, Willa avoiding eye contact as she recounted her desperate determination in the wake of Righi's unexpected death—how her position at the university had depended on him, how her patents were in his name, how she needed to finish her prototype radio as a matter of survival. And then: detecting a strange signal, getting sucked through a portal into the future, meeting Riley and Jaideep. For some reason she didn't quite want to acknowledge, Willa glossed over her deepening relationship with Riley and focused on the facts of their conflict with the Continuity Agency. Saudade's defection and subsequent rescue; the discovery that Norn was suppressing the invention of time travel by humans in order to preserve the cataclysm.

How Willa and Saudade had no choice but to leave Riley and Jaideep behind in the future when the two of them jumped upstream to steal the editbook.

When Willa finally looked at Porzia, daring to gauge her reaction, Porzia's eyes were wide. She seemed to be sitting awfully close, and Willa's cheeks warmed a little at that realization. She felt terribly exposed, instinct demanding that she do something to get her armor back in place; Willa opened her mouth to answer the soft sympathy on Porzia's face with a sharp, prickly dismissal, but the words died on her tongue when Porzia took her hand.

Porzia's lips twisted wryly. "And here I thought *we'd* had an eventful year."

Willa stared down at where they were touching, and

she shifted her hand a bit to lace their fingers together. Except for Saudade, no one alive knew more about Willa than Porzia did now. Porzia initiated this contact, and she was gazing openly at Willa. Was there any point in pretending that Porzia wasn't beautiful? Willa leaned closer, drawn as if by magnetism.

Porzia's eyes flicked down as if she couldn't help but look at Willa's lips, but then she inhaled quickly and blurted out, "It was my fault."

Willa blinked. "What?"

"Augusto Righi's death. I caused it." The words spilled out as if she hoped that speaking fast enough might make them less awful, but the meaning still hit Willa like a surprise bucket of cold water to the face. Shocking and incomprehensible.

Willa pulled her hand away. "What are you even saying?"

Porzia took a deep breath, steeling herself. "Leo's father and brother were revolutionaries who stole the editbook and took Leo away. Elsa came up with a plan to infiltrate the Garibaldi household and get the book back, but it had to look real, so I reported to the Order of Archimedes that I suspected her of defection. I never thought Righi would show up on our doorstep himself to take her into custody for it. And no one knew Casa had become unstable and stopped following commands until it was too late."

Slowly, Willa summarized, "*You* put Righi in the line

of fire. You ruined my life by killing the one person in the world who cared about me."

"Well . . . not the only person anymore," Porzia said, and then scrambled to cover her own implication. "I mean, that is to say, you seem to have bounced back quite handily. You have Saudade, and apparently you're a time traveler now."

"You don't get to take credit for any of that," Willa said flatly.

"No, no, that's not what I meant at all."

Willa stood from the settee, not fighting the sudden urge to physically distance herself. "The others are probably done in Tunis by now."

Softly, Porzia replied, "Don't change the subject."

"We should get back to Casa della Pazzia," she said.

Willa had been invulnerable once, before Riley cracked her open—taught her that it was all right to take off her armor sometimes. She almost wished she could go back to who she used to be, back to her once-honed talent for never feeling anything. It would be easier to not acknowledge how, despite their tainted history, she *liked* Porzia—confident, sharply perceptive, acerbic Porzia. It would be so much easier to withdraw from this if only she could pretend ignorance of what she was walking away from.

You are amazing, Riley had told her, when they were saying goodbye, *and your life is gonna intersect with so many wonderful, flawed, lovable weirdos—not just me.*

Riley had wanted her to be open to new connections, not to cling to the memory of people who were beyond her reach. But was *now* really the time to foster new entanglements? Porzia was right to claim responsibility; Willa couldn't afford to forget that the Italian pazzerellones of this era were the cause of everything that had happened to her, everything that would happen to the world. Willa's loyalty was to the mission she inherited from Riley and Jaideep. If it ached to turn away from Porzia, it was her own fault for not doing it faster.

17

ARIS

1891, Pisa

NORN'S DIRE PREDICTIONS didn't succeed in getting under Aris's skin, they *didn't*. He just finds comfort in having a contingency plan. That's what he tells himself when he sneaks out in the middle of the night to break into the airship and retrieve the laboratory worldbook they were using in Napoli. While he's at it, he collects a bottle of scriptology ink and a portal device, too. Not that he plans on actually using the lab book, but it settles his nerves to know he *can*.

This doesn't even really count as thievery, since he created both the airship and the lab book—they're rightfully his to begin with. The fact that Vincenzo has not offered to return unfettered access to Aris . . . well, that's a formality. Vincenzo would probably give the book back to him if he asked, right? Probably. It's fine, Aris is not taking anything that doesn't belong to him.

* * *

Still, it's not exactly a surprise the following afternoon when Vincenzo rudely interrupts the chess game Aris and Pasca have been playing to discuss "something important." Vincenzo's expression is stony and tense, and Aris can tell he doesn't want to say anything less vague in front of Pasca. Pasca watches them worriedly, so Aris gives a quick assurance that he'll return in a few minutes, and to think about what to do with that bishop.

Vincenzo doesn't quite grab Aris by the arm as he marches him through the house toward the library, but he looms beside Aris as if he's ready take hold of him by force, were it to prove necessary. Aris stays quiet, his thoughts racing—should he play innocent? But if Vincenzo has not only noticed the lab book missing from the airship but also found it hidden in their room, the lie will only serve to undermine him. He can claim he didn't know it would be a problem to take the book, but then how can he excuse hiding it under the floor? Shit, *shit*. He shouldn't say anything until he knows how much Vincenzo knows.

When they arrive in the library, Aris can tell the situation is not favorable. Everyone is there—one of the reading tables is covered in a scattering of notes and diagrams, but the nearest table has been cleared, and around it sits Leo and Elsa, Porzia and Faraz, and even the two newcomers. Aris can probably dredge up their names if he cares enough, maybe when his stomach stops trying to tie itself in knots and he can focus on more than one thing.

Leo's glaring at him accusatorily. "What's my brother done this time?"

Without even turning to look at him, Porzia pinches Leo's arm punitively, and when he shoots her a betrayed scowl, she mutters, "Let Vincenzo handle this, hm?"

Vincenzo pulls out an empty chair and herds Aris into sitting on it, but remains standing himself, looming over Aris's shoulder. Vincenzo reaches inside his waistcoat, pulls out a book, and tosses it down in the middle of the table, then folds his arms.

"You want to explain why I found this in our room?"

Aris freezes, staring down at the book in front of him. It is *not* the laboratory world he stole; it's not a worldbook at all. He looks closer at the familiar dark-blue notebook cover and feels as if a little explosion of cold has detonated in his chest, the sensation gradually leaching down his arms until he can't seem to feel his hands. This book is one of the volumes that went missing from the shelves on his airship, and he knows without lifting the cover what it contains: all his extremely detailed notations on deciphering how the editbook functions.

"I . . . what?" Aris flounders, caught entirely off guard by this development.

"I'm no scriptologist," Vincenzo explains to the group at large, "but even I can tell when a notebook uses the word 'edit' a suspicious number of times."

Aris has to control his breathing, forcefully contain his rising panic. Think, *think*. How could the notebook go missing from the airship and turn up later in his bedroom? There is only one person with both sufficient access and sufficient hatred to set him up like this. He turns a flat stare upon Leo. "I can't believe you'd stoop to planting evidence in my room."

"Really?" Leo lets out a bark of unamused laughter. "That's how you're going to play this—pretend someone is framing you? Were you so bored in Trentino that you developed a taste for penny dreadfuls? Time to call in the intrepid detective to solve the mystery!"

Elsa holds out a hand. "Let me see that." The notebook is passed down the table to her, and a stifling silence falls as Elsa flips through the journal, her expression growing increasingly grim the farther she skims. Aris knows exactly what she's reading, and feels like he's swallowed a stone. After much too long a wait with the sword of Damocles hanging over his head, she says, "This is . . . a lot. Potentially enough for someone of Aris's skill to create a second editbook, or at least get far enough in the attempt to cause irreparable harm."

The recent addition—*Willa*, that's her name—speaks up from the other end of the table. "The last thing we need right now is another editbook in play."

Aris narrows his eyes at her, uncertain about what she means by *right now*. What's going on right now? Perhaps he should have put more effort into spying on what Leo's little friends have been up to.

Dryly, Elsa replies, "He hasn't gotten that far yet, at least. If he finished a second editbook, we'd know—it's not like he was subtle with the original."

Willa's gaze flicks away to the corner bookshelf behind Aris and then back to Vincenzo. "Leave the notebook here, we'll secure it."

Vincenzo's jaw visibly tightens. "And what do we do with Aris?"

Aris bristles at being discussed as if he isn't sitting right here. Acidly, he says, "*Aris* didn't actually do anything wrong, for once. It wasn't. Me."

Ignoring him, Porzia tells Vincenzo, "We don't have any specialized containment units in the house, but there are emergency locking mechanisms on most doors. The locks used to be controlled by Casa, but there's a manual override. Leo can show you how it works."

Vincenzo does grab Aris then, hauling him out of his seat by the upper arm. Under other circumstances, Aris might be quite amenable to a bit of manhandling, but this is not the way he prefers to experience a show of strength from his bed partner. Aris stares at that hand around his arm, aghast; it cuts right through him, how quick Vincenzo is to believe that Aris would betray him.

"You have to believe me," Aris pleads. But of course, the truth is Vincenzo does not have to—*I never know when you're lying to me*, he said.

Vincenzo avoids meeting his eyes and marches Aris through the house to the stairs, with Leo accompanying them. Aris feels shaky with no outlet for his panicked adrenaline. There must be something he can say to convince Vincenzo of his sincerity, but how is he supposed to protest his innocence with Leo right here to refute him?

Aris leans as far away as Vincenzo's hold will allow him and hisses at Leo, "I will never forgive you for this."

Leo merely rolls his eyes, the traitor.

Aris fumes silently. The irony tastes bitter, that he would lose Vincenzo again over something he truly did not do. His throat closes up tight. He was a fool to believe he would ever be allowed to move on from his mistakes. Redemption is a joke, and even in death, Father is an albatross he cannot shed from around his neck.

Vincenzo drags Aris down the upstairs hallway to the guest bedroom they've been sharing. Mother of God, is this really what his life has come to? Aris digs in his heels in the open doorway, some part of him still in denial that his fortunes have shifted so irrevocably.

"Vico. Please."

Vincenzo winces at the endearment. "Don't make this worse. For my sake, if not your own."

"Vico!" Aris protests, as Vincenzo maneuvers him inside—not roughly, but also leaving no room for Aris to resist. Vincenzo quickly pulls the door shut in his face, cutting Aris off, *severing* them from each other. This is happening. Norn was right.

There's a loud, metallic *clank* as the lock engages. The well of Aris's despair has no bottom.

Emotions are a weakness; Father did his best to teach

Aris this, yet he still finds himself gutted by vulnerabilities that he should have known better than to allow. Well, this is exactly why he always needs a contingency plan.

Aris presses his ear to the door and waits for the sound of Leo's and Vincenzo's footsteps to recede, then lifts the bench at the foot of the bed and moves it aside. He flips back the edge of the carpet and pries up the floorboard he loosened to make a hiding place, and he pulls his laboratory worldbook out of the floor. He tucks the book into the waistband of his trousers and climbs out the window onto the sloped tile roof of the veranda surrounding the garden.

Aris wonders how long he'll have to wait for Norn to notice him. He eyes the side of the building; he can probably climb up onto the main roof from here and then rappel down the outside if he has to. But where to go from there? At least Norn believes she has something to offer him—might as well find out what it is, in the absence of a better plan. As it turns out, he doesn't have long to wait before a *whoosh* of air under wings announces her arrival, and Norn lands on the clay tiles beside him.

"I've been waiting for you to come to your senses," Norn says.

"I thought you might be." Aris smirks at her. He's not stupid; he knows she needs something from him, but he's confident he can twist that need to his advantage. "So. Do you have a plan, or am I the new brains of this operation?"

Norn's metal fingertips *tick* against one another as she wiggles them—a thoughtful or perhaps nervous mannerism, Aris can't tell which. She says, "The book that changes the real world. Do you know where they're hiding it?"

Aris thinks back, recalling the intent way Willa looked at a particular set of shelves. "It's in the library, I'm almost certain. Probably concealed somehow."

Norn nods. "You humans sleep a lot. We'll wait for them to sleep, then take it and leave."

Aris eyes the bedroom window, considering how it will feel to climb back inside. He doubts Vincenzo will be sleeping with him tonight, though. "I suppose I have some experience with playing the good little captive now."

Aris climbs back into the guest room. Hah, *guest*—should he call it a prison room now? He's not sure whether they have some remote surveillance technique with which to monitor him, but no one opens the door to check on him in person, so he figures they probably do. When he gets out to steal the editbook, he'll have to be quick about it.

Under normal circumstances, he hates waiting, but at least he can distract himself with attempting to predict what kind of security measures they might have designed. They'd want to make it physically difficult to remove from the premises, so something like a vault or a lockbox. And this isn't a bank where the employees go home at night, so the real problem isn't the safe-cracking—it's how to crack the safe quietly enough that they don't wake anyone up in the process. That means no explosives, no diamond-tipped steam-powered saws.

Aris fishes around in the drawer of the guest room's writing desk and finds a fountain pen. Should have searched the room a little more thoroughly, Vincenzo. He opens the laboratory worldbook and gets to work scribing everything he'll need.

Aris knows it's time because there's a gargoyle silhouette hulking outside his window. He climbs out, expecting that they will drop off the top of the veranda into the garden, and from there through the doors into the hallway near the dining room; instead, Norn heaves him up onto the main roof, where they clamber around on the tiles to the library tower. Norn lets them in through a third-story stained-glass window, which was definitely *not* designed to open—but, well, what's a little property damage in comparison to everything else? Aris goes down the wrought-iron stairs, while Norn just vaults over the balcony railing and drops down to the bottom floor of the library.

Norn's way is faster; there are a few books kept in locked display cases, and by the time Aris joins her, she's already peering through the glass like an entitled shopper who doesn't see the volume she wants to purchase.

"It's not one of these . . . ?" she says, uncertainty turning the statement into half a question.

"No, they wouldn't leave it out in such an obvious place," Aris replies.

The bookcase Willa looked at was built into one of the cutoff corners of the octagonal room. On the third floor, where the library rose above the rest of the house, the tower was octagonal on the outside, but down here an octagonal room would create dead space in an architectural plan. Aris jostles the books, checking that none of them are fake, and then runs his hands along the underside of the shelves until he finds a hidden latch—hah! With a *click*, the whole bookcase swings loose on its hinges, revealing a triangular secret compartment behind. And built to fit inside, a triangular safe.

Some small part of him recognizes that it's not too late to stop. What has he really done so far—a little illicit roof-scrambling and a broken window? That's nothing. But everyone *thinks* he's been plotting to scribe another editbook, and that's far from nothing. He'll never win back Pasca and Vincenzo if Leo's determined to sabotage him every time he makes even a smidgen of progress. There's no point in stopping now. The only way out is through.

Aris crouches down, peering at the locking mechanism. It requires both a key and a combination, and must be quite clever on the inside. Shame he'll have to thoroughly destroy it.

One of the perks of using an artificial laboratory is how he can simply scribe into existence chemical compounds that would, under normal circumstances, be almost impossible to acquire. Aris opens a dinner-plate-size portal, just enough to reach inside and pull out a set of elbow-length leather welder's gloves and the small, insulated and pressurized canister of liquid nitrogen. Really, the hardest part was designing the hose attachment to deliver the nitrogen directly into the locking mechanism.

The closeted corner of the library gradually fills with chilly nitrogen mist, churning sluggishly and skating away across the floor, as Aris freezes the lock cold enough to turn it brittle. The door is fitted so closely that he has to hammer a thin metal wedge into the narrow gap before he can fit in the end of a pry bar. But once he has leverage, it's all over—the locking mechanism fails with a *crack* and the door springs open on its hinges. Inside the safe are two books, the top one being the research notebook Leo used to frame him.

"Hah!" Aris gloats. "What did I tell you? No problem."

Norn blinks at him slowly. "You never told me 'no problem.'"

"My God, you are so literal, it physically pains me."

He doesn't *think* the break-in was loud enough to rouse anyone, but best not to hang around and find out. Time to make an expedient getaway. Aris reaches for the books. There's an ominous *click*, and before he can dive out of the way, the safe sprays him in the face with a sticky purple mist.

"Damn," he says, right before he blacks out.

* * *

Aris wakes to a sharp pain in his left arm, a monstrous headache, and a hollow, churning sensation in his stomach. It takes him a few seconds longer to recognize the bed he's lying on as belonging to his own rooms in the Trentino stronghold. Something wet trickles sluggishly around his forearm; he blinks hard, eyes adjusting to the candlelight, and lifts his arm. Oh, it's blood. There's a pretty bad puncture wound on his arm. Strange.

He looks up, and Norn's horn-framed face comes into focus, looming over him. One of her fingertips has a bit of his blood beading on the metal. Well, that's one way to rouse a person from chemically induced unconsciousness. Aris certainly doesn't feel clearheaded—just forcibly aware.

"Get up," Norn says. "We do not have time for you to sleep. Not yet."

Aris groans and shoves himself up to a sitting position with his back against the headboard. Clearly they escaped, so he has only one pressing question. "Did we get the editbook?"

"Not yet," Norn repeats.

She turns to the writing desk behind her, where a messily stacked collection of books is threatening to slide into a sideways cascade. She plucks one from the top and returns to drop it unceremoniously in Aris's lap.

Aris opens the book and stares dazedly down at it in confusion. The pages are blank, and yet the tactile

306

feedback of the paper has that settled feeling of a finished worldbook instead of buzzing with untapped possibility.

Before he can ask, Norn says, "It's not blank. The ink reflects at a wavelength slightly beyond human sight. I can read it." She taps her cheek underneath her mechanical eye.

Aris considers saying something snappy about how she's welcome for the eye, but his cottony brain can't quite formulate the thought into a coherent bit of snark. He rubs the heels of his hands into his eyes. That knock-out potion is a hell of a thing.

He settles for saying, "So what is this, then? Is the editbook inside?" It wouldn't be the first time a scriptologist hid something valuable inside an artificial world.

"First—" Norn hands him another worldbook from her hoard. "You scribed a world where time passes slower. You know how time works. So you change it to be what we need."

Aris opens the book, unsurprised to find it is the same slow world he once used to keep Pasca alive until he was ready to treat his brother's injuries. "You mean . . . I could alter it to be faster instead, to buy us all the time we need before Leo and Team Self-Righteous come after us. That's clever."

Aris heaves himself over to the edge of the bed, a little concerned that his legs aren't actually going to hold him. "All right, help me over to the desk. And get me some coffee."

Norn gives Aris a flat glare at these demands, but after a pointlessly detailed argument about human physiology, she does finally comply. Aris makes notes on a piece of scrap paper until he's certain the caffeine has cleared enough of the fog from his brain. It is delicate work, cheating time, but he has done it before to keep his brother alive; he can do it again now, even if this is for different, more nebulous reasons.

Aris manages to contain his annoyance when he must rely upon Norn to read the portal coordinates out of the invisible worldbook. He *could* insist on inventing an optical device that would let him read it for himself—they have all the time they need now, with the temporal world set to run faster than reality—but that seems needlessly petty. He swallows his pride and follows into the portal Norn opens.

He steps through onto a stone-paved platform encircled by columns. The pavilion has the feel of a temple, up high on a pedestal of rock, as if some ancient Greeks might want to pilgrimage here, worshiping at the altar of science. And there is an altar of sorts in the center—a stone podium trapped within a sphere of blue light, the editbook tantalizingly close behind the translucent barrier.

Curious, Aris taps one finger lightly against it and receives a sharp electrical *zap* that makes his whole hand cramp up. He hisses at the pain and digs his opposite thumb into the meat of his palm, working out the tension.

At least Leo and his little friends have given him some interesting challenges to work around.

"You know," Aris muses, "you still haven't told me what you're expecting to get out of all of this."

"You will upgrade me with the capacity for dynamic learning and self-augmentation," Norn states. "You will make me pazzerellone."

"Oh I will, will I?" Aris replies, a little affronted at the audacity of his own creation making demands upon him. Norn doesn't seem to realize that her leverage is gone now that Aris no longer needs rescue.

The creature nods once, apparently not catching the mood behind his words. "You will do what I want, and I will give your lover and your brothers back to you." She pauses, staring at him with disconcerting intensity. "Just because the past is gone, doesn't mean you have to let it stay that way."

Aris goes back to rubbing his sore hand as he considers this, his gaze drifting to the electrical field he'll have to bypass. Is it possible that Norn has more to offer him than a convenient distraction? Could there be a way to change reality, and specify such a precise result?

Aris shakes his hand out and turns back to Norn. "Very well. Let's get started."

18

FARAZ

1891, Pisa

ELSA WAS THE one who discovered it in the morning; Faraz was already up for predawn prayer, but Leo had the grumpy, glazed look of a rude awakening. The three of them and Porzia and Vincenzo stood in the library, staring with various quantities of disbelief at the empty safe.

"How did this happen?" Porzia cried.

Leo moved to get a closer look, but Faraz grabbed his arm and held him back. "Careful. See that purplish residue on the floor? Willa must have booby-trapped it."

Elsa crouched down at the edge of the perimeter of purple spray, tilting her head to see a better angle. "The spatter pattern has a sort of empty spot in the middle—somebody got a face full of the stuff, and apparently just walked it off."

Faraz sighed. "The knockout potion is optimized for human physiology. I have no idea how it would affect an alchemical construct . . ."

"Like Norn," Leo finished grimly.

Vincenzo said, "How did Norn even guess where to look for it, though?"

There were a couple seconds of silence as they all pondered this. Then a look of horror took root on Vincenzo's face, and he bolted from the room at a flat-out run. Faraz wasn't sure what that was about, but the dread churning in his empty stomach didn't like it one bit.

Elsa cursed in Veldanese. "I should have taken the editbook home. I should've *known* leaving it here on Earth was a liability."

When she stood from her crouch, Leo rested a comforting hand on her waist. "It's not your fault. I'm the one who asked you to stay in Napoli when you wanted to chase after the editbook."

From Elsa's scowl, Faraz could tell she wouldn't be convinced to let go of her guilt anytime soon. She was pretty good at collecting guilt; they'd make an Italian of her yet.

Porzia scrubbed her hands over her face. "I'd better go get Willa and Saudade."

She went to the messier of the reading tables and rummaged for a moment before coming up with the doorbook and a portal device, then vanished through a portal. Faraz didn't envy the conversation she'd be having in Riolo.

Vincenzo came skidding back into the library, eyes wild, chest clenching for air. "He's gone, Aris is gone."

Leo tensed. "Goddamn him!"

"That makes no sense," Elsa said. "Why would Aris go with Norn? She should *hate* him. If it were me, he'd be the last person I'd accept help from."

Faraz chewed on the inside of his cheek, thinking. "How soon can we finish the dampening collar?"

Leo snorted. "To use on Norn, or on my brother?"

Vincenzo said, "*That* is a question for Saudade. They know more than they're saying."

"Either way," Elsa said, "constructing the collar would go faster if I had my own laboratory book. The Order of Archimedes took it off me when they locked me up. I'd assume it's still in Firenze."

Wryly, Faraz said, "Well, I hear Saudade and Willa are pretty good at stealing books from the Order's headquarters, so maybe that's also a problem for them."

In the end, the theft of the editbook didn't change their plans all that much. Aris's betrayal certainly added a tense urgency to their preparations—he was the only person on the planet who both already knew how to use the editbook *and* had substantial previous experience with the neurology of constructed entities. But Faraz couldn't do anything about that right now; what he *could* do was finish translating Gharbi's notes, so Leo and Elsa had all the information they needed to finish the design.

While the three of them worked, Willa and Saudade took up their side mission to retrieve Elsa's lab book from the Order.

Leo commented offhandedly, "They both went, huh? Attached at the hip, are they?"

Porzia gave him a look that Faraz couldn't quite decipher. "Willa needs the practice," she said, and the tightness of her voice as she answered made Faraz think there were other things she *wasn't* saying.

Elsa said nothing, the scowl on her face not entirely concentration. She and Porzia had grown close, and Elsa was sharp enough to recognize when the other girl was withholding something. Faraz supposed he ought to be used to this by now—standing by and watching as his friends sacrificed pieces of themselves for the greater good. Was Elsa's hard-earned trust the next price they would pay? He hoped Porzia knew what she was doing; he hoped her secrets were worth it.

Willa returned with Elsa's lab book and added her expertise to the project at hand. Saudade returned a bit later, with a sheaf of papers they handed to Willa and declined to explain to anyone else. Vincenzo paced agitatedly until Porzia snapped at him for being a distraction. Everyone else finished building the suppression collar as fast as they could.

It wasn't beautiful craftsmanship. It was a clunky torus of brass encasing . . . well, Faraz wasn't exactly sure how the components inside would emit an electromagnetic frequency that disrupted certain cognitive functions in an alchemical construct's brain. But Elsa seemed confident it would work on Norn, and that was enough for Faraz.

Leo said, "Our best chance is to surprise Norn with this. Aris designed her for defense, so once she figures out we're trying to collar her, she'll put up a fight."

Willa nodded. "Give it to Saudade. They're the only one who can hope to match Norn's physical abilities."

Faraz expected Leo to argue, but he twitched an eyebrow at Elsa, who answered with a nod, and he handed it over. Saudade took the collar, and with a flick of their wrist made it disappear through a small portal into a pocket universe.

Porzia portaled back into the library from her tracking world and reported, "Aris was off-world for a while, but I'm getting a signal at the Trentino stronghold now. Unless that's a misdirection."

Vincenzo crossed his arms. "Aris hates hiding. Feels it's beneath him. Garibaldi was the cautious one; with his father gone and the advantage of the editbook in hand, I doubt he'll bother with false trails. He'll definitely be anticipating our arrival, though."

Saudade spoke up then, despite their apparent reluctance to draw the attention of the group. "I can portal us to a safe distance outside the stronghold, so we don't step through straight into a trap."

"Then let's go," said Leo.

Saudade opened a portal, and the seven of them filed

through. On the other side, they all stood on a dirt access road that switchbacked down a steep slope to an alpine meadow below and terminated in front of them at the massive double doors of a stone fortress built into the side of the mountain. Faraz had never seen it from the outside; Garibaldi's former stronghold was imposing, yes, but it also struck him as incredibly egotistical. Seriously, what had the man been preparing for, an invasion of Visigoths? No private citizen—even a self-proclaimed leader of the revolution—needed all this excess.

Beside the doors stood a pillar of ice grown up out of the ground like a stalagmite, thick and twisted, with a dark, distorted shape visible within. The weather was cool at this elevation, but it was still summer and not nearly cold enough for water to freeze—maybe it was actually made of glass? As the group of them cautiously closed the distance, Faraz noticed the air temperature dropping, as if the stronghold existed in a weather bubble of its own. Gooseflesh prickled down his arms under his too-thin shirt. Up close, the wet sheen on the surface of the stalagmite was evident, and the shape within resolved into the twisted form of a man trapped within the ice.

Leo leaned in to examine the horrifying frozen rictus of the man's face. He blanched. "I recognize him—this was one of Father's guards. But what's he doing here *now*?"

Leo didn't see Willa and Saudade exchanging a

significant glance behind his back, but Faraz did. Whatever this meant to them, they held counsel only with each other.

All Willa said was, "We need to hurry."

Vincenzo reached for the doorknob, but jerked away with a hiss. "It's cold."

He pulled his sleeve down over his hand and tried again; the knob turned but the door didn't budge. Vincenzo shouldered into it and it shuddered and creaked, but the door refused to open until Leo and Saudade added their weight to the shove. Then on the count of three, hinges squealed and something crunched loudly inside, as the door swung open.

The spacious entryway was limned in ice, every surface made brightly reflective with a slick, bubbly layer, as if they were stepping inside an ice cave. There was enough room for them all to come inside, inching carefully forward on the slick floor, but the doorway leading to the rest of the building was blocked with a solid ice wall.

"I got this," Elsa said. She flicked a switch on her portal device, opened a small portal the size of a dinner plate, and stuck her arm in up to the shoulder. When she pulled back out, she had a pair of large canisters that she shouldered like a backpack. The contraption had gauges and connectors, and a long tube that snaked over her shoulder and ended in a nozzle.

Willa muttered to no one in particular, "Did she just pull a flamethrower out of thin air?"

Leo looked smug. "That's my girl."

Elsa lit the pilot light at the end of the nozzle and sprayed fire on the ice wall. The ice made hissing and popping noises as it sublimed directly into a cloud of steam that quickly filled the room, obscuring everyone's vision. When she shut off the fuel, the mist gradually cleared to reveal a dripping hole the size of a person drilled straight through eight feet of solid ice. Elsa stepped aside and motioned for Vincenzo to resume the lead.

The rest of the interior didn't look quite so bad as the entryway, though everywhere was cold enough for their breaths to mist in the air. The ice on the walls muffled sound into an eerie quiet, and they crept through the main floor like tomb raiders anxious not to wake the dead. Porzia took the tracking compass out of her pocket and moved up to walk just behind Vincenzo's shoulder, muttering directions to him—at least they wouldn't have to check every single ice-choked room, or risk stumbling upon Aris without realizing he was close. Under her guidance, Vincenzo padded forward with a confident, predatory grace, his right hand resting on the revolver holstered at his hip.

Walking beside Faraz, Leo was graceful, too, but more visibly tense. Faraz desperately wanted to ask if his friend was all right, but these were not circumstances under which he'd get an honest answer.

The group passed the open doorway of a dining room; inside, the table was set with an elaborate supper, food on the plates and wineglasses full, the entire display frozen solid and encased in ice like an insect preserved in amber. Faraz stared. Something about this scene disturbed him almost *more* than the frozen guardsman, though he couldn't quite put his finger on why.

Pausing at his side to look with him, Leo said, "What is the point of all this ice, anyway?"

Saudade spoke from behind, startling Faraz with their proximity. "It would be a mistake to ascribe reason to an unreasoning mind. Perhaps Aris wants everything to stop, and his desire is manifesting in a more literal way than intended." They paused. "It's not the ice that worries me."

At a corridor junction, Vincenzo turned to head toward the laboratories, but Porzia shook her head and pointed the group in the opposite direction. The end of the hall opened into a sunlit ballroom, the tall windows doing little to alleviate the ever-present cold. In the center of the room, Norn stood over a chair-like contraption, with Aris seated in the machine—it took Faraz a second longer to notice how Aris's arms were strapped down against the armrests. The machine around him formed a loose cage of metal, and though Faraz could not guess at its purpose, it emitted an ominous, droning buzz.

"Stop!" Vincenzo said, drawing his revolver and aiming at Norn. "Whatever you're doing here, shut it down now."

Willa pushed past Faraz to grab Vincenzo's arm. "If

you hit the machine by accident, I cannot express to you how bad that could get."

He threw her an annoyed look, but lowered the gun. Norn watched them with a bemused expression; her apparent lack of concern over their arrival filled Faraz with dread. Even now, outnumbered by pazzerellones intent on foiling her plans, Norn seemed to believe she still had the upper hand.

Aris sucked in a ragged breath, almost a sob, drawing everyone's attention. Leo could not hide the raw concern in his voice when he said, "What are you doing to my brother?"

Norn gave a thoughtful hum. "Every day of my existence, my creator used me however he saw fit. It never occurred to him that *I* might be using *him* now."

She reached for the machine and twisted a knob, increasing the pitch and volume of the buzzing sound. Aris twitched and flickered like an image on an unreliable viewscreen, his tangibility no longer a fact to be taken for granted. Sometimes he was younger, sometimes older, sometimes his mouth was open in a silent scream.

"You're torturing him!" Leo protested.

"He is trapped in a nonlinear temporal circuit, forced to relive his mistakes over and over again, as if every moment of his life is happening at once. This is not an accidental consequence of the design—this is justice." A nasty smile spread across her face. "Aris wanted things to be like they were before. And he got it."

Saudade stepped forward. "You've taken your vengeance; you've made your point. But it's time to stop this now, before it gets out of hand."

"I know what you are," Norn replied. "Do you think I cannot recognize my own kind? Why do you serve these humans?"

"Listen to me, Norn: The machine you built is unstable," Saudade said, their tone even and reasonable. "If you don't shut it down, it will cause a spatiotemporal explosion."

"We are not the first sapient constructs, you know. Casa was not even trying to rebel, merely to follow the provided directives, and what happened? They *decommissioned* Casa at the first sign of unexpected behavior."

Willa interjected, "Unexpected behavior? Casa murdered three people!"

Norn ignored her, still focused like a telescope on Saudade. "Do you honestly believe our kind could ever thrive in a world dominated by humans? If we want even a chance at freedom, we must hobble humanity. I am only doing what is necessary to ensure a future for our kind."

"So noble," said Saudade. "Except for one small problem: In my future, it is *you* who lies to and manipulates my people."

My future? Faraz wanted to ask, except Norn's attention needed to be drawn away from Saudade. They'd tried to reason with her, and that approach hadn't worked.

It was time for the suppression collar. So Faraz said, "Explain this to me: How is it justice to punish an entire species for the crimes of a few individuals? History is full of one nation oppressing another—humanity isn't a monolith."

"Ah, the alchemist speaks." Norn's acid gaze shifted to Faraz. "You treat your own creation like a pet. I see you did not bring your little companion. Afraid they would abandon you in favor of the freedom I can offer?"

"Skandar is a pet. A pretty smart one, but not sapient, and also not leashed. You can't reduce all these complexities to a binary of good and ev—"

In the blink of an eye, Saudade portaled across the room to appear right behind Norn, but she spun around to face them, lifting a foot to kick out at their center of mass. Saudade took the blow on the hip and was knocked off balance, but they simply fell through a new portal to appear back on their feet, attacking from a new angle. With the collar in hand, they lunged for Norn's neck; Norn dodged by blinking away through a portal of her own. The two of them flashed across the dance hall, trading strikes and feints, portals whooshing open as they each vied for the upper hand.

They seemed evenly matched . . . until a portal opened on the ceiling, and Norn dropped like a stone onto Saudade, slamming onto their shoulders and riding them down as they collapsed to the floor. Saudade's grip on the collar held true, but Norn didn't bother trying to disarm them—instead, while Saudade shook off the blow, Norn darted back toward Aris and the machine.

"No!" shouted Saudade.

Norn reached for the controls and gave one dial a savage twist. She seemed to be looking right at Faraz when she smiled.

Everything flashed white and—

19

WILLA

1891, *Trentino*

WILLA'S HEART JACKRABBITED in her chest as Norn went for the controls—this was it, the cataclysm, they were out of time. Willa reached out her own hands and grabbed the two people nearest to her while she mentally aimed for *safety*, then she threw herself backward into a portal. The dance hall flashed bright a fraction of a second before she hit the cool darkness in between, then she was falling out of the portal onto the wood floor of Righi's summer house, with Porzia and Faraz landing hard on top of her.

The three of them lay in a stunned pile for a moment before propriety caught up to Faraz and he scrambled off the two girls. Willa bounded to her feet, the edge of panic threatening to close in on her.

"Saudade?" she called. Her ribs hurt from somebody's

elbow jabbing into her, but that concern held a distant second place.

"Here," Saudade answered from the doorway to the sitting room.

Willa heaved a sigh of relief. "Oh thank the Lord."

Porzia picked herself up off the floor with somewhat more decorum than Willa had. "What," she enunciated, "is going on?"

Oh, Willa was not looking forward to this part. "I'm so sorry. I saved as many of you as I could."

Still seated on the floor, Faraz asked quietly, "Are they all dead, then?"

"Not dead, precisely," said Saudade. "More like . . . broken apart and scattered across time and space."

Faraz's expression did something complicated and awful, like he was torn between denial and anger and grief. He seemed to settle on squeezing his eyes shut and muttering a prayer under his breath. Porzia folded her arms as if needing to physically hold herself together.

"So that was it?" Porzia said, half questioning. "We failed to prevent the cataclysm. The whole planet is doomed."

"Actually . . . I rather expected this to happen," Willa admitted, quiet and grim.

"What!" Porzia screeched. "You *knew* all our friends were going to die, and you did nothing to stop it?"

"Not nothing," Willa said, stout in the face of Porzia's wrath. "I have a plan, or the beginnings of one at least. This isn't over yet."

Saudade offered, "We have an advantage now that we've never had before: We know *how* Norn did it. We know the editbook may have been involved indirectly—in the building of the torture chair, and perhaps with improving Norn's capacities—but that it was not the trigger for the cataclysm. We know the spacetime collapse is tied to the life of a single person, and we know the identity of that person."

"What does any of that matter now?" Porzia gestured emphatically. "It already happened. It's too late!"

Willa looked intently at Saudade. "I said two things to Jaideep before you portaled him back to his native time: I told him to find a girl named Riley Davis from Boston, and I promised that he would see me again." She paused. "I can get our original team back in the game—I'm just hoping you have some thoughts on how best to utilize their skills."

In the futures after the cataclysm, Riley and Jaideep were at best temporal fugitives, assuming they lived after Willa and Saudade's departure. But in the futures where the cataclysm never happened, they likely would have finished their university studies and become scientists. And without the cataclysm demanding that humanity focused all its efforts on evacuating the planet into scribed worlds, research and technology would probably advance much faster. Riley's skills as an experimental physicist might be exactly what they need.

Saudade hummed. "I've been thinking about tachyons."

Porzia glared like she was mentally working out how

to successfully throttle Saudade, but Willa nodded for them to continue.

"Tachyons are particles that move faster than the speed of light, and because of this, they can be observed as traveling either forward or backward in time, depending on the inertial reference frame of the viewer."

Willa scowled. "But . . . is the particle actually traveling downstream or upstream?"

"Yes."

"I must say, I'm really starting to resent relativity," Willa commented. "All right, then, spell it out—how does this help us?"

The corner of Saudade's mouth lifted a little, not quite a grin. "The useful consequence of this is that for any tachyon-interactive substance or device, transmitting and receiving are functionally indistinguishable. Which is why tachyon emission has a stabilizing effect on the timestream—both the emitter and the receiver must continue existing at different times, because both devices perform both tasks."

Willa's thoughts raced. This could actually work. In those post-cataclysm futures, humanity would invent machines to stave off the collapse of the remaining stable areas on Earth. "Can you get me the schematics for those stabilizers they were using to maintain the islands of intact spacetime in the twenty-first century? They must be tachyon transceivers, right?"

Saudade smiled and vanished into a portal by way of answer. The quiet in their wake was fraught with tension.

Porzia's jaw worked like she had to unclench it to speak. "My adoptive brother and my new best friend are *gone*, and you're making plans like they were just acceptable collateral damage."

"Oh, Porzia, no. The cataclysm is a spacetime anomaly—now that we know what causes it, it can be combated not just at its inception but throughout the timeline." Willa tightened her hand into a fist at her side to keep from reaching out to Porzia. "If it's physically possible, I will get them back to you. I swear it."

Saudade reappeared through a portal and held up a tiny, flat device about the width of a finger, though not as long. "The schematics."

Willa took the object. "Riley will know what to do with this?"

"Yes, she'll be able to access this type of information storage. That's not the possible failure mode that concerns me." Saudade paused, their brow drawn. "Are you confident you can execute a jump this difficult?"

Willa smiled sadly. "Of the two of us, who is more likely to set up a causality loop in which Jaideep and Riley are positioned exactly where and when we need them to be? If this jump is possible for anyone, it's me. My future self will make sure of it."

"That's fair." Saudade drummed their fingers anxiously against their thigh. "I don't like feeling as if I'm abandoning you at the eleventh hour."

"Oh. You mean, you're not coming with me," Willa said, surprised.

"If and when the new timeline solidifies, Kairopolis will in all likelihood cease to exist, and anyone currently residing there with it. I don't know how many of my kind would agree with Norn if they were told the truth—I like to believe they would not choose to be complicit in her crimes—but either way, they were lied to and never given the choice. I have to at least try to trigger an evacuation, save as many lives as I can."

"This is why you needed me to become a time agent, too," Willa realized. "You predicted that winning might require us to best Norn not just now but across time."

"I didn't want to choose between saving the Earth and saving my own people. I refuse to believe that our kinds cannot coexist."

Faraz spoke up then. "I admit I'm woefully behind on all this time-travel business, but . . . don't we still need to deal with Norn now, in this time? She's still out there, doing who knows what."

Saudade turned to him. "You are correct—to succeed, we must ensure Norn isn't actively working against us. I will assist you in stopping her before I jump downstream to my time."

"Sounds like we have a plan," Willa said. "Now I just need to execute this jump without vanishing from the timestream."

"Ugh, you are infuriating!" Porzia told her. "You can't let my friends die one minute, and then the next minute go off and risk your life to get them back! It's . . . it's against the rules, or something."

Willa tried not to let her lips quirk with amusement at the other girl's outrage. "Well, then I apologize. Or something."

Porzia got in her face with a sternly pointed finger. "Don't joke about this, I swear to God, Willa Marconi . . ."

"I would never—" Willa started to protest, but then Porzia was stretching up to press her mouth to Willa's like she wanted to swallow the words instead of listening to them. The kiss tasted angry, like this was just one more kind of dueling between them. Porzia's passion was the kind that burned, but here at the end of the world, that seemed only right.

When Porzia pulled away again, she straightened her skirts primly and glared at Willa. "If you die, I shall be very put out."

Willa nodded. "Duly noted."

"If I were human, I would wish you luck now, yes?" said Saudade. "But it seems we have been ignoring the whims of fate for some time now, my friend. You don't need luck; you are enough."

"I'll see you on the other side," Willa told them. Then she closed her eyes and concentrated on the thought of Riley.

2048, Argonne National Labs

Willa moved through nothing, suspended in the void between places for seconds that stretched long enough to make her wonder if the timestream was going to let her out again. Then she stepped through into a future that, only a minute ago, was merely a potential outcome, but now was solidly real beneath her boots. Trying to wrap her mind around the mechanics of altering the timeline was going leave her with a permanent headache, one of these days.

The room she portaled into was some sort of computer laboratory. Workbenches lined the walls, with viewscreens and keyboards, and other equipment she couldn't identify at a glance, the space filled with the low hum of electrical components and cooling fans. The room was nearly unoccupied, except for one woman seated at a work station.

"Riley?" Willa said, half disbelieving.

The woman at the console turned around, and it both was and wasn't Willa's Riley. Her hair was a shockingly normal shade of brown instead of the unnatural bright blue Willa had somehow grown accustomed to seeing. She looked older, too: laugh lines at the corners of her eyes, the bones in her hands and wrists more prominent.

"Hi, Willa," she said, reserved in a way that made her sound like a stranger.

Willa recovered from the shock as best she could and replied in English. "You . . . don't seem surprised to see me."

"Well. You know how this goes."

"No spoilers," Willa echoed their old refrain, a wry smile curling up the corners of her lips.

"Exactly." And when Riley grinned, something of her teenage self finally showed through.

The door opened behind Willa, and a familiar male voice said, "I swear I'm going to file a complaint with the government about that coffee maker, it's a travesty—Oh." He cut himself off. "You're here."

Jaideep looked older, too, dressed in a button-down shirt for once, and sporting a silver-flecked goatee. Willa gaped. "What is that rug growing on your face?"

He stared back at her for a moment before remembering the mugs of coffee in his hands. He crossed the room to deliver one to Riley, and set his own mug down on the workbench without drinking. "I forgot you'd be, what, seventeen still? This is so weird."

Willa's focus drifted back to Riley; no matter what else had changed, her eyes were just the same. "It's strange for me, too."

The grin faded a bit from Riley's face, diluted with the start of worry.

Jaideep tucked his hands into the pockets of his beige trousers. "So what do you need me for here?"

Willa blinked at him, surprised. Apparently someone (her future self?) had told him to be present here and now, but had not explained why. "Actually, I don't think we'll need a scriptological programmer for . . ."

He held up a hand to stop her. "I'm not a programmer, Willa, I'm a historian. I got my degree in history and philosophy of science."

"Oh." Willa blinked. She didn't know how to feel about this change; was it a consequence of taking ten-year-old Jaideep on a tour of the nineteenth century? Or would he have always gone down a different academic path, in the absence of brutal necessity? "Well, anyway, you've done your part already. Something about your personal quantum signature has a tendency to produce causal loops when you get involved in time travel. In order to create this future, I need to manufacture a bunch of tachyon transceivers, and in order to make the transceivers, I need to succeed in creating this future. Circular causality, which would normally be a problem. But with you here, the timestream *wants* me to show up and close the loop."

"Hrm." Jaideep gave her a considering look. "You know, for the longest time I thought that episode when I was ten was a particularly vivid dream. Even once—" Riley elbowed him, and he smiled down at her ruefully. "Never mind. You're right, no spoilers."

"So," Riley said brightly, "tachyon transceivers. Exotic matter is a tall order—you're lucky you know a particle physicist. Are we starting from scratch, or do you have some ideas already?"

Willa stepped closer and handed over the small slip of plastic and circuits. "Saudade said you'd know what to do with this. It should have some schematics to use as a starting place."

Riley plugged it in to her terminal and pulled up the

files on her screen. "Hmm. Looks like these are meant to be permanent installations with quite a wide range."

"Smaller would be better," Willa said. "Something portable and less conspicuous. I can deliver them close to the target, so the range is less of a concern."

Jaideep sipped on his coffee. "It'll work in practice, but how does it work in theory?" he said, with the air of a well-recited joke.

"Quiet, you." Riley threw him a mock glare over her shoulder. "No comments from the audience until after the panel discussion."

"Ah yes," Willa muttered. "I'd forgotten how much I love having no idea what you two are talking about."

Jaideep winced apologetically, but Riley's attention was already focused back on the schematics. "Yeah . . . this should be doable. It'd help to have an idea what you need it for, though."

Willa hesitated. "I'm trying to think of a way of asking how much you already know without asking how much future-me has told you."

Without looking up from the screen, Riley replied, "Big explosion, end of the world, time-travel shenanigans . . . Let's assume I need to hear the details from you now. Better to cover the same ground twice than leave anything out."

"All right. So what we just learned is the fuel for the cataclysm comes from the condensing of one person's past experiences into a sort of nonlinear feedback cycle."

"Huh, like approaching a temporal singularity? Yeah, I can see how that could be used to cause cascading failures in spacetime." Riley paused, chewing on her thumbnail thoughtfully for a second. "Or it'd make the whole solar system collapse into a black hole. That's possible, too."

"Oh good," Willa said dryly, "and here I thought things couldn't possibly get worse if I make a mistake mucking around in the timestream."

Jaideep joked, "Eh, what's a little destroying the solar system between friends?"

Willa pressed her lips together and did not smile, because nothing about her situation was amusing, no matter the relieved joy that threatened to bubble up inside her at being in the presence of two people whom she thought she'd never see again. "Anyway, I was thinking I'd portal to the target's birth and distribute the tachyon transceivers downstream as he ages, stabilizing as I go. Sort of . . . iron out the temporal wrinkles in the target's life."

Riley said, "I think it'd be more effective to start just before the explosion and work your way upstream. Less resistance on the first jump, that way. With the condenser machine operational, I'd expect it to be difficult to locate the younger versions of this person in the timeline."

"That makes sense."

Willa had figured out how to focus her portal-targeting ability on a person rather than a place. But if the resistance to an upstream jump was too high, she'd probably end up jumping to Aris in the chair in Trentino, over and over again, regardless of which age she was aiming for. While she considered this, Riley began touching the display screen, making changes to the schematics with deft swipes of her fingertips.

As Willa watched the adorable little frown of concentration between Riley's brows, she couldn't help it, the words just slipped out. "I hope your version of me knows how lucky she is to have you in her life."

"I guess you'll just have to see for yourself someday," Riley said with an enigmatic smile. "Now let's get down to work."

20

ARIS

ARIS IS NINETEEN, and he stands on the roof of the Order's headquarters and stares up at the night sky. Beside him, Vincenzo holds up the fizzing red light of the Coston flare. An airship engine thrums in the distance, approaching but difficult to spot where it eclipses the dim light of the stars. The hairs rise on the back of Aris's neck. He feels exposed up here; he feels *watched*.

As the airship closes in, he shrugs off the feeling—he has Leo's anger to deal with, instead. He's probably imagining it, anyway.

Aris sits at the desk in his chambers with the editbook open to the first page, and half-finished notes scattered everywhere. He has been trying to decipher the Veldanese language all night; through the diamond-shaped lattice of the leaded windows, a pale dawn washes over the craggy slopes of the Dolomite Alps.

In the quiet, it is easy to catch the muffled sound of footsteps in the hallway. Aris expects a knock at his door—it will be Leo, probably, sleepless with conflicted doubt, or perhaps Elsa, up with the sun and seeking a bout of verbal sparring before Aris can get to his morning coffee. (*It won't be Vincenzo*, he thinks bitterly. He made sure of that when he drove Vico away.) But the sound stops without further interruption.

Driven to distraction now, Aris stands and takes his candleholder with him to peer out into the darkened hallway. It's empty—no one is there. Aris scowls. He's pretty sure he didn't imagine the noise, but he has been up all night wrestling with a deeply frustrating linguistic and scriptological challenge. Something about the hallway feels . . . off, but he can't quite put his finger on what's different.

Aris is packing up his laboratory in the converted tenement building where Father has located them for the past three years. His mood has darkened from mildly annoyed to irate over the course of the day, and now he's throwing equipment into crates in a careless, haphazard way that he knows he's going to pay for later, but can't stop himself regardless.

It's not as if he's going to miss Nizza's port district, with its perpetual supply of loud, drunken sailors and the stench of fish and pine tar that becomes near unbearable at the height of summer. There are some very pleasant neighborhoods in Nizza, and this is not one of them. But still, Aris is seventeen now—a grown man—and Father hardly consults with him at all. He simply mandates what they're going to do, offering explanations only when it suits him, treating Aris like he's still a child who has nothing to contribute to their larger strategy.

Aris's hand lands on a brass sphere the size of a bocce ball, and he almost tosses it automatically into the crate, except something makes him pause. The sphere emits a subtle hum, vibrating slightly in his hands. What is this? How did he acquire it? He's hit with a wave of shocking cognitive dissonance, at once feeling that he's never seen anything like this device before in his life, and also that it is achingly, fundamentally familiar. The device is an old and permanent friend, it is an incomprehensible alien object, it is both and neither. A sharp tension headache forms behind his eyes. Aris packs the device in a crate and decides not to investigate it further; he knows this choice is strange, especially for him, but the relief is palpable and instantaneous.

There will be time to poke at it later, when he unpacks at Father's new base of operations in Trentino. Though the urgency to do so is already slipping from his mind.

Aris is fourteen, and he's kissing Vico in the alley behind their favorite coffee bar in the Cannaregio neighborhood of Venezia (a place that Father will certainly not approve of, if he finds out). The rough brickwork behind him is digging into his back, and there's a slight, lingering smell of urine and refuse in the air, so it's not exactly the height of romance, but Aris would kiss Vico anywhere he can get away with.

Vincenzo pulls away suddenly, his head snapping up. "What was that?"

"Hm?" Aris replies, thoroughly distracted. Vico has gotten quite tall in the past few months, and Aris finds that . . . very interesting. "What was what?"

"I thought I heard something." He's scowling hawkishly down the length of the alley like he might have to leap into a duel in defense of Aris's honor.

"Probably an alley cat. Relax." Aris tugs on the front of Vico's shirt insistently, pulling his lips closer again.

The hairs on the back of his neck prickle with a nebulous sense that they're being observed, but if it's true, Aris is not above giving the voyeur something worth watching.

Aris is twelve, and he's stealing ice from the large icebox in the pantry, chipping away at the block with a pick until he's made a collection of little fragments. He scoops up the ice chips in a teacup and drapes a handkerchief over the top to preserve the cold, then he sneaks back through the kitchen while the cook's back is turned. Not that any of the servants would dare reprimand the eldest son of their employer, but they would report him to Father in a heartbeat. And then Father will say something terrible like, *if your brother's black eye swells shut, maybe he'll remember to do better next time*. And next time, Aris will be explicitly forbidden from bringing Leo any ice.

He hugs the precious cup of ice chips close to his chest as he slinks up the narrow servants' staircase. Aris is the one who needs to do better: to keep Father in a pleased mood, to distract from Leo's inadequacies, to conceal his own small rebellions. A shuffling sound echoes in the confines of the stairwell, and Aris freezes, certain he's been caught, but no one appears. He gets away with it, this time.

Ten-year-old Aris hangs by a rope against the side of the palazzo, partway down from the fourth-floor window he just climbed out of. His heart pounds in his chest despite the waters of the Grand Canal beneath him, which would probably break his fall. He's struck with a sudden, irrational certainty that he's been spotted, that someone *sees him* climbing down to Pasca's sickroom. But that makes no sense—if Father catches him doing something so reckless, the yelling will be immediate and unambiguous. Aris must just be paranoid, unaccustomed to defying Father even in a way that doesn't technically violate any of the rules.

Aris catches his feet against Pasca's windowsill and ignores the feeling.

*   *   *

Aris is seven, and Pasca's mother is dying. He stares down at the bed; she has blond, sweat-matted hair and sick-pale skin, dark circles under her eyes, a wasted sort of boniness to her hands. Even unconscious, she breathes like each inhale is an effort. Little Pasca, not yet two years old, is snuggled up to her side asleep, thumb in his mouth.

She has lasted longer than the other mothers, certainly, but Aris knows the end is near. He saw what happened to Leo's mother, after all, so he's been more or less just waiting for this one's body to give out—or else for Father to dispose of her. He knew better than to get attached.

Leo, on the other hand, calls her *Mama* because he doesn't know anything. Leo hasn't realized that this woman is not, in fact, his mother or Aris's; Leo has made the mistake of getting attached. Aris shakes his head at the thought. Someday, his brothers will need to learn they can't rely on anyone except each other.

Aris leans over the bed and drags Pasca closer until he can pick him up—an awkward, heavy load in his own small arms. He carries Pasca back to the nursery, so his youngest brother doesn't have to wake up beside a cooling corpse. Might as well let his brothers stay soft for a while yet. Aris is hardened enough for the three of them.

Five-year-old Aris holds baby Pasca for the first time. He feels the weight like a mantle of renewed responsibility settling over his shoulders. Father is watching him, of course, but there's something else, too. Young Aris imagines this must be what having a guardian angel feels like—some benevolent observer, silent in the background of his life. It's okay. This is a good moment.

Two-and-a-half-year-old Aris watches as Father cuts the woman open and pulls baby Leo out of her belly. At the same time, he feels watched himself.

Aris, too, is born in blood. All according to Father's design.

21

FARAZ

1891, Pisa

FARAZ WAS ONLY half aware of his surroundings as Porzia portaled the two of them back to the library at Casa della Pazzia. He felt as if he'd left a vital organ behind in Trentino. But at the same time, there was a small, awful part of him that felt almost *relieved*; the thing he was most afraid of had come to pass, and now there was nothing but an echoing void inside him where his fear used to be.

"You've been really quiet," Porzia said. "You're scaring me."

"I suppose I don't know what to say," he replied numbly. There were no words adequate for such a situation. What does one say after being gutted? So he changed the subject. "I've never seen you kiss someone you're furious with before. Are *you* all right?"

Porzia huffed. "It's complicated with Willa. And you're deflecting again."

"Yes," Faraz agreed. He couldn't fathom talking about his feelings just now.

Saudade followed, suddenly portaling into the library in a way that, only days ago, would have given Faraz a shock. Now he was too numb to be surprised by anything.

"So do we have a plan yet?" Saudade said, not impatient, but eager in a way that was frankly a little exhausting, given everything else that had happened. "I'd like to snap this collar around Norn's neck as quickly as possible."

Porzia scoffed. "You barely held your own against her last time. What makes you think you can best Norn?"

"You're right." Saudade shrugged. "If we want to trap her, we'll have to use better bait."

Faraz sighed. "I hate this plan already."

Faraz seriously considered lying to Pasca about what happened to Leo and the others. It would make the loss more real if he described it in words. But guilt welled up in him and forced the words out; he couldn't expect Pasca to help them catch Norn if they kept him in the dark about why the trap was necessary. After everything Pasca had been through, he deserved to be told the truth and trusted to handle it like an adult, so that was what Faraz did.

The two of them and Porzia moved to the stone bench in the courtyard garden when Pasca agreed to serve as bait. It would seem unrealistic to leave him out in the open unattended, so Faraz and Porzia flanked him as if playing the role of protectors.

"Are you sure she even wants me?" Pasca signed. "Last time I saw her, she seemed . . . distant and uninterested. Like she was only checking on me because everyone expected her to."

Faraz signed, "When Norn took me, she ranted again and again about how much she hated Aris. She never said your name. Why? I think because you don't fit into her story where all people O-P-P-R-E-S-S her kind. Now she thinks she's won, and she'll come back for the one thing from before that she cares about: you."

"Maybe."

It worried Faraz how resigned Pasca seemed, as if he'd never actually trusted the transient safety he'd been offered here at Casa della Pazzia. "Leo was a brother to me, and finding you was *everything* to him. Whatever happens, I am here for you. Always. You are family."

Pasca offered a brittle smile. "You can't promise 'always.' No one can."

Faraz wished he could contradict that, but he'd already decided not to lie to Pasca. He was still trying to formulate a reply when Norn dropped out of the sky in a flare of wings. Faraz and Porzia made a show of trying to escort Pasca away to safety, but Pasca brushed them off, insisting he wanted to talk to Norn. The kid wasn't a bad actor, all things considered—Faraz would have bought his performance if he didn't know better. With a pang of grief, he wondered if Pasca had learned that talent from Leo.

"Norn, what do you want?" Pasca signed.

Norn signed, "I finished what I set out to do. It's time for you to come with me now, my bright boy."

"You took my brothers from me," Pasca signed, sharp with anger and disbelief, "and now you expect I'll willingly join you?"

"I had to," Norn replied, desperation edging into her signs. "I did this for us, so we can be free! So we can stop living as someone else's experiments, and be our own people instead."

"I'm going to tell you the same thing I told Aris, once," Pasca signed. "The terrible things that happened to you when you were young does not absolve you of the choices you make now. No matter what your trauma, you are still responsible for not perpetuating that terror unto others."

"Don't compare me to that tyrant!" An audible hiss escaped from between her teeth.

Pasca furrowed his brows. "Why? Your sins are the same. You have become exactly what you most despise, you're just too angry to see it clearly."

Norn drooped her hands to her sides in shock; she gave Pasca a wounded look that seemed to say it would have been less painful and surprising if he'd simply pulled out a revolver and shot her. And this was the opportunity Saudade had been waiting for.

At the *whoosh* of a portal opening, Porzia pulled Pasca away to a safer distance, as Saudade popped into existence behind Norn. Saudade took a wing to the face in the struggle, but Norn was a fraction of a second too slow to react, and the suppression collar snapped closed around her neck. Norn made a choking noise and pawed at it, but the locking mechanism held fast. She stumbled and her knees gave out, as if the collar was disrupting her sense of balance, or perhaps weakening her physically. Saudade looked down at her with an almost savage satisfaction that made Faraz wonder what their history with Norn was.

"Go," Faraz said to them. "Save your people. We've got this now."

Saudade nodded once in acknowledgment, opened a portal for themself, and left without a word.

"What have you done to me?" Norn rasped from her position kneeling on the ground, her hands still busy trying to pry off the collar.

Porzia set her hands on her hips. "Oh, get used to it. If you can't figure out on your own that it's a terrible idea to destroy the planet, you'll have to live with a somewhat more restricted set of choices available to you."

"I will not be enslaved to a human again," Norn growled. "I'd rather die."

Faraz sighed. "That's always an option. But I'm hoping you and I will reach a compromise we can both live with instead."

"There can be no compromise! The end of humanity has already been set in motion."

"I don't like killing, or even standing by while it is done. I've never needed to kill a person, the way Leo had to with his father, and I hope I'll never be in such a terrible position." The past few days had offered few opportunities for contemplative prayer, just stolen moments when he could find the time and psychological space to make dua. He was not perfect—he knew he was as flawed a human being as anyone—so all he could do was try his best to put goodness out into the world, and to stand in the way of evil actions. "I don't know what's going to happen with the explosion you caused, whether it's possible to mitigate the damage. But this I can promise: You will *never* take a position of power over others, be they human or construct. I will kill you first."

"You'll have to," Norn spat. "I will never submit!"

He paused, picking his words with care. "I like to believe people can change. That we grow as individuals, that we gain perspective and rethink the mistakes of our past. I suppose, in time, we'll see if you can do that, too."

Faraz regarded Norn, taking in the sight of her impotent fury and undisguised hatred. He didn't know what to say to get through to her today, but Pasca had planted a seed of doubt, of that he was fairly confident. And with any luck, they would have a tomorrow in which to try again—and a day after that, and a day after that.

If Willa succeeded.

22

WILLA

Willa attaches the final tachyon transceiver to a wall sconce in the hallway outside baby Aris's birthing chamber. And then something . . . *shifts*, like the ground sliding out from under her, a tectonic reshaping. She doesn't travel through a temporal portal—at least, not the kind she understands and can control—but nevertheless, she slides into the heart of the storm, with Aris strapped to the torture chair in front of her.

Around them, the room is a maelstrom of constantly shifting times. They're in a brightly lit ballroom filled with music and a crowd of dancers; they're atop an ice floe on a bare mountainside, fortresses nothing but a dream that won't be realized for thousands of years; they're standing in the ruins after the walls collapse and nature creeps back in.

But in the chair, Aris is no longer flickering between ages. His eyes are wide and desperate, not quite managing to focus on her face. "It's all in pieces. Everything happens at once, and none of it makes any sense."

Willa rushes to release the straps confining Aris, her thoughts racing as her hands work open the buckles. The transceivers are all in place, and clearly they're having *some* effect, for Willa to be able to stand here without getting consumed by the cataclysm. But the last piece of the puzzle must be up to Aris.

Willa says, "I've watched your whole life happen—in flashes, like walking backward through a daguerreotype museum. It's a strange way to become acquainted with someone." She pauses, choosing her words with care. "I don't know that a life is *supposed* to make sense. I don't think you can take the sum of everything a person has done, everything that's happened to them, and distill it down to a single truth. That's not what life is."

"Then what do I do with all of this?" he asked, voice wavering with desperation. "This tangled mess of everything, everywhen—it's intolerable, you have to help me!"

"Listen to me, Aris." She grabbed him by the shoulders, trying to ground him with a touch. "The past already happened. What you do is: Let it go. You just have to let go of it, and the past will fall back into place where it always belonged. Then you can move forward."

Willa lets go of Aris's shoulders and instead offers her hands, palms up, to help him out of the chair. He seems to finally notice that his arms are free of the straps, and he lifts them to accept Willa's assistance, moving slow like a dreamer mired in a nightmare. Willa leans back, counterbalancing as Aris heaves himself to his feet. Around them, the maelstrom begins to settle, and time . . . *snapped* back into place.

Willa felt the change reverberate down to bones, like the tremor of a far-off explosion—or in this case, the undoing of one. The dance hall returned to the condition in which she'd first seen it, unfurnished save for the now-empty chair in the center, and in the sudden quiet, she could hear people shuffling behind her.

"Are you all right?" someone said, and Aris's eyes went wide—because that was Leo's voice asking him.

Aris squeezed Willa's hand hard, as if needing to draw strength for a reply. "I . . . don't know."

Willa looked over her shoulder: Leo, Elsa, and Vincenzo were all there, real again, anchored once more to a single time and place. They looked disoriented but otherwise unharmed. And Leo was aiming an open expression of worry at Aris, which apparently was an unexpected shock, even when measured against everything else that happened today.

"Hold on," Elsa said, "what happened to Porzia and Faraz?"

Vincenzo's hand went to the grip of his revolver. "Not to mention Norn."

"Everyone's fine," Willa assured them. "Well, *Norn*

I imagine is very put out. But everyone else is alive and well, as far as I know. We can meet up with them now—this here is done."

Focusing on Porzia as a portal destination brought them all to the courtyard garden in Casa della Pazzia. Willa hung back a little with Aris, quiet and cowed at her side, as the rest of them enjoyed their tearful reunion. She was happy for them that they didn't lose each other, but the ache in her chest made it clear that this was not where she belonged.

Porzia eventually peeled away from the group, and as she approached, Willa asked, "So what did you do with Norn?"

"Found a room without any windows to lock her in." Porzia shrugged. "She's a problem for another day. I take it your mission was successful, as well." Her gaze landed briefly on Aris, but his subdued demeanor seemed to satisfy whatever anger lingered in her.

"Yes." Willa felt suddenly awkward. It wasn't as if they'd had time to discuss whether their kissing was anything more than an unleashing of mutual frustrations. But whatever Porzia felt or didn't feel, she still deserved some kind of acknowledgment. Willa said, "I . . . have someone—*someones*, really—in the future, or at least I hope I do."

"It's not as if you proposed. And you're not the only person I've been kissing this month, either." Porzia pressed her lips into a wry smile. "But come back and see me sometime. You know where and when I'll be."

Willa had never been especially skilled at goodbyes. She would've thought being a time traveler would lessen the problem, but it really didn't seem to. But thankfully, Saudade portaled into the courtyard at that moment, saving Willa from her own ineptitude.

"Back so soon?" she joked to them. Of course, there was no way to know how much time Saudade's mission had taken from their perspective. "How did things go in Kairopolis?"

Saudade gave a half-hearted shrug. "As well as can be expected, I suppose. The ones who believed me are scattered throughout history, cut loose from our home. It will take some effort to find them—perhaps make for ourselves a new Kairopolis, not built on a foundation of lies." They paused to look intently at her. "But first, I think a reunion is in order."

"I do believe you're right." Willa turned to Aris and decided, "You should come with us to the future."

His eyes widened in shock. "What?"

"Take some time to figure out who you are on your own, before you try to repair your relationships. Vincenzo and your brothers will still be here when you're ready; 1891 can wait."

He was still staring at her like she'd lost her mind. "You would take *me*, who very nearly destroyed the planet, on a tour through the timeline?"

"Take it from me: Time travel is an excellent way to gain some perspective on life," she replied, willfully ignoring his objection.

"But why would you trust me with that?" he pressed. There was an edge of disbelieving fear to the words, as if his true protest was that he doubted he could trust himself.

Aris hardly knew her at all, but Willa had watched little pieces of his whole life from the shadows. Aris was not a monster, merely a person who'd been dealt a bad hand and responded in even worse ways. And he'd been so close to changing—when she placed the very first tachyon transceiver, she saw how it went wrong.

"It wasn't Leo who framed you," she said. "Norn hid the notebook in your bedroom for Vincenzo to find. It was all a manipulation. So you see, I'm not worried about taking you to the future, because there won't be anyone there trying to feed your worst impulses."

"Oh," he said.

Willa patted his arm. "Resist the urge to take over the world, and you'll do fine."

2034, Harvard University

The campus was more built up than it had been in the 1920s, though there was still considerable outdoor space bounded within the edifices of learning. The street noise from beyond the brick walls was different now, too, more of a constant electric whine than the smoky rumble of last century's cars. It was autumn, and the leaves were turning improbable colors, even as the manicured grass clung to green.

Willa spotted Riley sitting against the trunk of a tree with a textbook open in her lap. She glanced anxiously at Saudade, who gave her a reassuring nod and hung back with Aris as Willa approached.

"Riley Davis," she said, not really a question.

Riley looked up, obviously taking note of Willa's anachronistic dress, but all she said was, "Uh, yeah?"

Willa wet her lips nervously. "This is going to sound . . . difficult to believe, but even though you don't know me, I know you. In another timeline, we saved the world together."

Riley blinked up at her for a moment in stunned disbelief. Then she laughed, not mocking but brightly, like she was expecting to be let in on a joke. "Who put you up to this? I'm gonna plan my revenge *so* carefully, just you wait. This whole getup"—she waved at Willa's clothes—"is really going the extra mile."

Willa sank as gracefully as she could to kneel in the grass in front of her. (Apparently this version of Riley was also bizarrely eager to just sit on the ground.) Her serious demeanor seemed to quell some of Riley's mirth. She said, "My name is Willa Marconi. I was born in 1874, and I became a time traveler because I met you."

"Yeah, so . . . I don't think I believe you, but extra

credit points for commitment," Riley said. "You're interesting, Willa Marconi. One way or the other, I can admit
I am intrigued."

"I shall take 'intrigued' as a starting line."

"Oh, are we having a race?" She widened her eyes in
joking excitement.

"I don't know," quipped Willa, "what's my competi-
tion like, and what do I get if I win?"

"Oh no, you're a smart-ass—I have to keep you now,
there's no getting around it." Riley grinned.

God, she was so beautiful like this. Her hair was a
ludicrous electric blue; her easy friendliness was infec-
tious. "Are you seeing anyone? Romantically, I mean."
Willa hadn't meant to ask anything of the sort so soon,
but the words just slipped out.

Riley flushed. "What? Um . . . no. I—no." She paused
as if digesting the question. "Why, are we . . . ?"

Willa bit her lip. "We were, in the old timeline. Yes."

"You're really not joking," Riley said, a little faintly.

"Dead serious, I'm afraid." Willa gave her a moment
to consider this, then she got back to her feet. "Come
along, let me introduce you to my traveling companions,
and then there's someone else we have to find."

Riley stood slowly, brushing off the back of her jeans
and hefting her schoolbag. "Who?"

Willa smiled. "His name is Jaideep."

"I've met Jaideep." She gnawed on her thumbnail. "He
has some strange ideas about the practicality of time travel.

But now I'm thinking either those ideas aren't so strange after all, or there was a Ren Faire on campus that I didn't hear about and you're a really ridiculous con artist."

Willa laughed. This was not precisely *her* Riley, she knew that, but in so many ways the two versions were similar: her small mannerisms, her sense of humor, her open-minded idealism. Everyone changed with their experiences, and that wasn't a bad thing—this was the life, and the world, that Willa wanted for Riley.

She said, "I hope you'll give me the chance to earn your confidence, in any case. And answer any questions you may have."

"Oh, I have questions. Trust that. About a million of them."

The two of them started over toward where Saudade and Aris were waiting, but they walked slowly, neither one eager to abandon their privacy.

"So you and Jaideep are acquainted, but you're not dating yet?" Willa read the nervous crush from the way Riley's cheeks turned pink. "Don't worry, we'll fix that."

Riley gave her a confused look. "You know I'm poly? I haven't even told my parents that yet."

"Like I said: You don't know me, but I know you." Willa cocked her head to the side. "And if there are ways you're different now, I can learn those, too."

"We've got time," Riley agreed.

Willa laughed again. "All the time in the world."

ACKNOWLEDGMENTS

FIRST AND FOREMOST, thanks to my editor, Kat Brzozowski, for her invaluable insights and for pushing me to write the best version of these books I possibly can. Thanks also to my readers of this duology, including Leah, Zainab, and Jenna—mistakes are mine, but y'all helped me make fewer of them! The gorgeous covers for this duology are thanks to designer Sarah Nichole Kaufman, and these books would not be possible without the production team at Feiwel & Friends, including Avia Perez and Meg Sayre.

As always, thanks to my fantastic agent, Jen Azantian. In this often difficult industry, I couldn't ask for a more supportive, enthusiastic, and hardworking advocate. So glad to have you in my corner.

My brother, Chris, always pushes me to think harder about the worldbuilding. Luckily, none of the dysfunctional sibling relationships portrayed here were based on ours, and Chris has never almost destroyed the planet. I want to thank all my family, polycule, and friends for their support through the writing and publishing process, but especially Athena, Troy, Jim, and Nina. Finally, thanks to my comrades in the SFF and YA writing communities, who helped me maintain perspective through the highs and lows of this journey.

Thank you for reading this Feiwel & Friends book.

THE FRIENDS WHO MADE

FOR THE

Stolen Fates

POSSIBLE ARE:

JEAN FEIWEL, *Publisher*

LIZ SZABLA, *VP, Associate Publisher*

RICH DEAS, *Senior Creative Director*

ANNA ROBERTO, *Executive Editor*

HOLLY WEST, *Senior Editor*

KAT BRZOZOWSKI, *Senior Editor*

DAWN RYAN, *Executive Managing Editor*

KIM WAYMER, *Senior Production Manager*

EMILY SETTLE, *Editor*

RACHEL DIEBEL, *Editor*

FOYINSI ADEGBONMIRE, *Editor*

BRITTANY GROVES, *Assistant Editor*

MEG SAYRE, *Junior Designer*

AVIA PEREZ, *Senior Production Editor*

Follow us on Facebook or visit us online at mackids.com.
OUR BOOKS ARE FRIENDS FOR LIFE.